PASSIONS OF WAR

Recent Titles by Hilary Green

The Leonora Saga

DAUGHTERS OF WAR ★
PASSIONS OF WAR ★

WE'LL MEET AGAIN
NEVER SAY GOODBYE
NOW IS THE HOUR
THEY ALSO SERVE
THEATRE OF WAR
THE FINAL ACT

★ *available from Severn House*

PASSIONS
OF WAR

Hilary Green

This first world edition published 2011
in Great Britain and in the USA by
SEVERN HOUSE PUBLISHERS LTD of
9–15 High Street, Sutton, Surrey, England, SM1 1DF.
Trade paperback edition first published
in Great Britain and the USA 2012 by
SEVERN HOUSE PUBLISHERS LTD.

Every effort has been made to trace the copyright owner of the poem beginning 'I wish my mother could see me now' on p.171. Anyone claiming copyright should contact the publisher directly.

British Library Cataloguing in Publication Data

Green, Hilary, 1937-
    Passions of war. – (The Leonora trilogy)
    1. World War, 1914-1918–Medical care–Fiction. 2. First
    Aid Nursing Yeomanry–Fiction. 3. Balkan Peninsula–
    History–War of 1912-1913–Fiction. 4. Soldiers–
    Serbia–Fiction. 5. Love stories.
    I. Title II. Series
    823.9′2-dc22

ISBN-13: 978-0-7278-8104-5 (cased)
ISBN-13: 978-1-84751-402-8 (trade paper)

All Severn House titles are printed on acid-free paper.

Severn House Publishers support The Forest Stewardship Council [FSC],
the leading international forest certification organisation. All our titles that
are printed on Greenpeace-approved FSC-certified paper carry the FSC logo.

Typeset by Palimpsest Book Production Ltd.,
Falkirk, Stirlingshire, Scotland.
Printed and bound in Great Britain by
MPG Books Ltd., Bodmin, Cornwall.

These books are not romantic fantasies but are based on solid historical fact. They were inspired by the lives of two remarkable women, Mabel St Clair Stobart and Flora Sands. Stobart, who features as a character in this book, was the founder of the Women's Sick and Wounded Convoy in 1912, led a group of nurses to care for Bulgarian soldiers during the First Balkan War and returned to help the Serbs during World War I. She gave an account of her experiences in her books *Miracles and Adventures* and *The Flaming Sword in Serbia and Elsewhere*.

Flora Sands was the daughter of a clergyman and an early member of the FANY – the First Aid Nursing Yeomanry. In 1915 she volunteered to go to Serbia with Stobart, was separated from her unit and joined up with a company of Serbian soldiers, with whom she endured the terrible hardships of the retreat through the mountains of Albania. She later returned with them to Salonika and took part in the final advance which ended the war. She was the first woman ever to be accepted as a fighting soldier and ended the war with the rank of sergeant. Though she does not appear as a character in these books, much of the action is derived from her experiences, which are recorded in her own memoir *An English Woman Sergeant in the Serbian Army* and by Alan Burgess in *The Lovely Sergeant*.

I should like to thank my husband David for his help and patience, particularly in matters to do with the computer, and for proofreading.

The poem beginning 'I wish my mother could see me now' was written by an anonymous FANY and is quoted by Pat Beauchamp Washington in her book *Fanny Goes to War*.

One

June, 1914

'I'm going back to Belgrade.'

Leonora looked up from her book and regarded her fiancé with a frown. 'Why, Tom?'

'I'm going to try to talk some sense into that mutton-headed brother of yours.'

'In that case, I wish you luck,' Leo responded dryly. 'But why now, all of a sudden?'

Tom sat down opposite her. 'I don't like what I'm hearing from various sources out there. You remember I told you last summer, when we were there, that Ralph was getting mixed up with some dangerous people? I get the impression that something is brewing and I think we should try to get him away before it blows up in his face.'

'What do you mean by "various sources"?'

'Max, for one. As a newspaper man he has contacts all over Serbia and beyond and there isn't much he doesn't get to hear about. But some of the fellows I got friendly with last year, while we were staying in Belgrade and who I still correspond with, are telling me that they are worried, too.'

'What do they think is going to happen?'

'No one seems to know for sure. But you remember Dragutin Dimitrijevic, Apis, as they call him?'

'Only too well! He's a nasty piece of work. Isn't he the head of that group that call themselves the Black Hand?'

'That's right. They are dedicated to the creation of a Greater Serbia, to include Bosnia Hercegovina. And from what I hear they are plotting some act of provocation that might provoke a war.'

Leo sighed. 'Haven't they had enough fighting? I should have thought that two wars in the last two years would have been enough to sicken them of it. When I think of all those brave men, Bulgarians and Serbs, who suffered so terribly side by side and then were ordered to turn against each other, I could weep. And all those people involved in the siege of Adrianople, on both sides, who went through hell so that the Bulgarians could occupy it. And then look what happened. A few months later, at the Treaty of Bucharest, it is handed back to the Turks. It's so futile! And now they want to start all over again.'

'You have to remember Serbian society is dominated by the military. As far as they are concerned, they had two very good wars. First they got rid of the Turks, then they beat the Bulgarians in a war that lasted less than a month to hang on to Macedonia. Now they are determined to get Bosnia back.'

'But I can't believe Ralph would let himself get mixed up in something illegal,' Leo objected. 'He may be a bit too easily dazzled by military heroics, but he's not an idiot.'

'No, of course not. But there is such a thing as guilt by association,' Tom said. 'At the very least, it will do his army career no good.'

'That's true,' Leo agreed. 'But I don't give much for your chances of changing his mind, and anyway, he can't leave even if he wants to. He's been posted as a military attaché and he has to stick to his post. Regular soldiers can't just come and go as they please.'

'He must be due for some leave, surely,' Tom said. 'He hasn't been home for over a year. Failing that, at least I may be able to persuade him to distance himself from that crowd.'

Leo looked at him and saw the determined set of his features, so different from the easy-going, almost vapid expression she remembered from two years ago. 'When will you leave?' she asked.

'Tomorrow morning. If I get the first ferry I can catch the Orient Express from Paris that evening.' Leo's lips twitched and he raised his eyebrows. 'What?'

'I was just thinking, eighteen months ago I bet you would have thought catching the Orient Express was about on a par with flying to the moon on a broomstick.'

He laughed. 'That's very true. When Ralph sent me off on that wild goose chase to look for you after you ran off to nurse the Bulgarians I was terrified. But I have you to thank for broadening my horizons – among other things.' He reached out and touched her hand. 'Will you come with me?'

She shook her head. 'No, I can't, Tom. You know that. I should almost inevitably bump into Sasha and that would just be too painful for both of us. You do understand, don't you?'

'Of course,' he answered. He stood up. 'Well, if I'm going to catch that ferry I had better go home and tell Peters to pack a bag for me. You will be all right until I get back?'

'Of course I shall. But you take care, Tom. Those men are dangerous.'

'Don't worry. I'll see you in a week or two.'

He bent and kissed her cheek and she watched him go out of the door with a twist of anguish at her heart. For a year he had been her rock and her haven, something to cling to in a world that had fallen apart around her. Two years ago, when Ralph was determined that she should marry his closest school friend, she had despised him. He had seemed so ineffectual, with his vague ambition to be a painter and his unquestioning devotion to her brother, but now his gentle companionship was more precious to her than anything. But her pain was not simply due to his prospective absence. She had learned to live with solitude. It was the thought that he would be in Belgrade, that he would breathe the same air and tread the same streets as Aleksander Malkovic, a joy that was for ever forbidden to her.

She was jolted out of her unaccustomed descent into self-pity by the sound of the telephone. Her grandmother had always refused to have an instrument installed but it had been one of Ralph's first actions on becoming master of the house. Leo was often grateful for it but its ring still made her jump.

Beavis, the butler, appeared at the door. 'Miss Langford is on the telephone, miss.'

'Thank you, Beavis.' She passed him into the hall and reflected as she did so how radically his manner towards her had changed. When her grandmother had been alive she had been aware that he regarded her with disapproval, but now he was as respectful to her as he had been to the old lady. At first she had wondered if it was due to the accounts of her exploits that had reached the English press but later she realized that it was simply the fact that now, in her brother's absence, she was mistress of the house. It had taken her some time to get used to this new status but at least she no longer had to think up excuses for her actions or account for her whereabouts.

She took up the telephone and spoke into the mouthpiece. 'Hello, Victoria?'

'Are you coming to the drill tonight?'

'Yes, I'll be there.'

'Good. I'll pick you up about a quarter to seven.'

'Thank you. I'll see you then.'

'Yes, till this evening. 'Bye.'

It was more than a year since Leo had returned from Serbia. Almost immediately on her return Beavis had informed her that Victoria had called repeatedly over the previous months, asking for news of her. While she'd been away he had been able to tell her that Leo was in Belgrade with her brother, but nothing more. Leo's first instinct on arriving back at 31 Sussex Gardens, after the devastating discovery that Sasha was engaged to marry someone else, had been to shut herself away and see no one, but then she remembered how close they had once been. It was Victoria who had first introduced her to the FANY: the First Aid Nursing Yeomanry, whose purpose was to bring help to soldiers in the front line. And it was Victoria who had been her companion on the long journey to Bulgaria and in the months when they had struggled to care for the soldiers wounded in the war against the Ottoman Turks. They had parted on bad terms but she needed a friend, more than ever before, so she had sat down immediately and wrote a note asking her to call the following morning.

It had not been until she had heard Victoria's voice in the hall that she had experienced a twinge of doubt. Was it really possible to pick up the threads of their previous relationship, after the bitterness of their parting at Adrianople?

Beavis announced, 'Miss Langford, miss,' and Victoria entered and stood still, just inside the closing door. She was wearing a simple dark blue tunic dress with a peg-top skirt over a plain white blouse, and her normally sparkling blue eyes were shadowed with doubt. For a moment neither of them spoke, then Victoria said, 'Thank you for your note. I was afraid you would never want to see me again.'

Her words broke through the constraint Leo was feeling and she crossed the room and took hold of her hands. 'Of course I want to see you. Why shouldn't I?'

'I don't know how you can forgive me for the way I behaved,' Victoria said. 'I am so ashamed of leaving you like that, all alone.'

'I wasn't all alone,' Leo said, suddenly aware that she had been partly to blame. She had concealed the true state of affairs from Victoria and left her to shoulder all the guilt. 'Come and sit down. There's a lot I need to tell you.'

She led her friend to a sofa and they sat side by side. Victoria said, 'I was so relieved to learn from Beavis that you were safely in Belgrade. I had been picturing you lying in that awful hospital tent, dying of typhus. I knew I should have stayed but I just didn't have the courage. I always thought of myself as rather brave, you know, but I couldn't face the squalor and the disease any longer. I had to get away. I'm afraid I don't have your capacity for self-sacrifice.'

'It wasn't self-sacrifice,' Leo said. 'That's what I need to explain. I didn't stay at Adrianople out of a sense of duty or compassion. I stayed because I wanted to, because there was something, someone, there that I wanted to be close to.'

'Someone?' Victoria had queried. 'Who? It wasn't Luke, was it? You weren't secretly carrying a torch for him while I . . .'

'No!' Leo interrupted her, remembering the red-headed New Zealander who had volunteered as a stretcher-bearer. She had disapproved of Victoria's affair with him and it had opened up a rift between them which still needed to be bridged. 'No, I was fond of Luke, but we can come back to that. He wasn't the reason I wanted to stay.'

'Who, then?'

'Do you remember Colonel Malkovic?'

'Wasn't he that insufferably arrogant man we met in Salonika that first evening? The one who wouldn't let us go to the front?'

'Yes, that's right.'

'You can't mean you . . . you had fallen in love with him!'

Leo took her hand and gripped it tightly. The desire to pour out the story of the last few months was overpowering. 'Sasha's not arrogant, Vita. He's proud and reserved, but he's also strong and brave and kind. Let me explain . . .' As succinctly as she could she told the story of her meeting with Malkovic at Chataldzha, when he had mistaken her for a boy, of the expedition into the Turkish trenches, of how she had encountered him again at Adrianople and ultimately become his secretary. 'So you see,' she concluded, 'all the time you thought I was sacrificing myself nursing typhus patients I was actually having a wonderful time, riding out with Sasha and talking and playing cards and . . . well, getting to know him and realizing he was the only man I could ever think of marrying.'

'I don't understand,' Victoria had said, frowning. 'You're engaged to Tom Devenish. I saw the announcement in the paper yesterday. I admit I was surprised, knowing the way you feel about him. What went wrong?'

'You remember how Sasha mistook me for a boy at Chataldza because I was wearing breeches? I didn't dare disillusion him because I knew he'd be furious with me for deceiving him. Then Ralph turned up at Adrianople and gave the game away.' The momentary euphoria that her recollections of the days spent at Sasha's side had produced dissolved, as she told first of Tom's arrival, then of Ralph's, and Sasha's fury when she was unmasked.

'And that was the end of it?' Victoria had asked.

'Oh, no, far from it. You see, we met again in Belgrade and when he saw me as a woman he realized that he was in love with me, too. But he's not free, Vita. He's been betrothed to a girl he hardly knows since he was fourteen and he can't break it off without creating a blood feud between the families. His honour won't let him do that. So there it is. There's nothing to be done and we both have to learn to live with it.'

'And does that mean marrying Tom? I can't see how that solves anything.'

Leo shook her head. 'I'm not marrying Tom. The engagement is a matter of convenience for both of us. Ralph wouldn't let me come back to London unchaperoned and I had to get away from Belgrade. I couldn't bear to stay there when I might run into Sasha at any moment, at a ball or a reception. So Tom has made himself responsible for me, which means that Ralph trusts him again. He was livid with him to begin with because he found me first at Adrianople and didn't immediately give me away to Sasha and drag me back home. You were absolutely right there, incidentally. It is Ralph he loves, not me — although we have actually become very fond of each other in the last few months.'

Victoria shook her head again, slowly. 'What a tangled world it is! Poor Leo! I'm so sorry for you. But what a mess it all is. There's you, hopelessly in love with Sasha and Tom equally hopelessly in love with Ralph and poor Luke in love with me. I treated him atrociously, Leo. When he proposed to me I just panicked. I couldn't face the prospect of marrying him and going to live in New Zealand, so I cleared off and left him to it. I should never have started the affair in the first place. You were absolutely right about that, but at the time I just wanted to grab whatever comfort I could in the middle of all that misery and I didn't think about the consequences. I wonder what happened to him.'

'He's back in New Zealand,' Leo said. 'I gave him my address before he left Adrianople and there was a letter waiting for me when I arrived home.'

'Is he all right?'

'As far as is possible with a broken heart. He'll survive, and I suppose I shall — somehow.'

Victoria squeezed her hand. 'If there is anything I can do to help . . . What are your plans now?'

'I don't have any.'

'Come back to the FANY. It will do you good to meet up with all your old friends.'

'You've rejoined, have you?'

'Well, technically we never left. I tried to contact Mabel Stobart when I got back but she has gone off to Canada to visit her son and the Women's Sick and Wounded Convoy seems to have been disbanded. As far as I can see, Stobart was pretty disillusioned with the reception she got when they came back. I mean, if anyone deserved a hero's welcome she did, but really, except for a few people, no one seems to have noticed what we all did. It certainly doesn't seem to have made any impression on the powers-that-be. But the FANY are going from strength to strength and Ashley-Smith is convinced that if war does come we shall be allowed to play our part. So why don't you come along to the next drill?'

This time Leo shook her head. 'I'm not ready for all that yet. I just need time and peace to sort my life out. I think I shall go up to Bramwell Hall, our place in Cheshire, for a while. Maybe when I come back to London I'll rejoin.'

A year had passed since that conversation. Leo had done as she had suggested and spent several months at Bramwell. She rode out over the Peckforton Hills on Amber, the little chestnut mare her father had bought her to sweeten the pill of being left behind in England when she was fifteen. When the weather was poor she spent long hours studying the history of the Balkans and practising her Serbian. Quite what her object was in doing this she could not explain, except that it seemed a last, tenuous link with the happiness she had once dreamed of.

Since the death of her grandfather, Bramwell had been cared for in the absence of the owners by a married couple, James and Annie Bartlett. Both had been born on the estate and had risen from scullery maid in Annie's case and under groom in James' to the position of housekeeper and estate manager. They had been kind to the wild fifteen-year-old who had been deposited in the household five years earlier, and they extended the same unspoken sympathy to the sober young woman who had returned from the horrors of war. Leo found herself cosseted and spoilt as she had never been before.

Sometimes Tom came to stay, and sometimes Victoria came, but mostly she was alone and slowly the wounds healed and she ceased to wake every morning with that hollow sense of loss.

Tom, meanwhile, was busy making finished pictures from the sketches he had drawn during his horrendous weeks on the battlefield and arranging the exhibition he had planned with

Leo. It was the opening of this that finally persuaded her to leave her sanctuary and return to London. The pictures created a sensation, but it was not the kind that they had hoped for. He was variously accused of 'sensationalism'; 'gothic exaggeration'; 'an almost pornographic delight in violence and suffering' and an attempt to undermine the morale of the nation. Dispirited, he packed the pictures away and vowed never to exhibit again.

Over the winter Leo slowly picked up the threads of her old life again. Most of it was centred on the FANY, where she found old friends and a renewed sense of purpose. With rumours of impending war with Germany growing stronger week by week all the members were confident that if the crisis came they would be ready, and that their services would be welcomed by the military hierarchy. Leo found it difficult to take the practice drills seriously and from time to time she attempted to point out how very different the experience was under real war conditions. She tried to bring home to the others the horror of some of the wounds they would have to deal with, and the effect of living with the noise of the guns and the pervading dirt and stench. But she had the impression that many of them thought she was 'shooting a line' in order to bolster her own standing within the corps, so she gave up.

She continued to attend the drills, however, and as winter gave way to spring and then summer corps morale received a boost during the annual camp, when they were inspected by the commanding officer of the Royal Army Medical Corps and given an excellent report. There was a general feeling that they were ready to swing into action as soon as the call came.

As the months passed Leo had to fend off frequent enquiries about when she and Tom were going to get married. At first she told people that she still needed time to recover fully from the effects of her experiences in the Balkans but that story began to wear thin when it was clear that, physically at least, she was back to full health. Then, in a moment of inspiration, she hit upon the perfect excuse. 'It all depends on my brother,' she would say. 'Of course, he must be there to give me away but at the moment his duties are keeping him in Belgrade. We are waiting for him to finish his tour of duty.'

Now Tom was heading for Belgrade with the object of persuading Ralph to apply for leave. If he succeeded it might save Ralph from possible disgrace but it would certainly pose new problems for the two of them.

Two

Driving through the streets of Belgrade from the station to the hotel where Ralph was staying, Tom was assailed by conflicting memories. There was the police station to which he had been taken when he was arrested and accused of spying; but here was the house of a family who had made him welcome on his return months later, where he had passed many pleasant evenings; and that was the town house of the Countess Malkovic, where he knew Leonora had had her final encounter with Sasha. But he was concentrating on these recollections only as a distraction from the throb of excitement that he could not quite subdue. Very soon he would see Ralph again. Over the past year he had made a conscious effort to detach himself, to find a life that did not include Ralph. Once, in Athens, he had thought himself free of that enchantment. He was determined that this time he would not let it take hold of him again.

He had telegraphed ahead and Ralph had booked a room for him, and there was a note at the reception desk saying that he was on duty but would return in the late afternoon. Tom followed the bellboy upstairs and discovered that the room was part of the suite that Ralph had taken for himself and Leo the previous summer, so they would have adjoining bedrooms. He unpacked, washed and changed his shirt and decided to use the time before Ralph's return to pay a visit to the Malkovics. Leo had not asked him to contact them and he suspected that she would have forbidden it, but he felt that he could not return from Belgrade without at least being able to assure her that Sasha was well.

He presented his card to the butler who opened the door, and asked to see Count Aleksander. The man obviously remembered him from the previous summer but informed him regretfully that the count was not at home.

'He is with his regiment in Macedonia at present, but the countess is in residence. If you wish I can ask if she is at liberty.'

Tom remembered Sasha's mother as a warm, attractive woman who had always welcomed him, so he willingly agreed to the butler's suggestion. He was shown into an ornately decorated reception room where he spent some minutes examining a collection of dark oil paintings in heavy frames, until the butler returned to say that the countess would be happy to receive him. He followed the man up to the first floor, where he opened a door and announced: 'Mr Devenish, my lady.'

This room was much lighter, with long windows opening on to the garden, and decorated in delicate, feminine colours, but the figure which rose to greet him was not the imposing, well-upholstered one he was expecting. Instead he found himself facing a thin, pale-faced girl who appeared scarcely more than a child. She stepped forward and offered her hand.

'How do you do, Mr Devenish? We have not met, but I have heard my husband speak of you and I am very glad to make your acquaintance.'

Tom had addressed the butler in Serbian, having become reasonably fluent during his previous stay, but she spoke in careful, stilted English. Her manner and the words were perfectly correct, but he had the impression of a child playing at being grown up. For a moment he was disconcerted, then he realized what must have occurred.

'Thank you very much for agreeing to receive me at such short notice, Countess. I must offer my felicitations on your marriage. When did it take place?'

'We were married at Easter,' she replied. 'Unfortunately, my husband . . .' there was the barest hesitation in the use of the word, 'was recalled to his regiment almost immediately, so we have had very little time together.'

'That is unfortunate,' Tom murmured, 'but I suppose it is one of the penalties of being married to a distinguished soldier.' So, Sasha had fled his marriage bed at the earliest opportunity!

'Yes, you are right, of course,' she replied. 'Please, won't you sit down?'

Tom took the chair she indicated and she perched opposite

him, rigidly upright on the edge of her seat. He saw that her breathing was rapid and shallow and remembered what Leo had told him about Sasha's fiancée's delicate chest.

He said, 'How is the count? I hope he is well.'

'Thank you, yes. Last time I heard from him he was in good health.'

'And the . . . the dowager countess, his mother?'

'She is well, too. She is at the country house at the moment, with Adriana, her daughter.'

They made conversation for a few minutes more and then Tom rose. 'I won't take up any more of your time, Countess. Please give my regards to your husband when you write to him, and to your mother-in-law. I am sorry not to have seen them but I shall only be in Belgrade for a few days.'

On the way back to his hotel Tom was oppressed by a feeling of waste. He felt sorry for the fragile girl he had just left, and sorry for Sasha, bound to this pale child when he had found his perfect soulmate in Leo. He was sorrier still for Leo, stoically concealing her broken heart and determined to rebuild her life and sorry, finally, for himself, burdened with a love he could not acknowledge, let alone express.

He heard Ralph coming before he entered the hotel room: the rapid, energetic footsteps; the authoritative voice ordering tea to be sent up, in ungrammatical Serbian. Then the door opened and Ralph bounded in and seized him by the shoulders.

'Tom! My dear old chap! It's so good to see you. How are you?'

Tom gripped his upper arms briefly in response, and knew himself lost. 'I'm well, thank you. And you?'

'Fit as a flea, thanks. How about Leo?'

'She's well. She sends her love.' Tom stared into his face. 'You're growing a beard!'

'How very observant of you!'

'Why? It doesn't suit you.'

'Never mind that for the moment. When are you two going to stop shilly-shallying and name the day?'

'You know the answer to that. We are waiting for you to come home.'

'Don't wait. Name the day and then I can tell my superiors that I must have some leave to attend my sister's wedding.'

Tom's heart missed a beat. He had not thought of that and the last thing he wanted was to have their best excuse over-ridden. On the other hand, if it became really necessary to get Ralph out of Belgrade . . . As often before in the last two or three years he was oppressed by the sense that he was fated to marry Leo, whether they both wanted it or not.

Ralph was dealing with the waiter who had brought the tea. When the man left he waved Tom to a chair. 'Sit down, old chap. Have some tea and tell me what it is that has suddenly brought you back to Belgrade. I really thought once you got back to England nothing would root you out again!'

'I'm not so averse to travel as I once was,' Tom said, 'but I came because I'm worried.'

'What about?'

'About you.'

'Good lord! There's no need. I told you, I'm fine.'

'In health, perhaps. But I'm concerned about . . . the political situation here and your possible involvement in it.'

He saw a subtle change in Ralph's expression. The look of relaxed good nature was replaced by a hint of a frown and a narrowing of the eyes. 'I'm not involved with politics. I'm not allowed to be.'

'Yes, I understand that. That's why I'm worried about the sort of company you are keeping.'

'How do you know what company I keep?'

'I'm still in touch with various people over here: Max Seinfeld, for one. And they tell me you are mixing with a dangerous crowd.'

'Dangerous, in what way?'

'The Black Hand.'

'What does Seinfeld know about the Black Hand?'

'Oh, come on, Ralph. It's an open secret. Dragutin Dimitrijevic – Apis – and Tankovic and the rest have made themselves so powerful in the Serbian army that they're untouchable. Max thinks they are planning something, some-thing that could blow up in all our faces.'

'Like what?'

'He doesn't know, except he thinks it is something to do with Bosnia.' Tom leaned forward. 'The point is, Ralph, everyone knows that you have been associating with them. If they are going to do something violent it might be assumed that you were party to it. I've come to urge you to get out of Belgrade before it happens. Ask for some leave, you must be entitled to some. Come home, till all this blows over.'

Ralph put down his cup and leaned back in his chair. There was a look on his face that Tom had never seen before, a grave, calculating look that made him seem suddenly older. After a moment he gave a brief, wry smile. 'What an idiot you must think me! Do you really think I couldn't see what Apis and his cronies were up to? Do you think I hung around with them for the pleasure of their company?'

'Then why?' Tom asked.

'Because I knew they were dangerous lunatics! I thought if I could get close to them I might be able to pick up some information about what they intended and warn the authorities.'

'You were spying on them?'

'I suppose you could call it that.'

'Do you have any idea what they are planning?'

'I've been picking up clues for the last two or three months. I've seen Tankovic with some pretty unsavoury types who call themselves Young Bosnia. They are desperate to see Bosnia independent of Austria/Hungary and they will use any means that come to hand to achieve that. There's one called Gavrilo Princip, a little runt of a fellow with a fanatical look in his eyes, and another called Illic, who seems to be the leader. I'm pretty sure Tankovic has supplied them with weapons and training in how to use them, but I couldn't guess what for until a few days ago.'

'And now you can?'

'Archduke Franz Ferdinand of Austria is coming to Bosnia in two days' time to review the troops on manoeuvre there and afterwards he's due at a reception in Sarajevo. He must be the prime target.'

'Good God! Have you told anyone what you suspect?'

'I went to see our ambassador and told him but I don't think he took it seriously. After all, I have no proof. It's all speculation.'

'What about your contacts in the Serb military?'

'What would be the point? Apis is Chief of Military Intelligence so all I would be doing is exposing myself as a potential danger. Anyway, the Serbs won't shed too many tears over a rift with Austria.'

'Couldn't you warn the authorities in Bosnia, or even the Austrians themselves?'

'And be the cause of an international incident? There's nothing the Austrians would like better than an excuse to invade. I don't want that on my conscience.'

'If Apis and the rest suspected that someone had passed information to the authorities, could that be traced back to you?'

'Possibly.'

'Then for God's sake, Ralph, that makes it all the more vital for you to get out of the country.'

'Not yet. There's no official approach open to me so that means I have to find some other way to put a stop to it.'

'You? How? What can you do, on your own?'

'I don't know yet. But perhaps I'm not entirely on my own any more. Can I rely on you, Tom?'

A sudden sense of déjà vu swept over Tom. How many times had he looked into those amber eyes, just as he was doing now, and been inveigled into taking part in some mad scheme that could end in disaster for them both? But he had never refused before, and he knew he could not now. He sighed deeply. 'You know you can – as always.'

Ralph leaned forward and gripped his wrist. 'Good man! You never know, one day the world may be grateful to us, because if this assassination attempt succeeds it could bring the whole of Europe to the brink of war.'

'But what on earth do you imagine we can do?' Tom asked.

'Probably nothing, but we have to try. I've already made a rough plan – well, a starting point, at any rate. Today is June the twenty-sixth, in our calendar, but in the Julian calendar, which was in use then, it's June the thirteenth. June the fifteenth is St Vitus' Day, Vidovdan in Serbian, which commemorates the battle of Kosovo against the Turks in 1389. It's a very important date for patriotic Serbs, so it is the obvious date for the assassination attempt. Now, I happened to hear Danilo Illic tell Tankovic that his mother keeps a boarding house in Sarajevo. I've arranged to take seventy-two hours leave, starting tomorrow, and booked a room there. You can join me. If there isn't a spare room we can always share.'

'You can't just turn up there and expect no one to smell a rat!' Tom exclaimed.

'Not as the British military attaché, no. I can't go in uniform, so I'm going to pose as an English student travelling in Europe during the summer vacation.'

'But surely you'll be recognized?'

Ralph rubbed his chin. 'What do you think this is all in aid of?'

'You really think growing a beard will be enough?'

'Look, I've never been introduced to these chaps. Tankovic always hustles them off to a private room. They have only seen me from a distance, and in uniform. I'm just the British officer who hangs around playing cards with Tankovic and his friends. I don't suppose they've given me a second thought. Why should they connect me with a scruffy, bearded student?'

'Aren't we a bit long in the tooth to be students?' Tom asked.

'Not in this part of the world. Being a student is a way of life here. People often go on until they are thirty or more.'

Tom sat back with a sigh. He knew it would be pointless to argue any more. Ralph had made up his mind and once he was set on some mad escapade there was no deflecting him. All he could do was go along and try to limit the damage.

Three

Madame Illic's boarding house was located in one of the less salubrious areas of Sarajevo but the room she showed them into was clean and adequately, if sparsely furnished. All the other rooms were taken but she made no objection to Tom sharing with Ralph. The prospect of sleeping with him in the one big double bed sent a shiver through Tom's nerves but Ralph seemed happy to accept it.

'It fits in with the picture we want to present, of two impoverished students hiking round Europe,' he pointed out.

They had dressed accordingly, though Tom had been forced to allow a good pair of trousers to be rubbed in the dirt and a shirt collar deliberately frayed. The rest of their essential requirements had been stuffed into two well-worn rucksacks that Ralph had acquired by some means.

Ralph threw his on to the bed. 'Right. Let's go and have a wander round and get our bearings.'

As they descended the stairs they heard voices in the hallway below and Ralph gripped Tom's arm and pulled him to a standstill. Two men crossed the hall and went out of the front door: one tallish and around thirty years old, Tom guessed; the other a thin, dark-haired youth.

'That's them,' Ralph whispered when they had gone out. 'The tall one is Illic and the other is Princip, the wild-eyed fanatic I told you about. Let's follow and see where they go.'

The two men led them to a café a few streets away. It was evening and the streets were busy with people going home from work or strolling out to enjoy the coolness after a hot summer day. It was not difficult to keep their quarry in sight without making it obvious that they were being followed. The restaurants and cafés were filling up but they found a table in a corner where they could see Illic and Princip, who had been joined by a third man in working clothes with a narrow, dark face. The three leaned close together, talking earnestly, but

Tom and Ralph were too far away to hear what was being said. After about an hour, they left and made their way back to the boarding house. Once inside, the three disappeared into Madame Illic's private sitting room, leaving Tom and Ralph as the only occupants of the small, dark lounge that was available for guests. It was not long, however, before the door bell rang and Tom saw, through the half-open lounge door, two more men being admitted by Illic and taken through to the private room.

Ralph got to his feet. 'That's two more of them – Grabez and Cabrinovic. I've seen them all hanging around Tankovic and the other Black Handers in Belgrade. I'm right, Tom! Something is about to happen. If only we could hear what's going on in that room!'

Before Tom could protest he slipped out into the hall and crept towards the door of the private room. After a moment, he beckoned urgently and Tom joined him.

'Listen!' Ralph whispered.

Tom strained his ears. At first all he could hear was a mumble of voices, then the sound of a heavy piece of furniture being moved, followed by an excited babble, quickly suppressed. Then, quite distinctly, he heard Illic say, 'Here, Gavrilo, you take this one. Careful! It's loaded!'

Ralph met his eyes and jerked his head back towards the lounge. Once there, he whispered, 'He's distributing guns! Now we've got something definite to go on.'

'So far we've only got what we think we have heard through a closed door,' Tom pointed out. 'It's their word against ours.'

'True,' Ralph agreed. 'We need to catch one of them actually in possession of a weapon. The only solution I can think of is if we can get one of them on his own, take him by surprise and search him. Then we could drag him in front of the authorities and get them to arrest the others.'

'That's crazy, Ralph!' Tom objected. 'How are we going to overpower a man armed with a gun?'

'He's not the only one with a weapon,' Ralph replied, patting his pocket. 'You don't really think I left my own pistol behind, do you?'

At that moment they heard the door of the private room

open and footsteps crossed the hall. There was a confusion of voices: 'Goodnight', 'Take care', 'Till tomorrow'. Then Illic's voice: 'You all know your stations. Make sure you are there in good time. Courage, boys! Not long now.'

The front door slammed and they heard Illic and Princip return to the private room.

'Quick!' Ralph said. 'After them!'

Before Tom could object he was heading for the front door. Outside it was now dark, except for the glow of infrequent street lights, but they were in time to see the three conspirators turning the corner at the end of the street.

'What are you going to do?' Tom asked, as they followed.

'I don't know yet,' was the terse reply.

They followed the three down the street until they turned abruptly and disappeared from view. When they reached the place, Tom saw that they had gone down a narrow alley where the houses on either side blocked out all but the faintest gleam of starlight.

'Ralph, this is stupid!' he said, as his friend plunged into the alley after them, but Ralph took no notice. The three men, who were all wearing dark clothes, had almost vanished but Tom could hear their footsteps moving away. Then they seemed to come to a halt and he perceived a blacker darkness ahead and realized suddenly that the alley ended in a blank wall. Ralph saw it at the same instant and came to a halt, but it was too late. There was movement behind them and a torch was turned on, focusing first on Tom and then on Ralph.

Illic's voice spoke from the shadow behind the light. 'You fool! Did you imagine that I would not recognize you because you have grown a beard?'

Tom looked at Ralph and had a ridiculous impulse to say, 'There, you see? What did I tell you?' But the words were immediately suppressed by the sight of a gun barrel glinting in the torchlight. Princip was standing beside Illic, his weapon trained on Ralph. Tom felt the others move closer behind him and cold metal prodded his ribs.

Ralph was saying, in English, 'I don't understand. I'm a student from England. What is this all about?'

Illic either did not understand or chose to ignore the remark. 'Search them!'

Hands quested through Tom's pockets and patted his body. A similar search soon produced Ralph's pistol. 'British army issue!' Illic said. 'As I expected. Move!'

The gun in Tom's ribs gave a sharp jab and he moved forwards. Together they headed back towards Illic's house, the men they had been following clustering close around them to conceal the weapons pressed into their backs. In the house, Illic opened a door that revealed a steep flight of steps leading down to what Tom assumed was a cellar. There was no light, and he almost missed his footing at the bottom and stumbled into Ralph, earning a muttered curse from one of his captors. He could hear Illic groping around and then the sound of a match being struck and a single candle guttered into life.

'Sit!' Illic barked, and Tom was pushed down on to what felt like a barrel, with Ralph close by. Illic lifted the candle and stood over them.

'Do you think I haven't noticed you hanging around Tankovic in Belgrade?' he asked Ralph. 'I didn't realize you were a spy until I saw you this afternoon in the café. What did you think you were going to do?'

Ralph shook his head, still pretending incomprehension. 'Look here, I don't know what all this is about, but we are British citizens. You won't get away with kidnapping us.'

For answer Illic struck him hard across the mouth with the butt of his gun. 'Stop this! I know you understand Serbian, and speak it. You masquerade as a British officer, but you are a spy. Who are you working for? Tell me! What are you doing here? Who sent you?'

'No one,' Ralph answered in Serbian. 'I knew you were up to something and I wanted to find out what it was.'

'What are we wasting time for?' Princip said, his eyes glittering in the candlelight. 'Shoot them and have done with it.'

'Not yet,' Illic answered. 'I don't believe they are acting alone. We need to find out who else knows about us.' He turned on Tom. 'You! Who are you? Where do you fit in?'

Tom had had time to think and had spent it desperately trying to concoct a story that might at least buy them a little time. 'You have got it wrong,' he said. 'He's not the spy. I am. My masters in London have heard rumours about the Black Hand and its intentions. They sent me here with a message for you. Britain and Serbia are allies, but if you are responsible for an act that plunges us into a war we will withdraw our support. Serbia will be left to fight alone. Is that what you want?'

For a second he thought he saw Illic's eyes flicker and he felt the other men stir uneasily in the darkness. Then Illic said, 'Why should we care? We have other allies. We defeated the Turks and the Bulgarians. We can defeat Austria.'

'And suppose Britain were to throw her support behind the Austrians?' Tom said. He knew it was an impossible scenario but he had seen that faint shadow of doubt in Illic's eyes. 'My government might be prepared to turn a blind eye to regicide and remain neutral as long as its own citizens are not involved. But my masters know where I am and who I am investigating. If we were to be harmed they might take a very different view.'

'He's bluffing!' Princip insisted. 'Shoot them. None of this will matter tomorrow.'

'Not to us, perhaps,' Illic said. 'But we are not acting for our own benefit. As you say, after tomorrow it will not matter who they tell. We are not butchers. Why should we stain our sacred cause with their blood? They can do us no harm locked in here. Come, we should get some sleep.'

He turned and made his way to the stairs and after a moment's hesitation the others followed. At the top of the steps Illic turned back. 'Goodnight, gentlemen. Sleep well. We shall not meet again.'

The five men went out and Tom heard the door slammed shut and the sound of bolts being shot home. In the faint light of the candle he stood up and turned to Ralph.

'By God, Ralph, you've got me into some pretty messes before this, but this is the last time, I swear it!'

Ralph came closer and gripped his arm. 'All I can say is thank God I brought you with me. That was a brilliant piece of play-acting. I didn't know you had it in you.'

Tom lowered himself back on to the barrel. 'Nor did I,' he said, shakily.

Ralph took the candle and climbed the steps and Tom heard

him testing the door, shaking it and putting his weight against it. 'It's no good,' he said at length. 'It's rock solid. We'll never break that down.'

He came down again and began to feel his way around the cellar, running his hands over the walls. Eventually he returned to sit by Tom. 'That's the only way out. We're stuck here till someone lets us out.'

'What do you think Illic meant when he said we should not meet again?' Tom asked, feeling a shiver run down his spine.

'And all that about it not mattering after tomorrow,' Ralph said, nodding. 'I'm afraid there's only one interpretation. They plan to assassinate the archduke and then commit suicide.'

'All of them?'

'It seems like it. They have a hero to imitate. Four years ago a man called Zerajic tried to assassinate the Governor of Bosnia. He missed and then put a bullet into his own brain. Boys like Princip see him as a martyr. Besides, Tankovic wouldn't want anyone left alive to implicate him. He's probably provided them with the means for a quick death.'

'You do realize what that could mean for us?' Tom said. 'They are the only people who know we are here. If they are all dead . . .'

'Cheer up,' Ralph patted his arm. 'Once we're sure they are out of the way we can kick up such a row that his mother is bound to hear us. There's no point until then. It might prompt Princip to come back and carry out his threats. I suggest we make ourselves as comfortable as we can and try to get some sleep.'

After grovelling around on the dusty floor for a while Ralph came upon some old sacks that smelt powerfully of stale beer and they lay down on them side by side. Ralph curled himself against Tom's back and put his arm across him.

'Might as well keep each other as warm as we can,' he said.

There was little sleep for either of them. Before long the candle burnt out, leaving them in pitch darkness. The floor was hard and cold in spite of the sacking and now they were silent they could hear rustlings and scufflings all around them. Once Tom felt something run across his legs. The hours passed slowly but eventually Tom surfaced from a deeper doze and saw that the cellar was no longer completely dark. Away at the far end there was a faint gleam of light that seemed to be coming from the roof. Ralph was asleep, snoring faintly, so Tom got up carefully and groped his way towards the light. Looking up, he saw that it was coming through a small crack and that what he had taken for a solid ceiling was, at that point, made up of boards. At that moment he heard the unmistakable sound of footsteps above his head and then what sounded like wheels.

He returned to where Ralph was lying and shook him awake. 'Listen, I think I may have found a way out.'

Ralph sat up immediately. 'Where? How?'

'Over here.' Tom led him to the point where the light was filtering in. 'You know what I think? This was once a beer cellar. It certainly smells like one and there are barrels here. Think of pubs at home. How does the beer get delivered?'

'Oh, I'm with you!' Ralph exclaimed. 'There's a trapdoor in the pavement outside and when the brewer's dray arrives they just open the trap and roll the barrels down into the cellar. So that trapdoor leads straight out on to the street.'

'If I'm right,' Tom agreed.

'I'm certain you are! What time is it?'

'Just after six a.m.'

'So not too many people about yet, with any luck. Do you think we can force that trap open?'

'I won't know till we try. First of all we have to find a way of reaching it.'

A further search of the cellar in the faint light revealed several empty barrels but even when standing on one neither of them could reach the trapdoor. They piled one on another and Tom made a stirrup out of his hands so that Ralph could climb on to them. That was far from ideal because now he was too high up and had to work in a semi-crouching position, but at least he was able to find the two bolts that held the door.

'They're rusted solid,' he reported. 'It's going to be the devil's own job getting them free.'

'Wait a minute,' Tom said. He groped around until he found the remains of the candle sitting in a puddle of congealed wax. 'Try working some of this into them.'

It took the two of them, working in turn, over an hour to free the bolts but eventually Ralph was able to report, 'Right, I can move them now. But when I pull them out the trap will drop down and it will be open to the street.'

'Just pray no one is about to walk across,' Tom said. 'Otherwise they might be joining us down here, with a broken leg.'

'Pray Princip or one of the others isn't standing guard with his gun ready,' Ralph retorted. 'When I open the trap, we need to be out as fast as we can. I'll climb out and then pull you up. Can you manage that?'

'I'll have to,' Tom said.

'Ready, steady, go!' Ralph said, and pulled out both bolts. The trapdoor dropped open with a creak of hinges, showering Tom with dust, and Ralph grabbed the edges of the opening and hauled himself up. His efforts dislodged the top barrel and Tom had to jump aside to avoid it. He heard a small scream and a woman's voice raised in remonstration and Ralph's apology in mangled Serbian. Then Ralph leaned into the hole and stretched out his arm.

'Come on, quick!'

Tom climbed on to the barrel that remained in place, grabbed Ralph's hand and jumped. His free hand reached the wooden frame round the opening, and he felt splinters pierce the flesh. He hung for a moment, kicking his legs, then Ralph hauled him up till he lay like a stranded fish across the edge of the trapdoor. He scrambled to his feet and looked round. There were few people about, and he remembered that it was Sunday. Two women, on their way, he guessed, to early mass, looked curiously in their direction but no one seemed inclined to question them.

Ralph was peering into the cellar. 'I don't see how we can fasten the trapdoor back in place, so anyone from the house would see at once that we had escaped. The best thing we can do is get away as quickly as we can and try to blend in with the crowd.'

'Once we're on the train for Belgrade we should be safe enough, shouldn't we?' Tom asked.

'Train? We can't just get on the train. For God's sake, Tom!

There's an assassination about to take place, unless we can find a way to stop it.'

Tom choked back a protest. 'All right. What do you suggest we do?'

'Inform the authorities. We must have enough proof now to convince them to take action.'

As they headed for the centre of the city the streets grew more crowded. People were heading for the Appel Quay, the road along which the archduke's motorcade would pass. Ralph stopped one man and asked what time it was expected.

'Soon after ten o'clock, if he keeps to the schedule,' was the reply.

Ralph looked at his watch. 'It's nearly nine. There's still time. Either the whole procession must be abandoned, or at least he must go by a different route.'

They had to ask the way to the town hall, where the reception was due to take place, and when they reached it they found all access to the building barred by the police.

'Listen to me!' Ralph said to the man barring their way. 'I am the British military attaché in Belgrade. I have urgent information regarding the archduke's visit. I must speak to the mayor at once.'

The policeman looked him up and down and Tom was suddenly aware of the picture they must present, dirty and unshaven, their deliberately shabby clothes further rumpled and torn by their efforts in the cellar.

'Do you have any identification, sir?' he asked.

Ralph put his hand to his pocket and swore. He had intentionally left behind anything that might identify him as a British soldier. 'No, I don't, because I have been kidnapped and locked up in a cellar. All my papers were stolen. There is going to be an attempt on the archduke's life. I must speak to someone in authority.'

The policeman hesitated, then called to a colleague and the two conferred in undertones. From the glances cast in their direction Tom inferred that they were being cast as madmen or troublemakers, but after a moment the second man went off into the building and the first returned to them.

'I've sent a message to the captain. You'll have to wait here until he's free to talk to you.'

'But don't you understand?' Ralph expostulated. 'It's a matter of the utmost urgency.'

'So you say,' the policeman said stolidly. 'But I've done everything I can do. It's against orders for me to let anyone into the building.'

Minutes passed and Ralph paced backwards and forwards, clenching and unclenching his fists. Tom kept watch on the crowd behind them, fearing at any moment to see Illic or one of his cronies. If their escape had been discovered he had no doubt that the conspirators would be looking for them, and this time they would not hesitate to shoot.

After a long wait a man in the uniform of a police captain came down the steps and Ralph repeated his story.

'Kidnapped, you say?' the captain queried. 'Have you reported this?'

'No! There isn't time. The men who kidnapped us are planning to assassinate the archduke. You must get a message to him. He must stay away from Sarajevo.'

The captain frowned at him for a moment and then said, 'You had better come with me.'

'At last!' Ralph exclaimed.

His relief was short-lived. They were conducted to a small office and told to wait while the captain went in search of his superior officer. More time passed. Eventually two men arrived: one a colonel in the police and the other, in civilian clothes, who introduced himself as the mayor's secretary. Ralph embarked on his story again.

'One moment,' the colonel interrupted, looking at Tom. 'Who is this?'

Tom gave his name and explained that he was a friend of Ralph's from England, simply here on a visit. The colonel appeared to regard this with some suspicion and Tom could understand why. Ralph outlined the reasoning that had brought him to Sarajevo and described the events of the previous evening, adding the names and descriptions of the five conspirators. There followed a lengthy and ponderous inquisition and it became obvious that the colonel viewed everything they said

with extreme scepticism. Tom saw that Ralph was struggling
to remain calm but as the minutes ticked by he grew more
and more frustrated. Finally, he jumped to his feet and thumped
the desk where the colonel was sitting.

'Do you not understand? There are men out there determined to murder the heir to the Austrian Empire, on the
streets of your city. It could start a war. Do you want that on
your conscience?'

The colonel looked at his watch. 'The archduke will already
be on his way. It is too late to stop him now. I assure you, all
precautions have been taken for his safety but I will go and
give orders for everyone to be on the alert.' He rose. 'I will
send someone to take down your statement regarding the
kidnapping. Wait here, please.'

'Wait!' Ralph stormed. 'Wait! Is that all you can say?'

But the colonel and the secretary had already left the room.

Ralph turned to Tom. 'Come on. There's no point in
hanging about here.'

'Will they let us leave?' Tom asked.

'We'll soon find out,' Ralph replied.

The corridor outside was empty, although they could hear
voices and footsteps from above, moving towards the front of
the building.

'This way,' Ralph said, heading in the opposite direction.

A few minutes later they emerged, unchallenged, from a
service entrance at the rear. As they turned towards the main
street Tom felt the ground under his feet shudder and heard
the noise of an explosion from somewhere not far distant.
Ralph stopped dead.

'What was that?'

'A bomb,' Tom replied. He had heard enough on the battle-
fields of Kosovo to be in no doubt. 'I'm afraid we're too late.'

'The bastards!' Ralph ground out. 'That stupid, bloody
colonel! They could have avoided this if only they had listened.'

'You did your best,' Tom said. 'There's nothing more we
can do now.'

In the main street there was chaos. Some of the crowd,
impelled by curiosity, were trying to hurry in the direction of
the explosion; others, terrified, were attempting to run the

opposite way. On the steps of the town hall, where the official reception party were waiting, there was much agitated waving of arms and running to and fro. Then, into this confusion, came the sound of engines and three motor cars appeared, driven at speed. In the first there were uniformed policemen, while the second contained high-ranking officers, to judge by the amount of medals and gold braid. The third car was a Graf and Stift cabriolet, its top folded back to reveal the moustachioed figure of the Archduke Franz Ferdinand with his wife at his side.

'They missed!' Ralph exclaimed. 'The incompetent idiots missed! Thank God!'

'Who are the other two with them?' Tom asked.

'The fat one is Potiorek, the Governor of Bosnia. I assume the other is an aide-de-camp.'

The three cars screeched to a halt at the foot of the steps and the archduke got out to be met by the mayor. Tom was too far away to hear what was said, but it was obvious from the archduke's demeanour that he was extremely angry – with reason, Tom reflected. The royal party and their entourage were conducted quickly into the town hall and the crowd on the pavement began to disperse.

'What now?' Tom asked.

'The archduke is entertained to lunch, there are the usual speeches and then he's due to open the state museum, but if they've got any sense they'll get him out of the city by the shortest route,' Ralph responded.

'I meant, what next for us?' Tom said. 'But do you mean there could be another attempt?'

'There are at least five men involved in the conspiracy, to our knowledge,' Ralph pointed out. 'I presume the entire Sarajevo police force is looking for them now, but if I was in charge I certainly wouldn't take any chances.'

'Well, I don't see that there is anything more we can do,' Tom said. 'Let's get back to Belgrade.'

'The next train doesn't leave until this evening,' Ralph pointed out. 'There's no point in sitting in the station for hours. Let's go and see what happened.'

They made their way through the crowd until they came to the road running beside the Miljacka River. Here there was a dense knot of people, but between their shoulders Tom saw a large crater in the road and beyond it another official car, its doors open, windscreen smashed and bonnet a twisted mass of blackened metal. On the far side of the road, by the river bank, three policemen held a bedraggled figure who was writhing in their grasp as if in agony.

'It's Cabrinovic!' Ralph murmured in Tom's ear.

'What happened?' Tom asked a man standing near him. 'Did you see?'

'That fellow threw a bomb at the archduke's car,' was the reply. 'It bounced off the hood and landed in the road behind.'

'What has happened to him?' Tom inquired, indicating the assassin. 'Why is he all wet?'

His informant gave a harsh guffaw. 'The fool swallowed something and jumped into the river. He obviously isn't a local or he'd have known it's only a few inches deep at that point. Some men dragged him out and gave him a good kicking before the police got to him.'

As they spoke a police motorcyclist forced his way through the crowd and circled the hole in the road to reach the damaged car. He dismounted and leaned into it, obviously searching for something, and finally straightened up with a sheaf of papers in his hand. As he passed Tom, heading back towards the town hall, Tom saw that they were wet with blood.

'Clearly someone didn't escape unharmed,' he said. 'What do you think those papers were? Documents of state?'

'More likely the archduke's notes for his speech,' Ralph replied with a humourless laugh.

They watched Cabrinovic being taken away and then Ralph yawned suddenly. 'Do you know, I am ravenous! We haven't eaten since last night. Let's find some food.'

'I don't think we are in a fit state to go into a restaurant,' Tom said, indicating their filthy clothes.

'True,' Ralph agreed. 'Let's see if we can find somewhere we can buy a sandwich.'

They walked a little further along the river, until they came to the Latin Bridge. Ralph pointed across the road. 'Look, there's a place – Schiller's delicatessen. We should be able to get something there.'

They bought sandwiches and sat at a small table in a corner to eat them. Tom felt himself grow drowsy after his broken night, but he could not relax. The image of Cabrinovic twisting and vomiting in his captors' grip alternated in his mind with the thought that Illic and the rest were still at large and might be looking for them. It must be assumed that their escape had been discovered by now. 'What do you think Cabrinovic swallowed?' he asked Ralph.

His friend shrugged. 'I'm not a medical man. I should have thought cyanide was the obvious thing, but that is supposed to work much faster – unless there was something wrong with it. I wouldn't put it past Tankovic to have supplied them with pills that had been kept so long they had lost their efficacy.'

'He looked so young,' Tom said. 'Just a boy, really.'

'They all are,' Ralph agreed, 'except for Illic. No wonder the whole plan has gone off at half cock, when you give bombs and guns to a lot of teenagers with hardly any training.'

'Look, can we get away from here and find somewhere quiet?' Tom said. 'My head is bursting.'

Ralph paid the bill and they were just getting up to leave when he grabbed Tom's arm. 'Keep your head down! Princip has just come in.'

'Where is he?'

'Over at the counter, buying a sandwich.'

'Is anyone else with him?'

'No, he seems to be alone. This is our chance, Tom. We'll wait till he leaves the shop and then grab him. His testimony will be enough to put Tankovic and all the rest of the Black Hand in the dock.'

Tom had his back to the rest of the shop and Ralph picked up a newspaper and held it in front of his face, glancing over the top of it every few seconds. After a moment he said, 'He's going. Come on.'

They rose and followed the slight figure out of the shop. He paused at the kerb, biting into his sandwich, and at that moment the official cars reappeared, heading out of the city. The two leading vehicles crossed the bridge, the Graf and Stift following, with the archduke and his wife and the governor;

the aide-de-camp now standing protectively on the left-hand running board.

'My God, that was close!' Ralph said, adding abruptly: 'Now what? What the devil . . . ?'

The Graf and Stift was reversing, bringing it back to a point immediately opposite the delicatessen. Paralysed, as in a nightmare, Tom saw Princip drop his sandwich and reach into his pocket. Drawing his pistol he stepped forward, close to the right-hand side of the car and fired once. The archduke jerked backwards, blood spurting from his neck. Ralph was already plunging towards the assassin and as Princip raised the weapon again, aiming at the governor, he attempted to knock the gun out of his hand. The weapon went off and Sophie, the duchess, collapsed against her husband. Several passers-by leapt on Princip and wrestled him to the ground, but not before he had crammed something into his mouth. Meanwhile, the car accelerated away, heading back into the city.

Ralph sunk to his knees with his head in his hands. Tom grabbed him by the arm and pulled him up.

'What have I done?' he cried. 'I meant to knock his arm up. Are they both dead?'

'I don't know,' Tom said. 'Perhaps not. They were both still upright. Maybe the wounds were not fatal.'

Princip was being dragged away, writhing and vomiting in the same manner as Cabrinovic. Tom looked at Ralph. He was deadly pale and shaking. 'Come on. We're going to the station. If we can't get on a train to Belgrade we'll catch the first one that comes along. The sooner we get out of this place the better.'

Four

On June 29 the following headline appeared on page eight of the London *Times*:

AUSTRIAN HEIR AND HIS WIFE MURDERED
SHOT IN BOSNIAN TOWN

Five hours later a telegram arrived at the hotel in Belgrade to which Tom and Ralph had returned that morning. Addressed to Ralph it read: *Leonora seriously ill. Imperative you return immediately. Victoria*

When the two men reached Sussex Gardens, weary and travel-stained after three days and nights with little rest, they found Leo fully dressed, sitting at her writing desk in the morning room. Tom hurried towards her.

'Leo! What are you doing? Why aren't you in bed?'

Leo stood up and took his hand. 'I'm sorry, Tom. I'm afraid I deceived you. But I had good reason.'

'Deceived!' her brother broke in. 'Do you mean you're not ill? What was that telegram all about? Was it some kind of a joke? I bet that Langford woman was behind it.'

'Victoria sent the telegram,' Leo agreed. 'But it was my idea.'

'I don't understand,' Tom said. 'Why?'

'Have you any idea what you have put us through?' Ralph demanded. 'We have had a horrendous journey. Everyone is trying to get out of Serbia. There were no berths left on the Orient Express from Belgrade. We had to travel third class on a local train as far as Vienna, sitting up all night. Then when we picked up the Express there, it was packed. The whole of Europe seems to be on the move.'

'To say nothing of our anxiety about you.' Tom put it quietly.

'Well, that too, of course,' Ralph added.

'I know,' Leo said, squeezing Tom's hand. 'And I really am sorry. But as soon as I saw the headline in the paper I knew it was vital to get you out of Serbia as quickly as possible. It was the only way I could think of to make sure you got leave straight away, Ralph.'

'But what made you think we needed to get out?' her brother asked.

'It seems to me that Austria and Serbia could be at war at any moment and then it would be almost impossible for you to travel. And Tom told me you were mixed up with this Black Hand gang. It was them, wasn't it, behind the assassination? So if the Austrians demand that they are handed over to justice . . . I mean, I know you couldn't have been really involved, but I just thought . . .'

Ralph and Tom looked at each other and suddenly they both laughed. Ralph put his arm round Leo's shoulders. 'Oh, little Sis, you don't know the half of it! Shall I tell her, Tom, or will you?'

Over the next weeks the whole country was gripped by frenzied speculation about the possibility of war. Ralph summarized the situation succinctly.

'If Austria declares war on Serbia the Serbs will invoke the mutual defence treaty they have with Russia. France has treaty obligations to Russia, and we have agreements with the French that commit us. And the Germans are itching for a fight so that will be all the excuse they need to come in on the Austrian side.'

'And the whole of Europe is plunged into chaos,' Leo said.

'It might not be a bad thing, in the long run,' Ralph declared. 'It's time the Germans were put in their place.'

That seemed to be the general view in the country and Leo felt increasingly that only she and Victoria and a few others who had seen war at first-hand understood the implications. One of the voices raised against the prevailing mood belonged to someone they knew well. Mabel Stobart, the founder of the Women's Sick and Wounded Convoy, with whom they had worked in Bulgaria, had returned from Canada and involved herself in local politics, becoming a councillor for Hampstead Garden Suburb. Leo and Victoria had kept in touch and been invited to her home on several occasions, where they met several other influential women who were all opposed to war, but their voices were drowned by the increasingly bellicose chorus.

On 23 July the Austrians sent an ultimatum to Serbia, demanding among other things that a full investigation into those responsible for the assassination should be carried out by Austrian police officers on Serbian territory. The newspapers reported that Serbia was mobilizing troops but on the 27 July *The Times* carried an article detailing the Serb reply, which accepted all the Austrian demands except one. The following day Austria declared war on Serbia.

Leo followed these developments with anguish, knowing that Sasha was bound to be at the forefront of the fighting. When the papers reported on 29 July that the first shells had fallen on Belgrade she wept helplessly, not only for him but for all the friends she had made there. She remembered them as cultivated and courteous people, with great warmth and zest for life, but also an intense pride in their nation and its history and she knew that they would fight to the last man.

On 3 August the news came that Germany had declared war on France and invaded Belgium.

On 4 August Leo received a note from Mabel Stobart, asking her to attend a meeting in the Kingsway Hall which was billed as 'Women's Protest Against War'. Arriving with Victoria, she discovered that the hall was packed and a number of the women she had met at Stobart's house were on the platform, together with representatives from Finland, Hungary and Switzerland. Stobart was one of the speakers, forcefully putting forward the point of view that the two younger women had often heard her express in Bulgaria – that war was a barbarity and an expression of the double standards of morality which prevailed for men and women; that while women were expected to nurture and protect, men were allowed to kill and destroy. A resolution, passed unanimously, declared that 'Whatever its results, the conflict will leave mankind the poorer, will set back civilization, and will be a powerful check to the amelioration of the conditions of the masses of people on which the real welfare of nations depends'.

As the meeting broke up news arrived from the Palace of

Westminster that the government had decided to declare war
on Germany and her allies. Leo and Victoria were standing
with Mrs Stobart when it arrived and they were immediately
approached by a woman they knew as Lady Muir McKenzie,
a prominent peace activist.

'What will your plans be now?' she asked Mrs Stobart.

'I have always believed,' was the reply, 'that women can and
should take an active part in national defence, but in the relief
of suffering and care for the wounded.'

'Then I will support any efforts you make in setting up
women's units for that purpose,' Lady Muir McKenzie
responded.

'And you can count on us to join you,' Leo added.

As they drove away, Victoria said, 'I don't think you should
have promised to join Stobart. We're FANYs first and foremost.
I know we went off to join Stobart's lot two years ago, but
that was because the FANY weren't involved.'

'And what makes you think this time will be any different?'
Leo asked.

'It has to be!' Victoria exclaimed. 'Otherwise, what is the
point of all the training we've done?'

'Ashley-Smith isn't even around to take charge,' Leo pointed
out. 'She has gone off to South Africa to see her sister.'

'Never mind. Franklin will do what's necessary. After all,
we've got Sir Arthur Sloggett, the Chief Commissioner of the
Red Cross, on our side now. You remember how impressed
the surgeon general was when he inspected us last summer
camp. He got Ash an interview with Sir Arthur and she said
she felt convinced he would find a use for us if the time ever
came.'

'Well, it's come now,' Leo said, 'but I'm not so sure that
attitudes have changed that much.'

Leo found more urgent concerns waiting for her when she
reached home. Beavis handed her a note. *All leave cancelled. We
are to hold ourselves ready to embark for France at a moment's notice.
Will try to get home to say goodbye if possible. Don't worry about
me. It will all be over in a few weeks. Take care of yourself. Love,
Ralph.*

Leo could imagine her brother making his preparations, excited, nervous perhaps but eager to find himself doing what he had trained for all these years, and the image made her choke with distress. Although at twenty-three he was two years older he seemed such an innocent with his bright self-confidence, and she knew he was destined to be horribly disillusioned. She could not share his belief that the war would be over so soon and now it seemed to her that everyone she cared for was about to be swept up in its chaos.

Her breakfast next morning was disturbed by the sound of music and cheering. She rang for Millie, newly promoted to parlour maid, and asked her what was going on.

'It's the soldiers, miss!' the girl told her, her face flushed with excitement. 'The streets are full of people cheering them as they march off to the war.'

Leo was scanning the newspapers in the morning room when Beavis announced, 'Mr Devenish, madam.'

Glancing up, she had a momentary illusion that Beavis had gone mad and announced the wrong man, as she saw khaki breeches ending in polished boots with spurs. Raising her eyes she realized that she was the one who was mistaken.

'Tom?' She got up quickly, unable for a moment to find words. 'What have you done?'

'I've joined up,' he said. It was a statement of fact, without emotion.

'But why? You hate the idea of war, as much as I do. What ever possessed you?'

He came closer to her. 'It isn't quite what you think. I'm going to be a war artist.'

'Is there such a thing?'

'Apparently. I had a letter from a man called Charles Masterman, asking me to go and see him. It seems he came to my exhibition and was favourably impressed. Now he has been appointed head of the War Propaganda Bureau.'

'Propaganda?' Leo said doubtfully.

'I know what you are thinking. I told him I was not prepared to be the tool of some government machine churning out pictures to glorify war. He said that isn't what he wants. He wants pictures that show the reality of war, so that people at home will understand what the troops are going through. That seemed to me to be an honourable endeavour.'

'Of course it is,' Leo responded warmly. 'But was it necessary to join up to do that?'

'It seems I couldn't be given access to what is happening at the front unless I'm in uniform. And I felt I had to do something, Leo. I can't sit at home in safety while Ralph and men like him face the danger. Anyway, I suspect it won't be long before none of us has any choice in the matter.'

'Conscription, you mean?'

'It's bound to come, in my opinion.' He smiled at her. 'And there is a bonus to doing it this way. They are making me a second lieutenant and I was asked which regiment I wanted to be attached to. So, obviously I said Second Battalion, the Coldstream Guards.'

'Ralph's battalion!'

'Exactly. So I'll be able to keep an eye on him, at the same time as making my pictures.'

'And he can keep an eye on you,' Leo said.

'Either way, we'll be together.'

She took his hand. 'That's something, at least. It's the only bright spot I can see in all this horror.'

He nodded and pressed her fingers. 'There's one more thing I want to talk to you about. This engagement of ours . . . We both know it was a matter of convenience, for both of us, and up to a point it has served its purpose. But now . . .' he hesitated, 'now I think it may be time to . . . well, wipe the slate clean and start afresh. God knows how long this war will last, and it's entirely possible that I may not survive.' She made to protest but he silenced her with a quick gesture. 'Let's be realistic, Leo. What I am trying to say is this: I don't want you to be tied to a spurious engagement that was never intended to result in a marriage. You should be free.'

'Free?' she queried. 'Free for what – for whom? You know where my heart is.'

'Come and sit down a moment.' He drew her towards a sofa and she sat beside him. 'There's something I haven't told you. When I went to Belgrade I called on the Malkovics.'

'You saw Sasha!'

'No. He was with the army in Macedonia. But I was received by the countess.'

'I always liked Sasha's mother. How is she? Had she heard from him?'

He shook his head slowly. 'It wasn't the dowager countess. It was the new one.'

For a moment she was puzzled. 'The new one?' Then it hit her. 'Sasha's married. Of course, I should have known.' She removed her hand from Tom's and pressed her palms together. She knew it was foolish to feel hurt, but the news had reopened a wound she thought had begun to heal. 'He said it couldn't be delayed much longer, but I hadn't realized it would happen this quickly. When did the wedding take place?'

'At Easter. But, if it's any comfort, Sasha left for the front almost immediately.'

She glanced sideways at him, wondering what the implication of that comment was. 'What is she like, his . . . wife?'

'Very young: almost a child.'

'He said she was eighteen.'

'She may be, but she looks and sounds much younger than that. Oh, she carried out her duties as a hostess perfectly, but it was like a schoolgirl repeating a lesson. And she is very pale and thin – not strong, I imagine.'

Leo nodded silently, despising herself for the flicker of hope that news had ignited. She took a deep breath and forced herself to say, 'Thank you for telling me. But it doesn't make any difference to what we were discussing before. I have no wish to be "free", as you put it. But at least this resolves the problem of finding excuses to delay the wedding. Let us just say that we have decided it would be better not to make any irrevocable commitments until the war is over.'

'What will you do, when Ralph and I have gone?' he asked.

'Oh, I shall find war work of some sort. Victoria is convinced that the FANY will be given a role of some kind. If not, I'll go to Mabel Stobart. She is already starting to organize some kind of women's national service unit. Don't worry about me.'

He sighed and shook his head. 'That's just it. I know you.

I know what you did in the Balkans. Of course I shall worry.'
He stood up. 'I had better go. I have to go and see my parents
and put my affairs in order.'

'You will come and say goodbye, before you leave for France?'

'If I can, of course – and I'll bring Ralph.'

She reached up and kissed his cheek. 'Dear Tom! There was
a time when I thought you a very lukewarm suitor and the
whole idea of an engagement between us filled me with despair.
It's ironic, isn't it, that now I know there can never be any
question of marriage I have come to regard you as one of my
dearest friends?'

'That is all I could ever wish for,' he said. 'And a far better
outcome than I ever imagined.' He kissed her in return. 'I
won't say goodbye now. I'm sure there will be another chance.'

When he had gone Leo sat down again at her desk but she
could not concentrate on the papers. She went upstairs and
put on her hat and set off for FANY headquarters.

'He said what?'

'When Dr Elsie Inglis offered to take a medical team to the
front Sir Arthur Sloggett told her to "go home and sit still.
We don't want any petticoats here".' The speaker was Edith
Wharton, a long-established FANY. 'So I don't give much for
our chances of getting a different reaction.'

'I don't believe it!' Victoria drummed her fists on the table
in despair. 'After all the work we've done, and after what we
went through in Bulgaria. How can they treat us like that?'

'All right, all right! We all know that you two have seen
active service,' someone said cuttingly. 'There's no need to go
on about it. It doesn't entitle you to special treatment.'

'I'm not saying it does!' Victoria exclaimed. 'I'm angry for
all of us. It's just that I thought we'd proved something out
there – and now it has just been forgotten.'

'Well, there's one comfort,' Lilian Franklin put in. 'Ash is
on her way back.'

'Already?'

'As soon as she heard that war had been declared she cabled
ahead to Cape Town and booked her passage home. She only
spent four hours ashore.'

'That's great news!' Victoria exclaimed. 'If anyone can get things moving, she can.'

Leo said nothing. It was true that Grace Ashley-Smith had made the FANY much more efficient since she took over two years earlier. But if the Corps was sent anywhere it would almost certainly be France or Belgium, and Leo's thoughts were on another battlefield, along the Danube and the Sava where the Serbs were fighting to preserve their homeland.

Ralph and Tom came to say goodbye on the evening of 11 August.

'We can only stay a few minutes,' Ralph told her. 'We entrain at midnight.'

It was an awkward half hour. Ralph was flushed with excitement, helping himself a little too liberally from the whisky decanter; Tom was grim and silent. None of them had much to say to each other and Leo had the impression that in one sense they had left already. Their minds were on what awaited them in Belgium and the only thing left to say that had any meaning was 'goodbye and God bless you'. To her shame, she felt relieved when the door closed behind them.

Five

The rusty crane creaked and swayed slightly as Tom climbed and the rungs of the ladder were slick from the cold drizzle that was falling. He gritted his teeth and fixed his eyes straight ahead of him, knowing that if he looked up or down he would be lost. He had hated heights ever since the day some of the boys on the estate had dared him to climb a slender poplar in the grounds. *'Go on! A bit higher! A bit higher! You're not scared, are you?'* He must have been about eight at the time. The higher he climbed, the more the tree swayed and when he tried to climb down he found he was stuck and one of the game keepers had had to scramble up to fetch him. The man had told his father, thinking it a joke, and Tom had been beaten for causing a nuisance – or was it for being a coward? He forced the thought to the back of his mind and climbed further.

At last he reached the little driver's cabin and once he was safely seated inside it he was able to look down. Below him stretched an industrial landscape of pitheads and slag heaps, interspersed with small red-brick villages divided by cobbled streets. The pits were silent today and the sound of church bells from the town behind him reminded Tom that it was Sunday. If it had been a weekday, he wondered, would the pits be working, ignoring the fact that they were about to be the epicentre of a battle? Certainly, in the town, as he passed through, the people seemed to be going about their normal Sunday activities as if what was happening did not concern them.

Tom raised his gaze beyond the pitheads to where the canal gleamed dully between its marshy banks. On the far side the ground was level, running back to woods about three hundred yards distant, indistinct in the morning mist. He strained his eyes, looking for any sign of movement, but if the enemy were out there he could not see them. Below him, between the mining villages and the canal, he could just make out the dark lines of shallow trenches dug into a ridge of coal spoil and the heads of men crouched in them. It seemed to him a pathetically thin line, more a series of isolated posts with nothing to back them – but apparently this was the best that could be arranged. Only yesterday, they had been marching forward, confident that they were advancing to join their French allies and roll back the German attackers. Then, suddenly, the orders had been countermanded. They were to stop where they were and dig in. No one seemed to know why. Tom took his sketch pad out of his rucksack and flexed his chilled fingers. If this was going to be the British Expeditionary Force's first battle, he would have a bird's-eye view of it. He headed the first page *Mons, Belgium – Sunday 23 August.*

A movement away to his right caught his eye. A company of cavalry came cantering out of the mist, heading towards the trenches. At first Tom thought they were British, a reconnaissance party coming to report; then he saw that the uniforms were wrong. French, possibly? Or Belgian? Then there was a boom that made him jump and he saw smoke billowing up from an artillery position on the right flank and a gout of earth shot up just in front of the advancing horsemen. 'Boche, by God!' he said aloud. The rest of the guns had joined in by now and Tom saw shells falling among the horses. For a brief moment it seemed the riders intended to come on, regardless, then they wheeled away and galloped off into the trees. 'First blood to us,' Tom muttered, sketching busily.

He had no time to complete the picture. As if the initial gunfire had been a starting signal, the air was shaken by a series of huge explosions and shells began to fall all along the line of the British trenches. The crane trembled under Tom with the violence of the impacts and he saw huge craters opening up to both sides of him. He strained his eyes towards the forest on the far side of the canal and saw that the mist was lifting and beyond the trees the ground rose to a low ridge, from where he could see the muzzle flashes of the German cannon. The noise was terrifying – a continuous roar as one gun after another spewed flame and then a sobbing whistle as the shells flew through the air and explosion after explosion as they landed. Tom had seen what artillery could do, on the road to Kumanovo, and heard it around Bitola, but he had never encountered a bombardment like this. Even with his limited experience, he could tell that these German guns were bigger and more powerful than anything the Serbs had possessed – or than anything his own country could produce, he suspected.

The bombardment went on for hours and Tom looked down at the devastation below him and wondered if anything could possibly remain alive. His hands were shaking and his head was ringing and all he could think of was that Ralph was down there, somewhere, with his men. They had parted quite casually that morning, as if what was coming was nothing more than an exercise. Is this where it ends? Tom wondered. All our high hopes wiped out, and Ralph with them, almost without firing a shot.

The rain had stopped and steam was rising from the marshes as the sun came out, and suddenly there they were! An ordered phalanx of troops in their grey uniforms, marching out, rank on rank, from the sheltering trees. They advanced in a solid block and Tom, staring down, thought what an unmissable target they would make, if only anyone were left alive to shoot. He visualized them pouring across the canal, through the trenches full of dead, and realized that soon his crane would be surrounded. Would they see him? If so, he could look forward to spending the rest of the war as a prisoner. Should he draw his revolver and hope to kill one or two, before they shot him down? For a moment he felt constriction in his throat, not at the prospect of captivity but at the thought that he should have been down there, with Ralph and the others, taking his chance like the rest of them. Perhaps his father had been right all along!

Steadily, the grey-clad figures advanced until they were less than a hundred yards from the canal bank. Then a voice rang out, '*Fire!*' and all along the trenches heads appeared, rifles were aimed and bullets tore into the massed ranks of the enemy. So rapidly were the shots repeated that the sound was continuous and the German soldiers fell like wheat before the harvester. Watching, Tom remembered that Ralph had told him that it was the pride of the infantry that they could fire fifteen aimed rounds per minute. For all his hatred of war, he found himself cheering as the German ranks wavered and then fell back. His cheer was echoed along the thin line of the trenches.

The sun rose higher and Tom began to sweat in the confined space of the cabin but the battle continued to rage below him and the crane shuddered with the impact of the German shells on the ground below. The German infantry made two further attempts to advance, but each time they were driven back, leaving the ground beyond the canal strewn with bodies. Tom worked feverishly, filling page after page with sketches. Then, looking to the west, he saw movement. Small groups of men were retreating towards him, each in turn providing covering fire while the others withdrew through them. With a sickening lurch in his stomach Tom realized that the enemy had succeeded in crossing the canal by one of the bridges. Below him, other groups were moving, slipping back towards the slag heaps and the buildings of the mining villages. It was time to leave his vantage point. With cramped and shaking limbs, he began the long climb down to the ground.

At ground level the cacophony of the bombardment was more deafening than before. At the whistle of an approaching shell he threw himself face down and felt the ground heave. Soil thrown up by the explosion pattered down on to his back. He scrambled up and, keeping low, scuttled in the direction of the mine buildings until he encountered a platoon of Coldstream Guards.

'I'm looking for Lieutenant Malham Brown,' Tom said. 'Do you know where he is?'

'Back there, sir,' the corporal said, nodding towards a long, low building. 'Casualty clearing station.'

Tom's stomach churned again. Somehow he had convinced himself that in the midst of all this desolation he would find Ralph unharmed. He turned and stumbled towards the building. It was a disused factory and Tom entered a huge, echoing room, empty except for lines of wounded men lying on the floor. There was no sign of any doctors or orderlies, and the prospect of trawling the lines in search of Ralph was too daunting, so he picked his way across to a doorway leading into a second room. This one, too, was full of wounded but there was more activity. Two doctors were at work at trestle tables on the far side and several orderlies with Red Cross armbands were bustling about with trays of dressings.

Tom waylaid the nearest one. 'Lieutenant Malham Brown? Is he here?'

'Over there, sir.' The man indicated with a jerk of his chin and Tom turned to see Ralph crouched beside a prone figure.

Ralph looked up as he approached and for a moment his eyes were blank, as if he did not recognize his friend. Then he said, 'Ah, Tom. You're still in one piece then,' in a flat tone that expressed neither surprise nor relief. His face was smeared with coal dust and spent powder but beneath the filth he was chalk white.

'And you?' Tom said breathlessly. 'You're not hurt?'

'Me? No, no I'm all right. Just checking on the lads, like this one.'

He looked down at the still figure on the stretcher and Tom saw that it was a boy who looked hardly old enough to enlist. One sleeve of his tunic was ripped and a rough bandage had been applied, which was already dark with blood. Ralph put his hand on the boy's other shoulder and pressed it gently. 'Hang on, old chap. The medics will be with you soon.'

'Don't worry about me, sir,' the boy whispered. 'I'll be OK. There's others worse off than me.'

Ralph straightened up and looked about him with the same blank, lost look and Tom said quietly, 'Is there anything I can do?'

'I need to get back,' Ralph said. 'We're withdrawing to the second line of defence. Stay here, will you, and help out?'

'Of course,' Tom agreed. 'If there's anything useful I can do.'

Ralph started to move towards the door, then he stopped and looked round the room. 'There are so many,' he murmured, as if to himself, 'so many . . .' Tom wondered if he meant the Germans or the casualties, but before he could frame the question Ralph shook himself like a dog and left the room.

Tom located one of the doctors, who was bending over a man who was clutching his belly and sobbing. 'Is there anything I can do, Doctor? I've no medical or first aid training but I'm willing to help in any way I can.'

The doctor looked up. 'Are you familiar with the concept of triage?'

'Yes, I think so,' Tom responded, recalling what he had learned from Leo outside Adrianople.

'Casualties are divided into three categories. The first – those that need immediate treatment if they are to survive; the second – those whose wounds are less serious and can wait for a while; and the third – those whose condition is beyond our help. In that room out there are the men who fall into the third category. If you really want to help you can go round them and note down names and numbers, so we can inform next of kin.'

He turned back to his work and Tom moved away towards the door. He felt sick, but he knew that to protest would be to brand himself as worse than useless. In the outer room two army chaplains were now at work. Tom's offer of help was accepted with relief and for the next hour he went from stretcher to stretcher. Soon the pages of his sketch pad were covered, not with drawings, but with names and numbers and units. Many of the men were beyond speech and he had to grope for dog tags to get the necessary information. Some of them asked when the doctors would attend to them, others knew that they were beyond help and begged Tom to write down farewell messages to loved ones. Many begged for water and Tom refilled his canteen again and again, raising their heads and holding it to their parched lips. Some asked him to pray with them. Tom had lost his faith many years earlier, but the familiar words of the Lord's Prayer came easily and the dying men seemed to find comfort in them. Others simply wanted him to hold their hands and more than once he felt the grip go suddenly slack and saw the eyes glaze over. When one of the chaplains laid a hand on his shoulder and said gently, 'There's nothing more you can do here. Thank you for your help,' he staggered out into the sunshine and sank down on a pile of bricks, oblivious to the noise of the battle going on behind him.

When he dragged himself to his feet he saw that the day was almost over and a bank of clouds had built up in the western sky: black clouds in strange, irregular formations, tinged luridly red at the edges by the setting sun. To Tom's overwrought

imagination they looked like winged creatures. *Angels of death,*
he thought. *I hope they are coming for the Boche!*

He found Ralph with his company. They had taken up a
position behind a broken wall and were preparing for another
German attack.

'For God's sake, Ralph,' he begged, 'give me a rifle. I can't
stand by and watch without doing anything.'

Ralph looked at him and Tom was relieved to see that the
blank gaze had been replaced by a look of grim determination.
'You've never fired a rifle, have you?'

'No, but I've used a shotgun. It can't be so different.'

Ralph turned to a soldier nearby. 'Give this officer a rifle.
There must be spares that belonged to one of our casualties.'

Tom was handed a gun and Ralph gave him brief instructions on how to load and fire it. 'If they come at us en masse
like they did before, you might at least take one or two out
before they overrun us,' he said grimly.

At that moment somebody said, 'Listen!' and in the sudden
quiet they realized the guns had fallen silent and from the far
side of the canal a bugle sounded.

'That's the cease fire!' Ralph said, incredulously. 'One more
push and they would have had us on toast, and they've decided
to pack up for the night. Praise God!'

The sentiment was echoed all along the line and the order
went round to stand down. Before long Tom found himself
squatting by a campfire, eating bully beef and drinking tea
strong enough to tan leather. He watched as Ralph made his
rounds, setting sentries and joking with the men. He had never
seen him in action as an officer before and it was clear that
he was very good at his job, but Tom knew the real Ralph,
underneath the uniform. Only he could guess what it had cost
him to throw off the numbness of shock that had gripped him
in the casualty station. At length, Ralph came and sat beside
him and offered him a swig of brandy from his flask.

'Rotten job I gave you back there.' He nodded towards the
disused factory. 'You all right?'

'Just about,' Tom said. 'I was glad to do something vaguely
useful, after sitting up in that ivory tower all day.'

'Were you able to make some useful sketches?'

'I don't know. I was too busy to think about it.' Tom reached for his pad and flipped the pages.

Ralph took it from him. 'Bloody hell, Tom! You could see all this? Down here at ground level we only knew what was right in front of us – but an overview like this . . . It could be immensely useful in planning future tactics. You'd better show these to the CO when you get a chance.'

It was too late to pursue the idea further and before long Tom rolled himself in his greatcoat and fell into an exhausted sleep. It seemed he had hardly dropped off before his batman was shaking him awake.

'Get up, sir! We're withdrawing. Orders have just come round.'

Tom blinked at him. 'Withdrawing? You mean retreating? Why?'

'Sorry, sir. That's just what I've been told. Lieutenant Malham Brown says he'll meet you at the horse lines.'

Stiff and chilled, Tom scrambled to his feet. The batman collected his belongings and followed as Tom plodded towards the area behind the lines where the horses were tethered. Ralph was already there, preparing to mount.

'What's happening?' Tom asked. 'Why are we pulling back?'

'Ours not to reason why, old chap,' Ralph responded. 'Buck up and get mounted.'

Dawn was breaking and as they moved out on to the road Tom saw that it was already crowded with men. They were not formed up in marching order, as they had been when they arrived, but were in small groups with men from different units mixed together. There was no sense of panic, in fact it was eerily quiet, a stream of ghostly shapes in the grey morning light.

'I don't understand,' Tom said. 'Have we been defeated? I thought we had held them back.'

Ralph looked at him with a hint of his old insouciant grin. 'Strategic withdrawal. The BEF is going to quietly melt away. If the Boche knew we were withdrawing they'd be after us like a pack of hounds, but this way, by the time they wake up to the fact, we shall be over the hills and far away.'

'Was it necessary?' Tom asked.

'The Germans were across the canal on both sides of us. If we'd stayed we should have been outflanked and surrounded. We have to find a better defensive position.'

At that moment gunfire broke out behind them and Tom looked at Ralph in alarm.

'Have they spotted what we're doing?'

'No, that's our own artillery. Those poor blighters have been told to stay and cover our retreat. They'll be lucky to get the guns away before the Boche overrun them.'

Tom scanned the line of men ahead of him. 'I can see some of our chaps, but they're all mixed up with men from other regiments.'

'We'll gather them together when we stop. Right now what matters is to put as much distance between us and the Boche as possible.'

As they rode on Tom felt sorry for the foot soldiers. On the march out he had been uncomfortable because, as an officer, he was mounted while they walked, but now the discrepancy was magnified. The men had fought all day, and they each carried a heavy pack as well as their rifles and he saw that some of them were already limping. Many wore bandages on heads or arms and some had to be helped along by colleagues. But in general they did not appear to be downhearted and he heard several asking Ralph why they had been ordered to withdraw.

'We was on top of them, sir,' one said. 'We ought to be going after the buggers, not running away.'

'We're not running away,' Ralph assured him. 'When we reach a better position we shall turn round and let them run straight into our trap.'

As they reached the outskirts of the town of Mons, Tom saw a sight that reminded him with a jolt of Serbia. The road here was crowded with refugees, mingling with the troops. They pushed handcarts and perambulators piled high with everything they could carry. Women carried babies on their backs and led small children by the hand. A young girl carried a birdcage in which a canary was singing, undisturbed by the tumult around it, and behind her a youth pushed an old man with a long white beard in a wheelbarrow. Some of them

struck off across the fields, heading for some refuge unknown
to the English soldiers, others plodded on, adding to the
congestion and slowing down the retreat.

All day they trudged along the straight, tree-lined road with
its unforgiving cobbles. Unlike the previous day, which had
begun cool and damp, the sun shone from a cloudless sky and
Tom saw more than one man cast aside his heavy greatcoat,
careless of how he would cover himself when night came. The
ration cart threaded its way through the crowd, handing out
tins of bully beef and hunks of bread. The men opened the
tins and shared them out and ate while they marched. One
young lad dropped out of the ranks and sank down on the
side of the road. Ralph rode up to him and shouted, 'On your
feet. You can't stop here. Do you want to be taken
prisoner?'

'It's me feet, sir,' the boy whimpered. 'It's these boots. Me
feet's bleeding.'

'You've got to keep going just the same,' Ralph told him.
'Up you get. That's an order!'

As the boy hauled himself upright Tom said quietly, 'I could
give him my horse. My boots are better than his for walking.'

'Don't be a fool!' Ralph replied in an undertone. 'Do you
think he's the only one? You can't give up your horse to all
of them. You're an officer now. Behave like one!'

From time to time they heard outbreaks of firing behind
them and once they saw a cavalry regiment cantering through
the fields alongside the road in the direction of the enemy. It
was clear that the Germans were in hot pursuit and only being
held back by a determined rearguard action. Dusk came, with
some relief from the heat if nothing else, and still they marched.
Finally, when it was fully dark, the order was given to halt and
fall out and the men stumbled into the fields and dropped to
the ground. Tom slid off his horse and handed the reins to his
batman. He felt almost as exhausted as the men and wrapping
his greatcoat around him he prepared to lie down. Then he
saw that Ralph was still on his feet, moving around among
the men, exchanging banter and murmuring words of encour-
agement. He wondered if he should join him, but he was a
newcomer, not a regular soldier, and he knew he did not have

the rapport with the men that Ralph had. So he sat and waited until eventually his friend came back and sank down beside him.

'So this is war,' Ralph grunted. 'Not quite the way I imagined it.'

'I did try to warn you, after what I saw in Serbia,' Tom replied.

'I know,' Ralph said. 'But then I assumed that – well, that it was a civilian's view of things. I'm beginning to understand now.'

Tom shook his head sadly. 'This is only the start. I'm afraid, like the Yanks say, *You ain't seen nothing yet!'*

'Spare me the details,' Ralph muttered. He pulled his coat over his head and was asleep almost at once.

They were on the move soon after dawn next morning and late that evening they entered the village of Le Cateau. A halt was called as they reached the village square and Ralph was summoned to a briefing with the senior officers. The men dropped to the ground where they were, leaning against each other or any surface that came to hand, some of them already asleep. Tom was muzzy-headed from lack of sleep and his eyes stung with dust and sweat, but he took out his sketch pad and began to draw the faces of the soldiers around him: streaked with dirt, gaunt with hunger and exhaustion, but still amazingly indomitable in their expressions.

Ralph returned after a short interval. 'Thank God! We're to stop here and dig in. Our orders are to hold the Boche back as long as possible.'

'That's asking a lot,' Tom said. 'The men are exhausted. They fought all day at Mons, they've had very little sleep and now they've marched the best part of thirty miles.'

'Exactly,' Ralph said. 'They can't walk any further, but they can lie in a field and fire their rifles.'

A group of senior officers entered the square and Tom recognized General Smith-Dorrien. The men struggled wearily to their feet and the general mounted the church steps to address them.

'Men, this is where we stop retreating and make a stand. Our job is to hold the enemy back so that the rest of our forces have time to regroup. You held them off at Mons. I know I can rely on you to do the same here.'

Tom felt a lump rise in his throat at the ragged cheer that greeted his words.

Ralph's company was deployed in a cornfield just beyond the village, with other units to left and right of it. The men got out their entrenching tools and dug shallow pits, as they had done at Mons. Tom scraped a hole for himself behind a stook of corn and unslung the rifle Ralph had given him. He knew he could not match the expertise of the infantrymen around him and he found it hard to imagine that he could attempt to take the life of a fellow human being in cold blood, but he was determined to share the danger and hoped to play some part in the action instead of being an observer. Ralph, having toured the lines, checking and encouraging, came to join him.

'Now what?' Tom asked.

'Now we wait,' was the reply.

The brief hours of darkness passed and then with the dawn they heard the sound of conflict from the other side of the village and a detachment of Uhlans, the German cavalry, were seen galloping away. Soon after that the artillery, most of whom had succeeded in withdrawing with their guns from Mons, opened up and the German guns replied. The bombardment went on until midday, tearing great craters in the level ground and wreaking heavy casualties. Tom saw the shallow foxholes on either side of him disintegrate into flying clods of earth, in which were mingled the remains of weapons, shreds of clothing and dismembered body parts. Then the guns fell silent and the grey-uniformed ranks of the German infantry advanced. Incredibly, to Tom, they still came on in solid blocks, presenting a target even he could not miss. Even more incredibly, as at Mons, from what appeared a scene of lifeless devastation, a scorching rain of bullets erupted. Working the bolts of their rifles until the barrels were red hot, the British Tommies poured a withering fire into the massed ranks and soon the field in front of them was strewn with bodies. But still they came on, the numbers apparently inexhaustible, tramping over their dead comrades and advancing ever closer.

Again and again Tom reloaded and fired, oblivious now to whether his bullets found a living target, until his arms ached so much that he could scarcely support the rifle. To one side, he saw an artillery battery. Half its crew were either dead or wounded, but the survivors scrambled from gun to gun to keep up the fire. The enemy was closer now and it seemed they must be overrun at any moment. Then a bugle sounded and Ralph leapt to his feet, defying the bullets that whistled past him.

'Fall back! Fall back!'

Those men who could still stand got up and, bent double, raced for the safety of some woods a few hundred yards away. Tom ran with them. Then a sight arrested him. A little to his right the remaining men of the gun crew were struggling to harness their horses to the gun limber. Two horses lay dead already, the others, terrified, reared and plunged. Without pausing for thought Tom changed course and ran to help. Catching the bridle of one horse, he succeeded in holding it until the straps attaching it to the gun had been buckled. Two other men harnessed the second beast and then one shouted, 'Jump up, sir! Save the gun!'

Tom did not wait for a second invitation, but vaulted on to the horse's back and dug in his heels. Crouching low, with the gun limber rattling and swerving behind him, he rode at a flat gallop for the trees. The men were regrouping in a clearing and as he arrived one ran forward to hold the horse's head. As Tom slid to the ground the second gun team came careering into the clearing and the sergeant in charge came over.

'Thank you for that, sir. I don't think we'd have got both guns away without your help. We can manage now.'

Tom went in search of Ralph, but the men were already moving out on to the road beyond the village and he could see no sign of him. A voice called, 'Over here, sir!' and he saw his batman leading his horse.

'Glad to see you're still with us, Matt,' he said, as he mounted, and the man grinned.

'You too, sir, if you'll pardon the liberty.'

'Have you seen Lieutenant Malham Brown?'

'No, sir. I lost sight of him in the retreat. I expect he's ahead of us.'

It took Tom nearly an hour in the gathering darkness to find Ralph, trudging along with the common soldiers with a bandage round his head. He looked up as Tom slid to the ground beside him and for a moment his eyes were as blank as they had been in the casualty station at Mons. Then his face lit up.

'Tom! Thank God! I thought you'd bought it!' He reached out and gripped Tom's shoulder and Tom slid an arm round him.

'What about you? Is the wound serious?'

'No, just a scratch.'

'Where's your horse?'

'Shot out from under me when I went back to round up the stragglers. I'll get a new one from the remounts when we halt.'

For a moment he let Tom support him. Then he straightened up. 'Well, we held them for a day. I just hope that's long enough. Sooner or later we've got to call a halt and face up to them properly, or they'll sweep us into the sea.'

Six

On the afternoon of 26 August the London *Times* produced a special edition. The headline read BROKEN BRITISH REGIMENTS. In a despatch from Amiens, the reporter described the German advance and British losses. New recruits were urgently needed to reinforce the troops, the despatch concluded. By the next morning the recruiting offices were besieged by men wanting to sign up.

For Leonora it was a time of torment. Her anxiety about her brother and Tom was exacerbated by her own enforced inactivity. While the hundreds of new recruits marched, whistling, through the city streets it seemed that the only contribution the women of Britain were to be allowed to make was to knit socks and pack up parcels of 'comforts' for their menfolk. Ashley-Smith was still on her way back from South Africa, and Mabel Stobart seemed to have disappeared completely. The FANYs busied themselves with stretcher drills and collecting equipment, but the chances of their being required seemed remote.

She received a letter with a New Zealand postmark:

> Dear Leo,
> This will only be a short letter as I don't have much time. I just want you to know that yesterday I rode into Wellington and signed up with the Wellington Mounted Rifles. It would only have been a matter of time before I was called up anyway, since I've been in the territorials since I was eighteen, but I wanted to get in as soon as possible. Looks as if this time I'll actually get to do some fighting instead of carrying stretchers. It's a different enemy this time, of course, but there are rumours that the Turks may come in on the side of Germany, so I might get to have another crack at them yet! I don't know if I'll make it as far as Europe. We're still waiting for news of embarkation. But if I do I hope I shall have a chance to see you − and perhaps Victoria, too.

*What are you doing? I'm sure neither of you will be content
to sit back and let the fellows do all the fighting. I shouldn't be
surprised if we meet up again on another muddy battlefield. If
I ever have the misfortune to get wounded, there's no one's face
I'd rather see looking down at me when I come round from the
anaesthetic!*

*I'll do my best to keep in touch, and look forward to hearing
from you.*

Yours affectionately,
Luke

One morning the telephone rang and Leo heard the voice of
James Bartlett, the estate manager at Bramwell Hall. It was
very unusual for him to ring and when he did his tone was
normally restrained and respectful. This time he sounded near
to tears.

'They're taking the horses, Miss Leo!'

'What? Who are, James? Taking them where?'

'The army, Miss Leo. They came this morning with a document — all very proper and legal — saying they are entitled to
requisition any horses.'

'Have they taken them all?'

'All of them, miss. Even your little chestnut mare.'

'They've taken Amber? But that's ridiculous! She's too small
for an officer's mount and anyway she'll bolt at the first sound
of gunfire.'

'I told them that, Miss Leo. But they wouldn't listen.'

'And they've taken all the farm horses?'

'Every one except old Bramble. They reckoned he was past it.'

'How will you manage?'

'God knows, miss — pardon the language. But there's one
good thing. Most of the harvest is in. There won't be so much
work for the horses until spring ploughing season. Maybe by
then it will be all over.'

'Maybe,' Leo said, without conviction. She drew a breath
and sighed. 'There's nothing we can do about it, James. You
must just manage as best you can. Buy horses if there are any
to be had, but I doubt if there will be. Is there anything I can
do to help?'

'No, no, Miss Leo. Don't you fret.' She could hear that he had himself under control now. 'I just wanted to let you know. As you say, there's nowt we can do except pray the war doesn't last too long.'

'Amen to that!' Leo said.

When she had put the phone down tears welled up in her eyes. She had maintained a stoic attitude to her manager, but the thought of her beautiful little mare, her father's last gift, being caught up in the chaos of the battlefield was almost unbearable. She bit her lips. First Sasha, then Ralph and Tom, and now her beloved horse had been swallowed up in this pointless war and it was quite possible that she would never see any of them again.

Acute as her anxiety was for Tom and Ralph, it was doubled by the news from Serbia. Max, who was still at his post as a correspondent for an American newspaper in Belgrade, wrote to her every week and in this way she had learned that for two weeks the city had been bombarded by the Austrian's heavy Krupp's guns from across the Danube and Sava Rivers, while the main element of the Serbian army, short of supplies and ammunition, had struggled back from the south where they had been guarding the borders of Macedonia. Then had come the news of the battle of Cer Mountain, at which the Austrians had been driven back by the Serbs under General Putnik and it seemed Belgrade had been delivered from the immediate threat. Max wrote, however, that the Austrians were still massed on the borders and he expected a renewed attack at any time. Sasha, he had found out, had survived that battle, but Leo could only wonder how much longer his luck would hold.

After a long silence, which stretched her nerves almost to breaking point, she received a letter from Tom.

17 Sept

My Dear Leo,
Please forgive me for not writing sooner. There really has not been a spare moment in the last few weeks. I can't go into details about places and dates but I think you will have read

*in the papers about the fighting around Mons. That was followed
by a 'strategic withdrawal' which involved marching for twenty
hours out of every twenty-four, until we were almost on the
outskirts of Paris. How the men did it I shall never know. It
was hard enough on horseback. Now, thank God, we have
stopped retreating and the German advance has been halted at
the Marne. Everyone is exhausted and we seem to have reached
a kind of stalemate, so there's no knowing where we might go
next.*

*I've seen things that have filled me with admiration, and
others that have made me despair. For those of us, like you and
me, who have some experience of modern warfare the positively
medieval ideas of some of our commanders are almost unbelievable. Would you believe that the French cavalry charge machine
guns, wearing their polished cuirasses and plumed helmets, as if
they were going on parade? And the ordinary French soldier
wears a red coat and blue trousers, as if the intention is to make
him a perfect target for enemy fire. I have seen them shot down
like a flock of pheasants.*

*Enough of this! I am well – surprisingly so, in fact – and
so is Ralph. He would write but he spends all his spare time
going round his men, listening to their troubles and cheering
them along. He is a very popular officer, justifiably. I will write
again when I can and meanwhile I enclose a few of my more
light-hearted sketches.*

With my love,
Tom

Two days later Leo learned from the papers that the Austrians
had successfully invaded Serbia and were besieging Belgrade.

One day Leo and Victoria arrived at FANY HQ with the rest
of the Corps to discover Ashley-Smith awaiting them with her
second-in-command, Lilian Franklin. In response to the chorus
of delighted greetings she said, 'Well, the good news is, on
the boat home I met a M. Louis Franck, who is the Belgian
Minister for the Colonies. When I told him what we were
hoping to do he said that the Belgian army would welcome
us with open arms. Apparently, there already is a British-run

field hospital in Antwerp and I have the name of the secretary. I'm going to see him tomorrow, to offer our services.'

At last it seemed that the period of frustrating inactivity might be at an end, but Leo's optimism was short-lived. The following day Ashley-Smith reported that the secretary had insisted that he had no need of the Corps' assistance, though he had grudgingly conceded that she might go out herself, if she could get a *laissez-passer* from the Belgian government.

'Of course, he was convinced I wouldn't get one,' Smith added grimly, 'but I've proved him wrong there.'

Two days later she left for Antwerp.

For a week the FANYs chewed their collective fingernails and waited. Then Franklin came into the room where they were gloomily rolling bandages, waving a telegram.

'She's done it! The Belgians have offered Ash a three-hundred-bed hospital and we are to go out there and help her to run it.'

The cheer that went up must have been heard, Leo reckoned, in the street outside. The rest of the day was spent in a flurry of packing equipment and personal belongings.

Next morning, Leo woke to hear the newsboys shouting in the street and caught the word 'Antwerp'. She sent Millie out to buy a paper and read the headline that put an end to their hopes. 'German Army At The Gates Of Antwerp'.

Antwerp fell to the Germans on 10 October and there had been no word from Ashley-Smith. The mood of euphoria evaporated, leaving Leo and the other FANYs more depressed than ever. Then, ten days later, Ashley-Smith walked into their HQ, spick and span in her uniform and apparently unharmed. She was at once besieged with questions.

'Where have you been?'

'How did you get away?'

'Did you see the Germans? How come you weren't interned?'

'If you'll let me get a word in edgeways,' she responded in her soft Scottish burr, 'I'll tell you. I was in Ghent, helping to rescue wounded soldiers. When the Germans overran us I was evacuated to a place called Eecloo but then I heard that there was a British officer in the Flandria hotel in Ghent who was too ill to be moved, so of course I had to go back.'

'Go back!' someone exclaimed. 'Weren't you terrified?'

'Oh, my heart was in my boots, all right. But the young man's relief at seeing me was enough to make it all worthwhile. I managed to get him into a nursing home but the next day it was taken over by the Germans to billet their soldiers. I expected them to arrest me at any moment, but no one bothered us.'

'Did the young officer recover?'

'No, sadly. I sat up with him for two nights but on the third morning he died. I stayed to arrange his funeral and then I went to the German CO and asked for a safe conduct out of the city.'

'Were you wearing uniform?' Leo asked.

'Oh, yes! It was very funny to see the German's reaction. I suppose a woman in any uniform is pretty surprising to them, but to see a woman in British khaki in an occupied city – well, I think the German word for it is *verbluffend*. Of course, they refused me the safe conduct, but at least they didn't arrest me. I swanked out as if I owned the place and, do you know, one sergeant drew his men up to attention and saluted me!'

'Good for you!' Lilian exclaimed. 'But how did you get away in the end?'

'I happened to have met a Belgian baroness and she managed to arrange for me to get out through Holland. So, here I am and the good news is . . .' she paused and Leo held her breath . . . 'the Belgians have taken over an abandoned convent school in Calais as a hospital for their troops and they want us to go out and help to run it. And, I have persuaded Sir Arthur Stanley, of the Red Cross council, to give us permits to cross the Channel on the Red Cross yacht.'

On 26 October the advance party of six FANYs, together with three qualified nurses led by the redoutable Sister Wicks, and two male dressers assembled on the docks at Folkestone. With them was Ashley-Smith's brother Bill, at the wheel of a brand new motor ambulance.

'How did you get it?' Leo asked. 'I thought there were hardly any in existence.'

Ashley-Smith winked. 'Friends in high places. I twisted a few arms.'

'I wish Victoria was here,' Leo said. 'She would be green with envy.'

Victoria had insisted on taking Sparky, her sports car, to France and, on being told that there was no chance of it being accommodated on the Red Cross yacht, she had declared that she would make her own way over and join them in Calais.

As they made their way towards the berth where they expected to find the yacht they passed a hospital ship and saw stretcher after stretcher being carried down the gangways and laid out on the dock. There, a small party of men under the command of a tall, thin colonel in the uniform of the Royal Army Medical Corps were collecting them and carrying them to a waiting train. It was a miserable day, with a cold drizzle falling, but the stretcher-bearers could not keep up with the growing number of casualties being unloaded from the ship.

'There are so many of them!' whispered Marion Wilkinson, one of the youngest recruits, to Leo as they marched past. 'Where have they come from, do you think?'

'Ypres, I suppose,' Leo said grimly. 'According to the papers there's a big battle going on there.'

'Where's that?'

'Belgium. Poor devils, they shouldn't be left lying in the rain like that.'

When they reached the designated berth there was no sign of the Red Cross ship. Enquiries elicited the information that it was detained in Calais because of bad weather in the Channel.

'Right!' said Ashley-Smith. 'Let's make ourselves useful while we wait. Forward march!'

The colonel was checking a list on a clipboard and looked up impatiently as the group halted and Ashley-Smith saluted smartly.

'Who the devil are you and what do you want? Can't you see I'm busy?'

'Yes, sir,' Ashley-Smith replied. 'That's why we are offering to help. We are members of the First Aid Nursing Yeomanry and we are fully trained in stretcher drill.'

'You? Carry stretchers?' He stared at them with an

incredulous smile that came close to being a sneer. 'How long
do you think you'd last, with those soft white hands of yours?'

'These soft white hands are probably capable of more than
you will ever guess,' Ashley-Smith responded curtly. She turned
to the others. 'Right, ladies. You know what to do. Let's get
busy.'

Leo normally worked with Victoria but in her absence she
turned to the girl beside her. 'Come on, Wilks.'

As they stooped over the first stretcher the man lying on it,
his head swathed in bandages, opened one good eye and
exclaimed, 'Cor blimey! Angels! I must have died and gone
to heaven.'

'Not yet, private,' Leo said with a grin. 'You'll have to wait
a long time for that. But we can get you to a more comfortable billet. Ready, Wilks? Lift!'

They had practised stretcher drill till their arms ached and
their hands were blistered, carrying volunteers provided by the
RAMC, but Leo was the only one apart from Ashley-Smith
herself who had ever worked with real casualties. After the
third or fourth trip she saw that Wilks was sniffing back tears.

'What's the matter with you?' she asked irritably. 'You're not
tired already, are you?'

'No! It's just . . . I can't bear to see them in such pain! That
boy just now with his eyes bandaged. He kept asking if he'd
ever see again . . .'

'I know,' Leo said more gently. 'It's terribly hard. But think
how much harder it is for them. The last thing they need is
us snivelling over them.'

'You're right.' Wilks sniffed and drew her fist across her nose.
'I'll try to be braver.'

A call interrupted them. 'Four bearers needed here!'

Leo and Wilks hurried over to where Franklin and another
girl were standing. On the stretcher between them was all that
was left of a man. Both his legs had been amputated and one
arm was wrapped in bandages, through which blood was
seeping. He was shuddering with pain.

As they bent to lift him the colonel noticed them. 'Oh,
getting tired now, are we? Needs four of you to carry one
man, does it?'

Franklin straightened up and fixed him with a look. 'No, that is not the case at all. You should know that a stretcher carried by four people is considerably less jolting than one carried by two. This man needs all the consideration we can give him.'

Having delivered that rebuttal she bent to the stretcher again and the four of them lifted it with great care and carried it to the waiting train, where Franklin sought out a doctor and insisted that he leave what he was doing to give their patient a dose of morphia.

Eventually, all the casualties had been loaded on to the train and there was still no sign of the Red Cross yacht.

'We could stand round here all night,' Bill Ashley-Smith said. 'How about trying the ordinary ferry?'

Two hours later the motor ambulance was winched aboard the regular cross-Channel ferry and they were on their way at last.

It was dark when they reached Calais, to be greeted with the mirror image of the sight they had left behind in Folkestone: lines of stretchers laid out on the dockside in the rain, waiting to be loaded on to a hospital ship. This time they did not wait to offer their help because they had been met by an official from the Belgian Red Cross who was waiting to conduct them to Lamarck, the convent school which had been converted into a hospital. Calais, less than fifty miles from the battle front, was seething. They passed along streets teeming with soldiers in the uniforms of three nations, horses, carts, gun limbers and refugees and arrived finally at a large, grey stone building. Leo's heart sank as they entered the courtyard, and looking at the others she could see that they were feeling the same. Everything about the place spoke of neglect and decay. The shutters hung at crazy angles from their broken hinges, the paintwork around the door frames was peeling and the courtyard itself was strewn with rubbish. There was one redeeming feature. Rising above the buildings on one side was the towering bulk of the cathedral, its stained-glass east window glowing softly from the lights inside.

The interior of the hospital was no more encouraging than

the outside. Immediately inside the gateway was a row of latrines, easily identifiable by the smell. At an angle to them was a large, stone-flagged kitchen and opposite that a big, draughty room from which a stone-flagged staircase led to the upper floors. In the rooms above straw palliasses were laid out side by side, crammed together as closely as possible, and every one of them was occupied.

They were introduced to the doctors, two Belgian and one English, and a small number of Sisters of Mercy who were struggling between them to cope with the influx.

'We are so thankful that you have arrived,' said one of the sisters, who spoke English. 'But I regret to say that there is no accommodation for you here. As you see, every inch of space is occupied. You must find somewhere to sleep in the town.'

That was easily said but hard to achieve in a city bursting at the seams with soldiers passing through on their way to the front and refugees streaming away from it. As they trudged round the streets Leo was reminded of the night she and Victoria had arrived in Salonika and she felt a pang of loneliness without her friend. All the main hotels were full and the owners of the boarding houses where they knocked regarded them with suspicion. Women in uniform were unheard of, and the landladies were unimpressed by the news that they were employed by the Belgian Red Cross. It seemed the citizens of Calais had little sympathy for their Belgian neighbours and made few distinctions between foreign nationals of any sort. As far as they were concerned, they might all be spies. By the time she finally found a house that was prepared to take her in, though only for that night, Leo was almost too tired to stand.

Next morning they all assembled at Lamarck. On the top floor there was a big room with a stove which had been set aside as a kind of common room and it was there that they were given their duties for the day. Leo knew that most of her companions were expecting to be used as ambulance drivers, collecting wounded from the battlefield, but she was not surprised to learn that they were to be enrolled as probationer nurses. They had been assigned to the various wards and were just about to leave when they heard a loud honking from the

courtyard. Leo ran to the window and looked out, to see
Sparky with Victoria at the wheel come to a standstill at the
main door. Having asked for and been given permission, she ran
down the stairs and threw her arms round Victoria.

'Oh, am I glad to see you!'

'I told you I'd make it. What's happening here?'

'You won't be overjoyed to hear me say it's like old times
in Macedonia – but at least we know what we're up against
and we can face it together.'

As they spoke a mud-spattered horse-drawn ambulance clattered into the courtyard.

'Oh, no! More casualties!' Leo said. 'We're bursting at the
seams already.'

The driver jumped down and hurried over to them, releasing
a babble of what Leo took to be Flemish and waving his hands
at the rear of the ambulance.

'What's he saying?' Victoria asked.

'No idea. Let's take a look.'

'Do you mean to say there's a language you don't speak?'
Victoria followed her to the rear of the vehicle.

Leo lifted the canvas flap and peered inside. By this time
they had been joined by one of the Sisters of Mercy and the
driver had accosted her with the same urgent appeal. Leo let
the flap drop and stepped back. 'Typhus. No doubt about it.'

'You have met this before?' the Sister asked.

'Yes, in Macedonia. What is the driver saying, Sister?'

'He says they have tried every other hospital in Calais and
none of them will take typhus cases.'

'Can we take them?'

'We shall have to, somehow.'

Behind her, Leo heard Victoria mutter, 'Oh, no! Not again!'
But she did not hesitate when the Sister instructed them to
bring the patient inside and Leo climbed back into the ambulance. Between them they lifted the stretcher with its writhing,
delirious occupant and carried him into the hospital.

Seven

Conditions in the hospital improved as the days passed. The Red Cross provided proper beds and appeals to charities in England produced bales of blankets, sheets and pillows. More recruits arrived and the FANYs swept and scrubbed until the wards were at least reasonably hygienic, if not exactly homely. They were less successful in improving their own living conditions. It seemed that none of the landladies who ran the boarding houses were prepared to put up English visitors for more than three or four nights, though they resorted to a variety of excuses to explain why their guests would have to move on.

One morning on their way to work Leo and Victoria passed an empty shop, which bore the name 'Le Bon Genie'.

'I wonder who it belongs to,' Victoria mused. 'If we could rent it we could live there.'

'We can't sleep in a shop window!' Leo protested.

'I'd rather do that than move every three days,' Victoria retorted.

Enquiries produced the answer that the tenants had fled the town and the owner was only too glad to rent the place to someone else. Sheets of brown paper were pasted over the windows and spare beds were carried down from the hospital, though there were so few of them that the night nurses simply fell into those vacated by the day shift. 'Just like good old Lozengrad,' Victoria commented.

The wounded arrived every night by the trainload and at dawn each day the FANY ambulance, which had now been joined by an assortment of other vehicles, including Sparky, set off in convoy for the station. Lamarck was not the only hospital, and the casualties had to be distributed amongst the others before Leo and her colleagues could begin their work on the wards. Periodically news arrived that a hospital ship was in the port and then all those able to be moved had to be loaded into the ambulances and driven to the docks, to make room for new admissions.

It was not long before the first typhus patients were joined by others, and Leo volunteered to nurse them, reckoning that her experience at Adrianople would be useful. Their care needed more labour than the other casualties. They had to be regularly sponged with cold water to reduce the fever and as there was no running water in the building it all had to be drawn from a well in the courtyard and carried up several flights of stairs. And since there were no chairs or tables the basins had to be placed on the floor, making the actual sponging a back-breaking occupation. Then they had to be fed with great care, sip by slow sip. They were often raving with delirium and could sometimes be quite violent. It was dispiriting work, since despite her best care roughly a third of the men died and it was not unusual to come to work in the morning and discover that the bed occupied yesterday by someone she had bathed and fed and comforted now held a new occupant.

One of the typhoid patients was called Franz. He had been a gunner and had served at the siege of Antwerp. In his delirium he believed he was still there and constantly counted his ammunition and shouted to his imaginary comrades. Occasionally he gave vent to a loud 'Boom!' which made everyone jump. One day Leo was feeding another patient when she heard him shouting.

'*Cochon! Bastard! Vous avez tuer mes camarades. Maintenant je vous etranglerai.*'

The words were followed by a muffled scream and Leo turned to see Franz grasping one of the nurses, a girl called Margaret, by the throat. She put down the bowl she was holding and ran across the ward, but before she reached him two male orderlies had leapt on him and wrestled him back on to his bed.

'Why did he do that?' Margaret panted, clasping her throat. 'I only wanted to feed him.'

'It wasn't anything you did,' Leo consoled her. 'He thought you were a German soldier.'

★   ★   ★

There was a rota for work on the night shift, and when her turn came Leo found it a relief. The pressure was less and she had time to chat to some of the men who were on the way to recovery. The ones who spoke French were glad to find someone who was able to converse easily in their language and she made efforts to learn a little Flemish, so she could communicate with the others. They told her about their families and many of them asked her to write letters home for them. They reminded her of the soldiers she had nursed at Adrianople. They expressed the same meek gratitude for everything she did for them and endured their suffering with the same mixture of stoicism and humour.

One night the relative peace of the night shift was shattered by a strange throbbing, buzzing sound. Leo turned to the orderly who was on duty with her but he indicated with a shrug that he had no more idea than she had what the noise might be. Leo glanced round the ward, saw that all the men were either asleep or at least resting quietly, and went out into the courtyard. The noise was coming from somewhere above her and for a moment she wondered if it was an aircraft, but very few planes flew at night. Then she saw a huge shape blotting out the stars.

'It's a Zeppelin!' she gasped to the orderly, who had followed her out.

'We should take cover,' he suggested, but Leo shook her head.

'I want to see what it does. Why aren't our people firing at it?'

At that moment a searchlight beam sprang up, criss-crossing the sky until it fastened on the Zeppelin, so that it hung above them like a great silver fish. Others joined it and star shells began to burst around it, green and blue against the night sky. Then the guns opened up but the huge craft continued serenely on its way.

'What is it doing?' Leo asked. The courtyard was crowded by now with staff from other wards but she got no reply except for heads shaken in puzzlement. Then she heard a whistling, rushing sound, followed by an explosion, and the ground beneath her feet shook.

'Bombs! It's dropping bombs!' the cry went up, but no one headed for the cellars. The spectacle of the silver craft surrounded by the brilliance of the star shells, which outshone any fireworks display Leo had ever seen, was too fascinating to miss. The Zeppelin circled over them a while longer and dropped two more bombs, then the engine note changed and it throbbed away towards the German lines.

Soon after that incident Lilian Franklin – 'Boss' to all the FANYs – called for volunteers to take a vehicle up to the front with comforts for the troops and possibly bring back casualties. There was no shortage of offers but Victoria was chosen to be the first, in view of her previous experience, and she naturally chose Leo to accompany her. Two other FANYs, Wilks and 'Nicky' Nicholson came with them. The rear of one of the ambulances was stocked with woolly socks and mufflers, chocolate and cigarettes and medical supplies and they set off through the crowded streets in high spirits. They had grown accustomed to the reactions of the local people as they went to and from the hospital. They varied from stunned amazement through to a condescending amusement to scandalized disapproval. Their uniforms came in for a great deal of comment but the fact that they drove cars was the biggest talking point.

As luck would have it, just as they crossed the Place d'Armes, the main market square, there was a bang and a jolt and the ambulance swerved to the left.

'Damn!' Victoria exclaimed. 'What a spot to get a puncture!'

They all climbed out and very quickly a small crowd assembled round them.

'Oh, how embarrassing,' Leo said. 'How fast can we change a wheel?'

'I like a challenge,' Victoria responded with a grin. 'Let's show the Frogs that we don't just drive the cars.'

She set to work while Leo leaned on the bonnet and translated, deadpan, the comments of the onlookers.

'*Zut, alors! Elle ouvre comme un homme!*' 'My goodness, she works like a man!'

'*Regarde ses bottes!*' 'Look at her boots!'

'*Et son chapeau! Quel chic!*' 'And her hat. What style!'

'*Crois-tu qu'elle peut nous entendre?*' '*Non, non. Les anglais ne parle que sa propre langue.*' 'Do you think she can understand us?' 'Oh, no, the English only speak their own language.'

The comments continued in this vein until Victoria completed the wheel change and they both climbed back into the cab. As they prepared to drive off Leo leaned out of the window and called sweetly, '*Mesdames et messieurs, le spectacle est terminé!*'

Victoria doubled up over the steering wheel. 'Their faces! How priceless!' And they drove on, laughing.

Once they were out of the city they found themselves on a long, straight road, dwindling into infinity through a flat, featureless landscape punctuated by small clusters of houses and the occasional church steeple. It was bordered on each side by deep ditches, full of mud at this time of year.

'I loathe these cobbled surfaces,' Victoria complained. 'They shake you till your teeth rattle.'

'The *pavé*, you mean,' Leo said. 'Well, it's not comfortable but at least it isn't full of potholes like so many English roads.'

'I blame the railways for that,' Victoria said. 'Now everyone goes everywhere by train no one bothers to keep the roads in good condition. We're all right on the cobbles but I dread to think what will happen if we end up in the ditch.'

She had good reason to worry. The roads were thronged with traffic. Columns of soldiers marched towards the front while refugees streamed away from it. There were farm carts pulled by oxen, guns on horse-drawn limbers, detachments of French cavalry resplendent in cuirasses and plumes and occasionally a staff car full of bemedalled officers. Overtaking, or passing another vehicle, was fraught with difficulty. At one point they found themselves behind an old shepherd, calmly driving his flock along the road.

Victoria, at the end of her patience, leaned out of the cab. '*Ecoutez! Allez* off the bloody *pavé, tout suite.*'

Leo chortled. 'Vita, your French is improving!'

At intervals they were stopped by sentries manning barriers constructed at angles across the road. They had been given a *laissez-passer* by the Belgian military command, and also told the password for the day, so these obstacles presented no more than an irritating interruption to an already tedious journey. They passed through Dunkirk and then Furnes, where they saw several buildings that had been damaged by shells and it was there that Leo heard again the sound she had heard for the first time when their ship docked in Salonika; a sound which had been the daily accompaniment to life at Chataldzha. She looked at Victoria and they nodded in mutual comprehension. From behind them a nervous voice asked, 'What's that noise? Is it gunfire?'

Leo turned round. 'I'm afraid it is, yes. But it's quite a long way off.'

Shortly after that they passed the first dead horse, its belly bloated, four legs sticking straight up in the air.

'What do you think? Killed by a shell or dropped dead from exhaustion?' Victoria asked.

Leo, thinking of Amber, had to swallow hard before replying. 'Who knows? I'm certainly not getting down to check.'

After that they saw more horses and the landscape became pitted with shell-holes. A column of walking wounded passed them, many of them limping, heads or arms swathed in bandages. The sound of the gunfire grew louder and then they all heard the whistle of a shell and an explosion somewhere just ahead. At that point the road made one of its infrequent bends, to by-pass a large farmhouse, and when they rounded it they saw a smoking crater almost in the centre of the road. Victoria stood on the brakes and Wilks and Nicky crowded forward to look over her shoulders. For a moment nobody spoke.

Then Victoria said, 'Oh well, there but for the grace of God . . .' and put the engine into gear.

Wilks said in a small voice, 'You don't think perhaps we should turn back?'

Leo was about to speak but Nicky's robust rejoinder cut her off. 'Good heavens, no! That's what we're here for, isn't it?'

There was just enough of the *pavé* left for the ambulance to edge past but it took all Victoria's skill and Leo found herself staring down into what looked like a bottomless pit of mud and praying that the wheels would not slip over the edge.

It was late afternoon when they finally drew up at a dilapidated building which was serving as a *poste de secours*, where the officer in charge was delighted to receive the medical supplies they had brought with them. The gunfire had stopped and he informed them that they could stretch their legs without fear as the bombardment had finished for the afternoon.

'How can you be so sure?' Leo asked.

'Because it happens like this every day,' he answered. 'The Boche have a schedule and they keep to it like clockwork.'

Leo looked across the darkening landscape. The banks of the Yser had been breached and the land around flooded to slow down the German advance and the light of the setting sun was reflected off the water, giving the whole scene an air of unreality.

'I don't understand,' Nicky said. 'I thought we were close to the front but I can't see any sign of either army.'

'That's because they are all dug in, in trenches,' Leo explained. 'Can you see those dark lines? They are full of men, but if they were to show themselves they would risk being blown to bits.'

They were told that they could not go up to the trenches until after dark so they sat drinking *marc* with the officer and his men until nightfall. Then they were instructed to follow one of them to a point beyond the village where a doctor would meet them. After that, they must walk in single file with at least twenty feet between them and be prepared to drop flat if the Germans sent up a star shell. They set off, each carrying a bundle containing woollen socks and mufflers, donated by knitters back in England, as well as a supply of bandages and other medical items. Along the way they passed silent lines of troops, heading for the trenches or going in the opposite direction. It was pitch dark by now and they were not allowed to show a light and Leo felt that she had trudged for miles, just keeping the shadowy figure of the doctor in sight. At last they came to the first trench and scrambled down a slippery plank into it. At once Leo's nose was assailed by a familiar stench of foetid water and human excrement and for a second she was back in the Turkish trenches with Sasha. She pushed the memory to the back of her mind and concentrated. Behind her, she could hear Wilks trying not to retch.

The first task was to assist the doctor with a number of wounded men. Then they set off along the trench to distribute the 'comforts'. It seemed to Leo that she had stumbled along for hours, up to the ankles in mud, ducking down every few yards to crawl through the entrance to a dugout where the inhabitants crouched like troglodytes around hissing paraffin lamps. Their gratitude for the gifts was touching. The socks were particularly welcomed and, feeling her own frozen feet, Leo could understand why.

When all the goods had been distributed they made their way back to the entrance, where two wounded men were waiting on stretchers.

'This is going to be tricky,' Victoria muttered. 'How are we going to get them up that slippery plank without tipping them off?'

'Tricky is an understatement,' Leo agreed. 'But it has got to be managed somehow.'

Somehow, between the four of them, they manhandled the stretchers out of the trench and set off, with aching arms, for the village. Halfway there a star shell exploded overhead, flooding the area with light, and they had to dump their burdens and lie flat until it died out. By the time they reached the *poste de secours* they were all ready to weep with exhaustion. One of the wounded men reached up and caught Leo's hand.

'*Merci! Merci, madame!*'

Leo stooped over the stretcher and managed a smile. '*De rien, mon brave.*'

Once they were safely back in the ambulance and on their way Leo voiced a thought that had been at the back of her mind since they left the trenches.

'Vita, do you think Tom and Ralph are living in the same conditions as those men?'

Victoria gave a small snort. 'Well, wherever they are, I imagine your brother's boots are not as shiny as they used to be.'

Leo looked at her. 'That's a bit hard-hearted.'

Victoria negotiated a pothole in silence. Then she said, 'Sorry. I suppose it was a bit uncalled for. But you must admit Ralph did need taking down a peg or two.'

Leo thought back to the scene at Adrianople, when he had discovered her in her male disguise. Than she remembered what Tom had told her about their exploits in Sarajevo. 'He can be a pompous ass at times,' she conceded, 'but he's very brave, you know. He'll be doing his bit with the best of them.'

The conversation lapsed, largely because Leo had to fight to stay awake. She tried to keep talking, because she was afraid that Victoria might drop off and drive them into the ditch, but she kept forgetting what she was trying to say. In the end, it was only the frequent need to whisper the password for the day to the sentries along the way that kept her from falling into a deep sleep.

Back at the hospital, Leo found a letter waiting for her. It was from Luke, telling her that he and his regiment were now encamped outside Cairo.

We're training with a load of Australians and people have started referring to us as ANZACs. We're not too sure about being lumped in with them — they're an uncouth lot, most of them. But they seem to be pretty tough, so on the whole we're glad to have them fighting alongside us. Anyway, now the Turks have come into the war, it means I'll have a chance to even some old scores.

A few days later, walking back to the Bon Genie with Victoria, Leo's gaze was attracted by a lighted shop window. In it was a replica of the Nativity scene. Leo stopped dead and caught Victoria's sleeve.

'Vita, what's the date?'

Victoria frowned. 'No idea. Why?'

'Look!' She indicated the window. 'It must be nearly Christmas.'

She opened the shop door and asked the woman behind the counter what the date was. The women stared at her with an expression that said plainly that these strange English girls were obviously mad, or heathens — or both.

'It's December the twenty-first, mademoiselle.'

'The twenty-first!' Leo repeated to Victoria. 'It's almost Christmas and we'd forgotten. We must do something for the patients.'

'Difficult,' Victoria said. 'There's nothing in the shops to make a Christmas meal and we couldn't give them all presents.'

'Perhaps we could get together and sing carols,' Leo suggested.

'Let's see what Boss says. She may have something up her sleeve.'

Lilian Franklin had given some thought to the festival and over the next three days everyone who had a moment to spare was occupied in wrapping presents, culled from among the various comforts sent out from England. So on Christmas morning every man received a parcel containing cigarettes and chocolate, often with a handwritten card from whichever nurse had been taking care of them. Leo's suggestion of carol singing was well received and after a few scratch rehearsals all the FANYs not actively required for duty assembled and toured the wards, singing 'Away in a Manger' and 'While Shepherds Watched Their Flocks by Night' and 'O Come, All Ye Faithful.' The patients were delighted and some of them joined in, singing along in their own languages.

Afterwards, Beryl Hutchinson, who had already established herself as one of the leading spirits in the group, said, 'You know, we were not half bad, even after only two rehearsals. I reckon if we put our minds to it we could put on a pretty good revue.'

'It reminds me of Christmas in Lozengrad.' Victoria said privately to Leo. 'Oh, no, you weren't there, were you?'

'No, but you told me about it,' Leo said. 'About how the local orderlies taught the men to wish you Merry Christmas and they all sat up in bed and chanted . . .'

'Melly Chissimas!' Victoria laughed.

'And Melly Chissimas to you, too!' Leo responded.

Further along the line of trenches that now stretched from the Channel to the Alps, in a dugout only slightly larger and more salubrious than the ones Leo had visited, Tom and Ralph huddled over a paraffin stove. Tom was sketching and Ralph was desultorily flicking through the pages of an old copy of *Punch*. Tom raised his head.

'Listen!'

Ralph cocked an ear. 'Sounds all quiet to me. I checked the sentries ten minutes ago.'

'No, I don't mean anything like that. Can't you hear it?'

'Hear what?'

'Sounds like singing.' Tom got up and lifted the tarpaulin covering the entrance. The sound was clearer now; male voices singing a lilting lullaby. 'It's coming from the German trenches! I've heard that tune before. I think it's a Christmas carol.'

Ralph joined him at the entrance. 'You're right.' Then he added gloomily, 'Can't think what the Boche have got to sing about.'

'As much or as little as we have, I suppose,' Tom said. 'I imagine they are just as fed up and homesick as we are. Maybe singing carols helps them to remember that somewhere out there people are still living more or less normal lives, putting up decorations, wrapping presents, all the usual things, and one day we shall be doing it, too.'

'Shall we?' Ralph asked.

'Of course. Next year we may all be home.'

'I doubt it. I shan't see another Christmas.'

'What on earth do you mean by that?'

'You know what the mortality rate has been among junior officers in these few months. I don't expect to escape much longer.'

Tom looked at him in dismay. 'You mustn't think like that! That's the way to get yourself killed.' Ralph shook his head without speaking and Tom, with a flutter of nerves at the pit of his stomach, laid his arm across his shoulders. 'Come on, old chap! You've borne a charmed life so far, and it's going to go on. We're going to survive this war and I won't hear you say otherwise.'

For once Ralph did not shrug away from the contact as he usually did, but leaned against him and gripped his shoulder in return. 'Good old Tom! I'm glad you're here with me.' He met Tom's eyes. 'I suppose it would sound daft to say "Happy Christmas"?'

'Not to me,' Tom replied, his voice suddenly husky. 'Happy Christmas, Ralph.'

Eight

'Ever been up in a balloon, Devenish?' the colonel asked.

'What?' Tom responded, aghast, then remembering his position, added: 'Sorry, sir. A balloon? No, never.'

'Well, you're going to have that pleasure tomorrow,' the colonel informed him.

'Me, sir? But I can't . . . I mean, I'm not very good at heights . . . Why me . . . ? He trailed into silence.

'Because we need your eyes up there. I've seen some of your drawings. You have a remarkable eye for detail and we need to know everything we can about the enemy dispositions. The Royal Flying Corps chappies do their best, but the photographs are very indistinct. From the balloon you should be able to get a pretty clear picture of the location of artillery emplacements, fuel and ammunition dumps etc. That's what we need from you, in as much detail as possible. Captain Manson here will brief you with the arrangements.'

Tom made his way back to the house where he and Ralph had been billeted in a mood of fatalistic depression. The Coldstreamers had been withdrawn from the line for a rest and until that morning he had been enjoying the chance of sleeping under a proper roof. Though even that was a doubtful pleasure, since the shelling had left huge holes in it, and as it was a single storey building there were only limited places where it was possible to avoid the unending rain. At least the big stove in the centre of the main room still worked and he had been able to dry out his clothes and boots.

After the initial fighting around Ypres both sides had dug in and the winter months had become an exercise in stubborn endurance. The days had passed in the unending routine of drills and inspections interspersed with periods of inactivity and boredom. Now it was March and everyone knew that the coming of spring meant the beginning of a new offensive.

The sickening knot in Tom's stomach was due as much to the anticipation of renewed fighting as to the prospect of going up in the balloon. He was not afraid so much for himself as for Ralph. He knew that his role as official war artist was supposed to keep him out of the fighting line, but he had learned already that the distinction was impossible to maintain; at least he would not be required to lead men into battle, as Ralph would be. He sensed that Ralph was chafing at the inactivity of the winter and eager for the fighting to start again but there was a fatalistic quality about that eagerness that disturbed him.

When he told Ralph about the balloon he saw his eyes widen and for a moment he looked as if he was about to voice a protest. Then his expression changed and he looked away, saying, 'You lucky bugger! I wouldn't mind going up in one of those things.'

'Well, you'd be welcome to take my place, if it was possible,' Tom replied. 'You know how I feel about heights. I shall probably be sick or start blubbing, or disgrace myself in some other way.'

'Oh, you'll be fine,' Ralph said dismissively. 'You'll soon get over it.'

Looking at him, Tom knew that neither of them was saying what was really in his mind; namely that balloons presented an obvious threat and were therefore often targeted by enemy aircraft. They had both seen what happened when a hydrogen filled balloon was hit by incendiary bullets.

The following morning was damp and chill, with a threat of snow in the air and Tom had hopes that the flight might be cancelled. He arrived at the site soon after dawn and shivered as he saw the vast, sausage-shaped balloon hovering a few feet above the ground, tugging at the mooring lines that held it. The basket below it looked improbably small by comparison. He had not eaten breakfast, as a precaution, and now he was unsure whether the nausea he was feeling was a product of nerves or hunger.

The pilot, who introduced himself as 'Wally' Wallace, was a man in his thirties with a large, drooping moustache and a quite unreasonably cheerful manner, or so it seemed to Tom.

'Ever been up in one of these before?'

Tom shook his head and tried to stop his teeth from chattering.

'Nothing to it, old boy! Climb in and hang on to that handle, there, and keep your knees bent during the take-off. Same when we land. Apart from that, sit back and enjoy the ride!'

'Once we're up, what's to stop us drifting away and ending up on the wrong side of the lines?' Tom asked.

'No chance of that,' the pilot replied. 'We shall be tethered to that cable there – see? – and that is attached to that winch. In the event of a problem, such as an attack by an enemy plane, we can be winched down in less than a minute. Planes won't risk coming down to less than a thousand feet, because of the ack-ack guns. Don't worry, we're well protected. Oh, here. You'd better put this on.'

He handed Tom a package resembling a rucksack. 'What is it?' Tom asked.

'Parachute, old boy. Don't worry, you won't have to use it, but we're supposed to wear them.'

Tom allowed himself to be strapped into the parachute and climbed stiffly over the side of the basket. He heard Wally shouting orders to the ground crew, who were hanging on to the ropes that kept the balloon from soaring away. He gripped the handle like a drowning man clinging to a life raft and shut his eyes. There was a slight jolt, a sense that his body had grown suddenly heavier and then a gentle rocking motion.

'Right, that'll do,' Wally said. 'Visibility's not too bad. You should be able to see all you need to see from here.'

Tom opened his eyes and looked down. Below him the landscape swayed gently as if the solid earth was tilting from side to side. He stared for a minute, then grabbed the side of the basket and leaned out, retching.

'Oh dear, oh dear!' Wally's voice came from behind him. 'Lost our breakfast, have we? Never mind. It takes some people that way to begin with but you'll get over it. Now, you'd better get your sketches done before the Boche decide to use us for target practice.'

Tom straightened up, the bitter taste of bile in his mouth, and reached into the case he carried on one shoulder to produce his sketch pad and pencil. He moved unsteadily to the side of the basket facing the enemy lines and forced himself to examine the scene below him. The basket had come to rest and the ground had almost stopped swaying and he was amazed at how far he could see. In the foreground were the British trenches: first the reserve line, then the support line and furthest away from him the front line, with a network of communication trenches. Beyond the front line was no-man's-land, a grey wasteland pitted with shell-holes and bisected by barricades of barbed wire. Beyond that was the first line of German trenches. Further away still was the village of Neuve Chapelle, the skeletons of houses abandoned long ago by their inhabitants. The landscape beyond the village was flat and featureless until it rose in a low ridge, the Aubers Ridge, which Tom knew would be one of the objectives in the next attack.

He lifted his field glasses and studied the village. He could see German strong-points, reinforced with sandbags, but it was another sight that made him catch his breath. In the middle of what had once been the village square, which was now a mass of rubble, the crucifix that had been its central point still stood, the figure of the Christ gazing out across the desolation as if, Tom thought, in despair at human stupidity.

He opened his sketch pad and began to draw and as he did so the usual morning artillery barrage from the German guns opened up. From his vantage point he could see from the muzzle flashes the exact position of each battery and he marked them carefully on his sketch. Working quickly, he drew in other salient features. There was a small wood, a farmhouse with a moat round it, several sunken roads which were a feature of the area and could be useful routes for an advance. He had almost finished when he realized that he was no longer feeling sick. When he was sure that he had included every useful detail he turned the page and raised his glasses once again, focusing on the crucifix. Here was an image that seemed to encapsulate everything he felt about the war and he was determined to capture it. He had only had time to make a preliminary sketch, however, when there was a sudden explosion of noise all round the balloon and puffs of white smoke filled the sky.

He heard Wally shout, 'Enemy aircraft! Hang on, we're going down!'

With a speed that made Tom feel as if his stomach was rising up into his throat, the balloon descended. He craned his neck to look upwards but the bulk of the balloon itself made it hard to see what was happening. Above the noise of the anti-aircraft guns he could hear the sound of an aero engine coming closer and then he caught a glimpse of a German biplane banking sharply as it turned away. The basket hit the ground with a bump that almost knocked him off his feet and he realized that he had forgotten Wally's instructions about holding on and bending his knees.

'Sorry about that, old man,' Wally said. 'Did you get all you needed?'

Tom assured him that he had and shook hands. 'Thanks for taking me up. It's been a memorable experience.'

'You're welcome . . . any time,' Wally responded cheerily.

'Not if I can help it,' Tom muttered under his breath as he walked away.

His relief was short-lived. After he had reported to the colonel and shown him the drawing, which was pronounced splendid and an excellent aid for forward planning, he was stunned into silence by the CO's next remark.

'Right! When the attack commences you will have a grand-stand seat. I want you up there again, watching and reporting back. The devil in these situations is that once an advance begins it's impossible to keep in contact. Half the time we, here at the command post, haven't the vaguest idea of what's going on at the front, and it takes too long for runners to reach us. Your observations will be crucial.'

The next two days passed in an atmosphere of growing tension. Everyone knew that a new attack was imminent, but no one knew when or where it would happen. Ralph spent much of his time with his men and Tom's admiration grew for the concern he showed for their welfare. He knew each one of them personally, remembered their families and their problems, looked after their health and made sure that they had the best of whatever was available in the way of food and comfort. When he was not with them, he was moody and restless. Tom tried to engage him in a game of chess, which had been one of their favourite pastimes in pre-war days, but he was unable to concentrate. He had brought a gramophone out from England and a collection of ragtime records, which he played over and over again, until Tom was forced to seek peace and quiet outside.

On the evening of 9 March Ralph came back from a briefing and Tom knew at once that they were about to go into action.

'This is it,' Ralph said, rubbing his hands. 'We go up the line at four thirty a.m. The bombardment will start at six thirty and this time the artillery are going to concentrate all their fire on the primary objective, which is the Boche first line of trenches. Once they have been reduced, we go in and the artillery moves the target to the next objective.'

'Which is?'

'The village and the Bois du Biez. Ultimately, if all goes well, we shall take the Aubers Ridge, which will deprive the enemy of the high ground. If we can do that we shall have cut through the German lines. So, this is the big push – and you'll see it all happening, you lucky devil! We poor bloody infantry never get to see the big picture. All we know is what's happening within about forty feet of us.'

'Well, I'll show you the pictures when you get back,' Tom said, trying to keep his voice even.

Ralph turned away, holding his hands to the warmth of the primus stove. 'Oh,' he said, as casually as if he was saying he would not be home for dinner, 'I shan't be back. I know that. I've been lucky so far but I know my number's up this time.'

Tom strode across the intervening space and grabbed him by the shoulders, swinging him round to face him. 'Don't talk like that! You can't know anything of the sort.'

Ralph shrugged and looked away. 'I do. I can't explain how. I just feel it.'

'That's nonsense! Can't you see that thinking like that is the best way to ensure that you don't come back? You have to make up your mind that you're going to survive.' He paused, struggling for words. 'Listen, what would you say to one of your men if he told you he was sure he was going to die in the next attack?'

Ralph's eyes swivelled from side to side in the effort to avoid Tom's gaze. 'I'd tell him to stow that sort of defeatist talk. But I'm not telling them how I feel. Give me some credit!'

'Do you think they can't guess? You don't have to put it into words. It's there in your eyes. They need you, Ralph! What will they do without their officer? You have to come back for their sakes. You owe it to them to do your damnedest to survive.'

For a moment Ralph continued to look from side to side as if searching for a way of escape. Then Tom felt his shoulders begin to shake and he ducked his head, but not before Tom had seen his eyes well up with tears. Without further hesitation, Tom did what he had longed to do so often before and put his arms round him. Ralph burrowed into his shoulder and Tom held him tightly, rubbing his face into the dishevelled chestnut hair. For a moment they clung together without speaking, then Ralph pulled away, blew his nose and walked out of the door. Tom took a step or two after him, then thought better of it and instead busied himself putting the kettle on the primus.

Ralph came back after ten minutes or so, huddling his greatcoat round his ears. 'Bloody hell! I thought it was supposed to be spring! It's snowing out there.'

'Never mind,' Tom said, carefully casual. 'Come and have a hot cup of tea.'

Neither of them slept much that night and it was still snowing at four a.m. when Ralph left to join his men in the reserve trenches. There was no repeat of the emotional scene of the previous evening. Ralph checked that his revolver was fully loaded, shrugged on his greatcoat and said lightly, 'Cheerio, old man!' and Tom replied, 'See you later.'

When it was light Tom reported to his position at the

balloon launching point, where Wally was waiting for him. This time he kept his eyes shut until he felt that the basket had stopped swinging and managed to avoid a repeat of the sickness that had overtaken him before. They had just reached their intended height when the British guns opened up in a barrage that was more intense than any Tom had ever heard.

'By George, they're giving the Boche a proper pasting!' Wally exclaimed. Tom agreed and wondered if the Germans had any idea what the sequel would be. He peered eagerly across the expanse of no-man's-land and saw the shells bursting on the trenches with their barbed wire entanglements. So far, so good. The sound of aircraft engines caused him a sudden lurch of alarm but Wally said quickly, 'It's OK. They're ours. See?'

Three planes bearing the red, white and blue roundels of the Royal Flying Corps, appeared from the south and began to patrol over the battleground. They were almost at the same height as the balloon and it was the first chance Tom had had to study one at close quarters.

'Those things look as if they're held together with paper and string,' he commented.

'You're absolutely right!' Wally agreed. 'Give me a balloon any day.'

'Just a minute! What is that chap doing?' Tom pointed to the nearest aircraft. The planes were manned by two men and, as he watched, the observer leaned over the side of the cockpit and dropped something. Seconds later they saw the puff of an explosion close to the German trench.

'A bomb, by God!' Wally exclaimed. 'That's the first time I've seen that.'

Before long the planes turned and headed for home but the barrage continued for half an hour. Tom was sketching busily when he was startled by the sound of a bugle and Wally exclaimed, 'There they go!' Staring through his field glasses Tom saw men scrambling up out of the front-line trenches and swarming across no-man's-land. There was something inhuman about the sight and he found himself thinking of ants or locusts – or maybe lemmings. The first of them was well across before the Germans, presumably startled out of their early morning lethargy, opened fire. Tom saw men falling and soon the ground was littered with bodies, but the wave of attackers rolled on and the leaders reached the German trenches. At that point Tom could no longer follow what was happening, or distinguish friend from foe. The infantrymen poured over the rim of the trench and what went on beyond it was hidden, even from his vantage point.

Suddenly, figures appeared on the far side of the trenches, running across the clear ground towards the village.

'By God, they've got them on the run!' Wally shouted. 'They've bloody done it. They've taken the first trenches!'

Today, as well as the line tethering the balloon to the winch, they were trailing another wire connected to a field telephone, through which they were to relay their observations to the ground. Tom wound the handle and when a voice crackled down the line in answer he reported that the first phase of the attack appeared to have been successful.

The British soldiers were surging towards Neuve Chapelle now and soon disappeared again amongst the ruined buildings. Other units were spreading out across the plain while more poured out of the trenches. Movement to the south caught Tom's attention.

'Where do that lot think they're going?' he asked. 'They're heading straight for a section where the wire hasn't been cut.'

He wound the telephone again and reported that one unit appeared to have lost their sense of direction and were heading for disaster, but whether the fact was passed on to HQ he never knew. Perhaps it was impossible to communicate with the wandering unit. Either way, he watched helplessly as the soldiers threw themselves uselessly against the strongly defended section and were cut down almost to a man.

The fighting around the village went on for another two hours but by midday it seemed to have died down.

'It looks as though we've done it,' Wally said with a cheerful insouciance that made Tom want to strike him.

'I thought we were supposed to move on to take the wood and Aubers Ridge,' Tom responded.

'Waiting for reinforcements, I expect,' Wally said.

The artillery barrage had refocused on the ridge but Tom, watching through his glasses, realized that many of the shells were falling short. He reported the fact, but it seemed to make no difference. Before long they saw several companies moving out of the village in the direction of the ridge, but the Germans were ready for them now and the wire, it seemed, was still intact. Tom saw more men fall and at length the remainder retreated to the village.

'Where are the reinforcements?' Tom demanded, of the air. 'God knows, I'm no military strategist, but it's obvious we can't hold on to the gains we've made without more men.'

When darkness fell the situation was more or less unchanged. The balloon was winched down and Tom went to the command centre to give a fuller account of what he had observed. He raised the question of reinforcements and was told that there had been a delay but they were on their way. No one seemed to know quite why or where the new units were at that precise moment. Tom went back to his billet but was unable to rest. Eventually, he made his way up the line to the forward dressing station, hoping and at the same time dreading to get news of Ralph. No one knew where he was, but it was assumed that he was with his men in Neuve Chapelle. Tom spent most of the night at the grim task of listing the names of the dead and dying.

After four hours sleep he was back at his post in the balloon, watching helplessly as attack after attack was thrown back by the German second line of defence. There was still no sign of the promised reinforcements. Then his glasses picked up movement on the Aubers Ridge and he saw, to his dismay, columns of fresh German troops advancing. He wound the handle on the telephone desperately.

'Tell HQ that German reinforcements are approaching from the ridge. I can't estimate numbers yet but there are a lot of them. Our men need backup urgently!'

He saw the final reserves brought forward and pushed into the line. The British forces were entrenched in what had been the enemy strong points and mounted a stubborn resistance and by evening it was obvious that a stalemate had been reached. The Germans were unable to push them back, but the advantage of the early success had been lost and the ridge had not been taken. What the cost in lives had been for the gain of a few yards Tom could not begin to estimate.

By noon the next day a truce had been declared so that both sides could bury their dead and Tom was relieved of his duty. He made his way forward, through the British trenches and across no-man's-land, stepping over bodies so mud plastered that it was hard to tell from their uniform which side they belonged to. In the German trenches there were more bodies, and burial parties were picking their way among them but Tom did not recognize any Coldstream uniforms. He asked several times for information but no one seemed to know where any particular units were. In the confusion they had become inextricably mixed.

He found some of Ralph's men eventually, hunkered down in a German dugout on the outskirts of the village.

'Where is Lieutenant Malham Brown?' he asked.

A corporal struggled to his feet. 'Sorry, sir. We've no idea. He was ahead of us when we pushed out of the first enemy trench but there was a lot of hand-to-hand business when we reached the village and I lost sight of him. We've scouted round but we couldn't find any sign of him. We think perhaps he pushed on towards the ridge without waiting for us.'

Tom understood the force of the cliché 'his heart sank'. It was as if some vital force was draining out of his body as he remembered watching the advancing lines thrown back time after time, and the landscape scattered with bodies.

'I'll keep looking,' he said thickly and stumbled on.

He found Ralph at last, standing under the crucifix in the village square, his uniform in tatters, his revolver dangling from one hand, his face blank and deathly white. He looked up as Tom approached and shook his head slowly.

'I don't know what to do, Tom.' He sounded like a bewildered child. 'There are too many of them.' He made a movement of his free hand to indicate the bodies heaped around him.

Tom took him by the arm. 'It's all right,' he said. 'You don't have to do anything. The burial parties will see to them. Come along. Your men need you. This way.'

Ralph looked at him and there was a hint of new life in his eyes. 'My men? They're not all dead?'

'No. I've seen some of them. Come on. I'll show you.'

He tugged his arm gently and Ralph roused himself as if waking from sleep and let himself be led away.

Nine

In Calais, as winter turned slowly to spring, life at Lamarck continued in the same routine. Casualties were collected from the trains and transported to the hospitals or, in the case of the most severely wounded, directly to the hospital ships in the harbour. The patients had to be fed and bathed, dressings had to be changed, and there was the occasional variation of a trip up to the front line to distribute comforts and collect casualties. The work was unremitting and carried out against a background of Zeppelin raids, limited rations and inadequate sleep. Amazingly, in the middle of it all, Grace Ashley-Smith found time to get married and became Mrs MacDougall – known from then on to everyone as Mac.

There were more vehicles now. They had three ambulances, converted trucks with canvas hoods and no windscreens; two lorries, which were used for carrying supplies; and of course Sparky, who was pressed into service to carry the less seriously wounded – designated 'sitters' rather than 'liers' (a terminology that gave rise to some considerable amusement among the troops). Leo saw less of Victoria these days, because as one of the most experienced drivers she was more often put in charge of this side of the work.

Every day at ten in the morning they all met in the common room at the top of the building, in the steamy fug produced by the freshly laundered sheets that hung on clothes horses around the big black stove. There, for a few precious minutes, they drank tea, ate biscuits and swapped stories. One morning Victoria rushed in, breathless with amusement.

'I say, girls, come and look at this!'

They crowded to the window and Leo saw in the courtyard below a quite extraordinary-looking vehicle.

'What on earth is it?' she asked.

'Mobile baths,' Victoria replied.

They all clattered down the stone stairs and found 'Boss'

talking to two unknown young women in FANY uniform.
The elder of the two turned to greet them.

'Good morning. I'm Gamwell – Marion – and this is my
sister, Hope.'

'Is it really a mobile bath?' Leo asked.

'Baths, plural,' was the reply. 'Come and have a look.' As
many of them as possible crowded into the vehicle and Marion
went on: 'It's a forty-horsepower Daimler engine and the chassis
has been specially fitted out. There's a boiler here – you see?
– with a tank and a pump, and six canvas baths on either side,
all divided off with these canvas screens.'

'That's marvellous!' Leo exclaimed. 'And it really works?'

'Well, proof of the pudding and all that . . .' Marion said
with a grin. 'But we've tested all the equipment and we should
be able to bathe twelve men every fifteen minutes – say forty-
eight an hour. And what's more, we can boil up their clothes
as well.'

'It's exactly what's needed,' Lilian Franklin said. 'Most of the
men are ridden with lice, poor things. No wonder there is so
much typhus.'

Leo found that the days began to blur into each other, each
of them a long round of back-breaking labour. To her intense
distress, she discovered that the resilience and self-confidence
which had carried her through the mud of Chataldzha and
the squalor of Adrianople seemed to have deserted her. Then,
she had been buoyed up by the excitement of strange surroundings and new experiences; and there had been, of course,
the vital frisson of knowing that Sasha Malkovic was somewhere nearby. Now, the work had become a matter of routine,
there were few distractions in Calais, and she was more acutely
aware than ever of the pointless waste and misery of war.

Her depression was deepened by the news from the front.
She knew from letters forwarded from Sussex Gardens that
Tom and Ralph were somewhere in the Ypres salient and
she dreaded going to pick up casualties from the train one
morning and finding one or both of them there. But her
worst imaginings were centred on what was happening in
Serbia. In November the Austrians had occupied Belgrade but

then, in a determined counter-attack, the Serbs had retaken it and pushed forward into Bosnia and Croatia. Max had ceased to write and she had no way of knowing whether he had been killed in the fighting, or had fled the country, or whether he was still at his post but unable to get letters out. Either way, she had no news of Sasha and no way of knowing if he was alive or dead.

Strangely, it was the behaviour of her colleagues that she found hardest to tolerate. At the outset, she had had private doubts about how some of her fellow FANYs, with their highly privileged upbringing, would react when faced with real casualties. It was one thing to be full of fun and enthusiasm at camp in England but could they cope with the real thing? She soon had to recognize that they coped superbly. Their main resource was humour – much of it of a fairly black variety. They had the capacity to transform even the most gruesome occurrences into jokes that left them all doubled up with giggles. All except Leo. She found herself unable to join in the laughter and every day it grated more and more on her nerves.

One morning in the common room she found herself screaming at the top of her voice. 'Stop it! Stop it! It's not funny! How can you laugh like that? You're like a lot of little children! Stop it, for God's sake!' In the stunned silence that followed she was overwhelmed by a wave of anguish. She clasped her hands over her ears and sank down on a bale of blankets that served as a stool, sobbing desolately.

Victoria was by her side instantly, wrapping her arms round her. 'Leo, don't, don't! Whatever is it? Come on, old thing, this is not like you.'

'It is, it is!' Leo sobbed. 'I'm such a bitch, Vita. I've been so full of my own importance, as if I'm the only one who knows what to do. And I'm the feeblest of you all. I can't bear it. I can't face it any more.'

Victoria's arm was removed and Leo felt her shoulders gripped by less kindly hands. Sister Wicks' voice cut through her paroxysms of self-flagellation. 'Now, that's quite enough of that. Pull yourself together. We've got enough to cope with. The last thing we need is you sobbing and screaming.' Then, as Leo looked up and gulped back her tears, she went on more gently: 'You're tired. We all are. But you're one of the strong ones. We need you to help the rest to keep going. Now, you've had your little outburst. Go and wash your face and get back to work.'

Later, Victoria sought Leo out on the ward. 'Are you all right?'

'Yes. I'm sorry about earlier.'

'What you said, about being the only one who knows what to do . . .'

Leo shook her head and brushed the back of her hand across her eyes. 'I'm so ashamed of myself, Vita. You know once, years ago, I heard my grandmother tell someone I was arrogant. And she was right. I've always had this idea of myself as being stronger and braver and cleverer than other people and I'm not. I can't compete with the likes of Mac or Boss or . . . or any of the others.'

'That's not true!' Victoria said, with quiet conviction. 'You've been terrific with the typhoid patients. Most of the others were scared stiff to begin with and they looked to you to show them what to do. They still do.'

Leo sighed. 'I don't know. Maybe I am just tired. It's all such a mess, such a waste.'

'I know,' Victoria responded. 'But what can we do? We just have to keep going and hope for the best. But just remember, you've got nothing to be ashamed of.'

Two days later Leo received a letter, forwarded as usual from Sussex Gardens. As soon as she had finished reading it she hurried to find Victoria, who was down in the courtyard with her head, as usual, under the bonnet of one of the ambulances.

'Vita, I've had a letter from Mabel Stobart!'

Victoria straightened up. 'Really? The last rumour we heard was that she'd been arrested as a spy by the Germans. Was it true?'

'I don't know, she doesn't say. The point is, Vita, she's going back to Serbia. She's got another convoy together and they're sailing from Liverpool on the first of April.'

Victoria resumed her work on the engine. 'Good for her!'
'But don't you see?' Leo persisted. 'We have to go with her.'
'Oh, no, we don't!'
'You mean, you won't come?'
Victoria stood up again. 'Leo, you are not seriously considering going back there, are you?'
'Of course I am. I must!'
'Why?'
'You know why.'
Victoria wiped her hands on a rag and reached out to touch Leo's arm. 'What's the point? The chances are you'd never catch up with him – assuming he's still alive. And even if you did, he's married. You know that.'
'Married to a girl he doesn't love.'
'But still . . .'
'It wouldn't matter! She won't be with him. She'll be on the family estate, or perhaps evacuated to Greece or somewhere safe. If I can just find him, Vita . . . if we can just have a few weeks, a few days even . . .'
'You mean, an affair?'
'If that's what you want to call it. And you can't criticize me, you of all people. Not after Luke.'
'I'm not criticizing. I'm just afraid that you'll go out there, into heaven knows what dangers, and then discover that he's miles away, or . . . or dead . . . or . . .'
'Or what?'
'It's been nearly two years, Leo. A lot can have changed in that time.'
'He won't have changed,' Leo said with conviction. 'And if I go, at least I shall be able to find out where he is, and if he's still alive. I have to go, Vita. You must understand that.'
Victoria sighed. 'I suppose so. You're not happy here, that's obvious. It's got to be your decision.'
'And you won't come with me?'
Their eyes met and Victoria shook her head slowly. 'No, I'm sorry, Leo. Not this time. I like what I'm doing here. You know I've always preferred the driving to the nursing, and I don't imagine the Serbs will have many motor ambulances. I know I can be useful here and I've always felt that my first

loyalty is to the FANY. So, no, I'm afraid I won't come with you.'

Leo held her gaze for a moment, tempted to try to persuade her, but what she saw convinced her that she would be wasting her time. She turned away sadly. 'All right, if that's how you feel. I'd better go and break the news that I'm leaving to Boss.'

Grace MacDougall was away, attending a meeting somewhere, so Leo had an uncomfortable interview with Lilian Franklin.

'I know you were involved with Stobart in Bulgaria, but you're a FANY first and foremost. I don't understand why you feel you have any obligation to rejoin her.'

Leo could not explain her real reasons so she said, 'I feel an obligation to the people I worked with out there. The Serbs are fighting the Austrians all on their own and we haven't lifted a finger to help, and their soldiers need nursing just as badly as ours.'

'But it was the Bulgarians you worked with, wasn't it?'

'It was both. They were fighting on the same side then. Now the Serbs are with us and the Bulgars have chosen to remain neutral.'

'But don't you have a duty to our men? Why do you want to go off and nurse the Serbs instead?'

'I'm not nursing "our" men, am I?' Leo pointed out. 'What is the difference between nursing Belgians or Serbs, when we are all fighting on the same side?'

That effectively finished the argument and Franklin conceded stiffly that, since Leo was a volunteer and under no obligation to remain, she could do as she pleased. The other FANYs were stunned to learn that she was leaving and it was equally hard to convince them that she had good reasons, since only Victoria knew the true story. One or two even implied that she was running away. Leo shrugged and would have ignored them, but Victoria leapt to her defence, with a graphic account of the conditions they had endured on their previous expedition. Leo left her to it and went to pack, although she had a suspicion, from the changed attitudes she met when she went to say goodbye, that her friend had dropped a few hints that there was more to her decision than they had been told.

Victoria drove her to the ferry. On the quayside they hugged each other and Leo murmured, 'I wish you were coming with me.'

'I wish you were staying here,' Victoria responded, 'but all I can do is wish you luck. I hope you find him – and if you do, don't let old-fashioned Victorian morality stand in your way. Take a leaf out of my book!'

'I shall,' Leo promised. 'Take care, Vita. For goodness' sake, mind how you drive. Stay on the bloody *pavé*!'

'I'll try!' Victoria forced a laugh but Leo saw that there were tears in her eyes. 'Take care, yourself.'

'I will.' They looked at each other in silence for a minute, then Leo said, 'I expect the war will be over by the time we see each other again.'

Victoria hugged her again. 'Then let's hope it ends soon! I won't say goodbye. Just *au revoir*.'

'*Au revoir*,' Leo echoed. Then she turned away and hurried up the gangplank without stopping to look back.

Mabel Stobart's convoy sailed from Liverpool on 1 April, with Leo among them. It was a larger group than the one which had manned the hospital in Lozengrad, including among others seven women doctors. They were not the only medical expedition on the ship. It was crammed with Red Cross volunteers and VADs, all bound for the same destination. The first few days were tense, as they had been told to anticipate attacks from the Germans' new submarines in the Irish Sea, but the danger did not materialize and on 8 April they reached Gibraltar. On 15 April they sailed into the harbour at Salonika. Standing on the deck, watching the towers and domes appear out of the mist, Leo was almost swamped by nostalgia. Two and a half years had passed since she last saw this sight but now she could hardly recognize the naïve, excitable girl who had stood there then.

The same contrast between then and now persisted as they went ashore. She remembered the irritation and disbelief with which she and Victoria had been met on that first occasion. Now, the group was expected and welcomed and their onward passage was smoothed by the new British military attaché,

Colonel Harrison, and Colonel Hunter, who was in charge of the Royal Army Medical Corps' mission. They were to go, they were informed, to Kragujevac, to the south of Belgrade, where they were to set up a field hospital.

They travelled by train, first to Nis, where they spent the night, and then on to Kragujevac, and all through the journey Leo was beset by contrary emotions. First she was reminded of the last time she had passed that way, sitting between Ralph and Tom, wearing the dowdy dress her brother had bought in Salonika to replace her boy's breeches and tunic, all three of them too angry and shocked to talk. But then she became aware of the beauty of the countryside: the green hillsides and deep pastures, the orchards awash with cherry and plum blossom, the storks sitting on their nests on the tops of chimneys in the villages they passed. That recalled the drive out to the Malkovic estate when they had been invited to the family's Slava day celebrations and the garden where she and Sasha had sat and talked and she had understood for the first time that he cared as much for her as she did for him. It was that memory that she clung to as the train chugged slowly towards its destination.

Her companions teased her for her silence and her abstracted manner but she smiled and said nothing. Some of them remembered her from Lozengrad, but they had never been at Chataldzha or Adrianople and never met Sasha Malkovic.

At Kragujevac they were met by the commander of the local garrison. There was already typhus in the town, so it had been agreed that the hospital would be set up on a small hill outside. They had brought specially made tents with them and a detachment of soldiers from the garrison was detailed to put them up. By the following day they were ready to receive their first cases.

As soon as she had the opportunity Leo asked one of the officers for news from the front line. He was cheerfully optimistic. It seemed the Austrians, who had been badly mauled during their last attempt to invade, were thinking twice about trying again. Besides, they now had a Russian invasion on their eastern border to deal with. The Serbian army was encamped along the border, ready to repel any further incursions, but everyone was hopeful that the danger was past.

'The only worry is the Bulgarians,' her informant explained. 'So far, they have stayed neutral but if the Germans can persuade them to come in on the side of the Central Powers we shall have a real fight on our hands.'

As casually as possible, Leo inquired for news of Colonel Count Aleksander Malkovic, whom she had met during a previous visit to Belgrade. He was with his regiment, she was told, on the border and, as far as anyone knew, in good health. Leo thanked the officer and made an excuse to hurry away, so that he would not see the relief on her face.

Ten

Eight days after Leo's arrival at Kragujevac Luke Pavel stood on the deck of the ship that had brought him from Egypt and gazed across at the dun-coloured cliffs and snaking ravines of the Gallipoli peninsula.

'Looks a pretty godforsaken sort of territory, Sergeant,' the young officer beside him remarked.

'Too right, sir!' Luke responded. 'There isn't enough vegetation to feed a goat up there.'

'You sound as if you know it.'

'I do. But last time I was here I was up there, trying to push the Turks into the sea, instead of down here trying to get at them from the beaches.'

'What the hell were you doing?'

'Working as a stretcher-bearer for the Bulgarians.'

'What made you want to do that, for Christ's sake?'

Luke was beginning to explain when his companion interrupted.

'Hold up! Looks like the Aussies are on the move.'

Luke watched as the first troop transports headed for the shore. The beach appeared undefended but beyond it the cliffs rose steeply and as the first men landed they were cut down by merciless fire from above. Soon the beach and the shallow water along it were choked with bodies and the beach itself was a chaos of milling men as more and more transports discharged their cargoes. Groups of men ran for the narrow ravines that carved through the cliffs and Luke saw that once there they had some shelter from the fusillade and that they were beginning to work their way upwards towards a ridge that resembled, from his angle, the trunk of a sleeping elephant. The objective, he knew, was to gain the heights above it, but he knew, too, how broken and contorted the landscape was, and how easy it would be to lose all sense of direction. He licked dry lips and swallowed. The Turkish defence was more determined than they had been led to expect and there was no artillery support from their own side. He knew it would be his turn to join the melee soon.

He had to wait until four thirty that afternoon and by that time the landing craft had to push through a tangle of floating bodies to reach the beach. Small craft full of wounded surged around them, begging the sailors to take the casualties on board. As soon as his feet touched firm ground Luke ran for the shelter of the cliffs. He had fixed his eyes on a ravine that seemed from the sea to lead inland and shouted to his companions to follow him. The gully was choked with undergrowth, all of it sharp with thorns designed, it seemed, to catch at clothes and boots, but here they were out of the line of fire and Luke scrambled upwards, the others following. At the top the ravine opened out on to a narrow ridge and Luke turned left, heading still for the higher ground. Some yards further on they came upon a company of Australians, sheltering behind rocks from sniper fire. Luke looked around him and realized that there were no officers in sight.

'What's going on, lads?' he asked breathlessly.

'Search me,' one responded. 'We were told to follow this ridge but there's no shelter from here on and the ragheads are well dug in up at the top.'

Luke peered round the rocks and ducked back as a bullet whistled past his head. The Australian was right. To press on was to court certain death.

A runner stumbled up the track behind them. 'Change of orders. This way is too exposed. You're to rendezvous with Captain Fraser's lot over there, on the parallel ridge.'

Between the two ridges was a deep valley. Somehow they scrambled down into it, but once there they lost sight of the ridge they were aiming for and found themselves wandering in a maze of gullies that ended in unscalable cliffs. By the time Luke and a small group of New Zealanders finally reached the ridge the sun was low in the west and they had lost contact with the rest of the men. Once again, they began to climb towards the summit, keeping low and taking advantage of every scrap of cover from the Turkish riflemen on the hills above.

In a brief lull in the fighting Luke heard another sound, the clatter of loose stones from ahead of him.

'Wait!' He waved the men following to stop and they crouched in the shelter of a rocky outcrop. The noise came closer. He could hear boots striking rocks and men panting. Several people were heading in his direction, but were they friends or foes? Then someone slipped and he heard a very recognizable expletive.

'Shit!'

Luke raised his head and called, 'Don't shoot! We're the Wellingtons. Who are you?'

There was a stunned pause, then a voice came back: 'Bloody Kiwis! What the fuck do you think you're playing at?'

There was a scuffle of boots and a small landslide of loose stones, and six men in Australian uniform scrambled into the shelter of the rocks.

'What are you playing at?' Luke retorted. 'We're supposed to be going up, not down.'

'Good luck, mate!' was the response. 'There's a sheer precipice a couple of hundred yards further on. The only way off this effing ridge is back down.'

It was almost dark now. Luke's throat burned with thirst and dust and he was suddenly aware of how exhausted he was. He looked at his men and saw that they were in the same condition.

'If we try to get back in the dark we'll end up wandering round in circles or falling to our deaths. We'll rest up here for the night and start back at first light.'

The Australians decided that this was good counsel, so they all settled down in the lea of the rocks. Luke tipped the last dregs of water from his canteen down his throat and opened his emergency rations. Several of the others had already eaten theirs, so they shared what was left amongst them. With darkness the sniping from above had stopped and they could hear occasional shouts from other areas of the broken terrain. In one or two places they could see lights from torches moving, but no one came close to them. Far below, they could make out fires lit along the beach and the riding lights of the ships that had brought them.

'What happened to your officers?' Luke asked the Aussies.

'Captain was shot before we got across the beach,' one said. 'Gawd alone knows what happened to the others.'

'What a bloody shambles!' Luke grunted and there were mutters of agreement all round.

Now the sun was down it turned very cold. They huddled together for warmth and tried to sleep but none of them was sorry when the dawn came. Cautiously, Luke raised his head and peered round. Immediately a bullet whistled past his ear and ricocheted off the rock.

'Bloody hell!' he muttered. 'Those Turks are sharper than we reckoned.'

It was agreed that there was no point in trying to continue up the ridge, so they began to scramble back the way they had come. In the valley they met up with some of their own men under their colonel, Malone.

'We'll try that ridge to the south,' he said. 'I sent up a scouting party and they say it leads to a kind of plateau.'

It was the beginning of three days of hell. In that parched and desolate landscape there was neither food nor water. Twice small provisioning parties reached them, but they never carried enough water to slake the raging thirst they all suffered. In the face of unremitting fire from above they fought their way up on to the plateau and made another attempt to gain the high ground. Men fell to left and right of Luke, a bullet grazed his cheek and another ripped through his trouser leg, but he was unharmed. For two more nights he crouched with the others, shivering, and waiting for the firing to start again at dawn. Finally, on the fourth day after they landed, a runner reached them. The attack had failed, and they were to withdraw to the beachhead.

Eleven

Early in May Luke and the rest of the Wellingtons were transferred from the chaos of what had become known as Anzac
Cove to another landing beach on the far side of Cape Helles,
where a second beachhead had been established. Their new
objective, they were informed, was the village of Krithia, which
stood between them and the mountain called Achi Baba. From
the top of Achi Baba, the allied forces would be able to
command the Dardanelles and enable the British and French
fleets to enter the Black Sea. On the day after their arrival,
Luke was summoned to the tent occupied by Colonel William
Malone, the Wellington's commanding officer. Luke liked
Malone. He was a strong leader, who could appear domineering
at times, but he understood soldiering and his men trusted
him.

Malone came to the point without preamble. 'Lieutenant
Franklin tells me you've been here before.'

'Not here, exactly, sir,' Luke replied. 'But inland, above here.
I was with the Bulgarians in 1912, when they were trying to
push the Turks into the sea.'

'In Krithia?'

'No, sir. Krithia was always in Turkish hands.' But as he said
it something flickered in Luke's memory. He had heard the
name of the village before.

'And you speak the local language. Is that so?'

'Yes, sir. My grandparents came from near here.'

'Could you pass for a local?'

Luke drew in his breath. Instinct told him to say 'no', but
there was a quiver of excitement in the pit of his stomach that
urged otherwise. 'Possibly, sir.'

Malone had been pacing around the tent. Now he stopped
and fixed Luke with his eyes. 'What I am asking, Pavel, is this.
We desperately need more information about the Turkish
dispositions. Would you be prepared to go in undercover and

try to find out as much as you can about their numbers and type of armament, position of guns etc.? It's asking a lot, I know. But it could save lives when it comes to the attack.'

For a moment Luke struggled to take in what the request implied. Then he said, 'I'll do my best, sir.'

As darkness fell, Luke, clad in rough peasant's clothing whose provenance he thought it best not to question, made his way to the forward trenches. The night was still and clear, with no moon, and the cloudless sky was brilliant with stars. As he crouched listening for any sign of movement a nightingale began to sing from somewhere above him on the hillside. The landscape was very different here from the cliffs above Anzac beach. Reconnoitring the area through glasses earlier, he had seen grassy slopes, dotted with orchids and rock roses. The village itself was set in a slight valley among mulberry and oak trees and surrounded by orchards of apricot and almonds.

Everything seemed quiet, so he hoisted himself up and wriggled on his stomach over the edge of the trench. Keeping low, he worked his way forwards until he was several hundred yards from the allied position. Then he stood up. He had decided that if he was challenged he would say he was a shepherd searching for a lost goat. He was guessing that the defending troops were not local and would not be able to recognize that he did not belong to the village. It was a gamble, but one that seemed worth taking. He kept moving up hill, pausing every now and then to listen, until he heard low voices speaking Turkish and knew that he was close to the first line of trenches. Making use of the cover provided by bushes and outcrops of rock he worked his way to his left, trying to establish how far the trench system extended. It seemed to be continuous until it ended in a steep drop into a ravine. Luke edged his way down the slope but, in spite of his care, loose stones rattled away from under his feet. Above him a voice shouted a challenge and he froze, until a second voice spoke. The tone was derisive and Luke understood enough Turkish to interpret it as 'Relax! It's only a goat!' He stayed still until he thought the Turks would have lost interest and then crept down the last few yards. The bottom of the gully was choked with prickly undergrowth, which made progress difficult, but he managed to work his way uphill until he became aware that the head of the valley was blocked by a looming dark shape. Crouching by a rock he made out, silhouetted against the stars, a sandbagged gun emplacement.

Luke backtracked a short way and then climbed cautiously out of the ravine on to the open hillside. He was now behind the Turkish lines and he wondered if this might be a possible route by which an attacking force might bypass the defences. A moment's thought brought the realization that troops could only advance in single file and to do so in silence, in the dark, would be impossible. Once detected, they would be sitting targets for fire from the trenches above and the guns at the top of the valley. He squatted under an olive tree and peered along the contour of the hillside. The Turkish trenches seemed to extend right across the peninsula, resuming again on the far side of the ravine. Any attack would entail a frontal assault, straight into the teeth of the enemy guns. Luke bit his lips and wondered whether he should now attempt to return and deliver that gloomy message. It seemed a pretty pathetic outcome to the expedition. *Surely*, he thought, *there must be some more useful information to be gleaned.* He looked up at the sky and realized that the short summer night was almost over and the sky in the east was paling towards the dawn. If he was going back, he would have to hurry. On the other hand, if he stayed he might see something that would be more helpful to the commanders planning the assault. He had seen that the villagers still went about tending their fields and their flocks behind the Turkish lines. There was no reason why he should not pass for one of them.

An hour later the sun came up and he heard movement and voices. From the reserve trenches the smoke of cooking fires rose into the still air, and he saw the tops of Turkish fezes moving backwards and forwards as watches were changed and the men on night duty were relieved. He tried to estimate numbers but all he could reasonably deduce was that there was a large force in occupation. A movement in the vicinity of the village caught his eye and he saw a group of women filing along to the rearmost trench, bearing baskets of what he took to be freshly baked loaves. Soon they were followed by men carrying hoes and bagging hooks and boys leading small flocks of goats and sheep. Luke got stiffly to his feet and sauntered as casually as he could towards an orchard on the slope ahead of him. From there, he reckoned, he would be able to look down directly into the trenches.

He was strolling through the trees when a voice stopped him in his tracks.

'Who are you?'

Luke looked up. A boy of about twelve was sitting in the branches of a mulberry tree. The language was the Macedonian Serb he had learned from his grandparents but a glance told him that the boy was dressed in Turkish style. He cursed himself for a fool. He knew that although the village was part of the Ottoman Empire the population was a mixture of Serbs and Greeks, with a few Bulgarians for good measure. But he had forgotten that some of them were ethnic Turks.

He forced a smile and responded, 'You haven't seen a stray goat, have you? She's brown and white, with a slight limp.'

'Whose goat?' the boy asked suspiciously.

'Mine, of course.'

'You're not from round here.'

Luke gritted his teeth. He had reckoned on passing as a local if challenged by the soldiers but had not expected hostility from the people in the village.

'No, that's right, I'm not. But you know what goats are like. They can wander for miles if the fancy takes them.'

'Where are you from, then?'

Luke racked his brain for the names of nearby villages and came up with nothing. He waved his hand vaguely inland. 'Back there.'

'I've never seen you before.'

'No, well, I've been away. I was in the war. Not this one, the last one.'

'Which side were you on?'

Luke struggled for an answer, then inspiration struck. 'Ours, of course.'

The boy was not fooled. 'I think you're a spy. I'm going to tell my father. He's the mayor.'

He was starting to climb down and Luke knew if he let him go he would bring the whole village out in search of him. He had to make a snap decision. As the boy's feet touched the ground Luke jumped forward and grabbed him.

'Don't be silly. If you go rushing off and tell everyone I'm a spy you'll just make yourself look a fool . . .' He was improvising frantically and the boy struggled in his grip, shouting, 'Let me go! Let me go!'

A man's voice cut across the tumult. 'Let the boy go! Put your hands above your head and turn round.'

Luke did as he was bid and found himself looking down the barrel of a shotgun.

The inside of the small hut was dark and smelt of animals. Luke heard the bar that held the door shut slotted home and a brief investigation convinced him that there was no other way out.

The man with the gun had turned out to be the boy's father and he had been accompanied by two others holding bagging hooks, so there had been no point in resisting. Luke had been marched up to the village and into the square, passing small groups of local people, mainly women and children, who stared at him with as little expression as cattle. One or two of them wore Turkish costume but the majority were dressed in the full skirts and bodices and headscarves of Serbian peasants. Once he thought for a second that he recognized a face in the crowd but when he looked again the woman had turned away.

He had been kept standing in the square until an officer arrived from the military camp to interrogate him. He tried to bluff him with the same story but it was useless.

'You are a spy! Who are you working for? The Serbs?'

It struck Luke that Serbia was a long way off and if he was working for them his captors might feel that they could execute him with impunity. On the other hand, the British forces were close at hand and might be expected to take revenge if he was harmed.

He said, 'No, not the Serbs. I'm a New Zealander.' The Turk stared at him blankly and he realized that he might as well have claimed to be a Hottentot or a mountain gorilla. 'I'm British,' he amended, nodding his head seaward. 'I'm with the British forces down there.'

The Turk took a step or two closer and stared into his face for a moment as if he were a rare and fascinating specimen. Then he turned away and said sharply, 'The colonel will wish to interrogate this man personally. He is away until tomorrow. Shut him up somewhere safe and keep him until the colonel gets back.'

So now he was shut in this little hut and there was nothing to do but wait. He settled down on the floor with his back to the wall and watched the thin line of sunshine that penetrated through a crack in the fabric move slowly across the floor. As the day wore on the heat in the confined space grew more and more oppressive. Luke's throat was parched and he could feel the sweat trickling down between his shoulder blades. He went to the door and banged on it.

'Water! Please, I need water!' He tried in Serbian and Turkish, but the only response was an unfriendly growl from outside. It answered one question, anyway. Someone was keeping watch.

More time passed and then he heard movement outside and a woman's voice, speaking Serbian.

'I have brought water and bread for the prisoner. Let me in.'

There was another growl in answer. 'Leave him be. No one is allowed in.'

'But if he does not have water he will die. What will the colonel say if he comes tomorrow and finds we have let the prisoner he wants to interrogate die?'

More grunting and then the bar was lifted and a small woman in black slipped through the door carrying a tray. She was wearing a headscarf and kept her head bent so that Luke could not see her face. She went straight to the back of the hut, where she knelt down and set the tray on the ground.

Looking up, she said very softly, 'I did not think we should meet again like this.'

Luke stared down at her, then suddenly he was on his knees facing her. 'Sophie! My God, it's you! What are you doing here? The last time I saw you, you were nursing the Serbs at Adrianople, during the last showdown.'

She reached out and put her fingers on his lips. 'Quiet! I can only stay a moment but I will come back tonight. There is one thing you must promise me. If I help you to escape, you must swear to take us with you.'

For a moment he could only look at her in silence. 'Us?' Who did she mean? Then he had a mental vision of himself and Victoria and Leo in the mess tent of the hospital at Adrianople and opposite them a laughing, round-faced girl and a small dark man. Iannis! Of course! Now he knew why the name of the village was familiar. Iannis came from Krithia. He nodded quickly. 'Yes, of course. If that's what you want.'

'It is vital, if I am to help you. I have your word? You will take us to the British lines?'

'Yes, I promise. But can you really get me out?'

'Trust me!' She rose and moved towards the door, saying more loudly, 'Eat! Drink! It is all you will get today.' The door opened and she was gone.

Luke lifted the cloth covering the tray and found a flask of water, a hunk of bread and some goat's cheese. The water was straight from the well, metallic tasting but icy cold. He took a long swig but forced himself to save some of it for later. Then he fell on the bread and cheese, aware that it was a long time since he last ate.

When his hunger was blunted, he sat back against the wall and thought about what Sophie had said. It was hard to recognize the girl he remembered in the hollow-cheeked woman who had just left him. Iannis was a doctor, he recalled, a Macedonian Greek, and had made his way through the Turkish lines to care for the Serbian and Bulgarian wounded in that first Balkan war. He and Sophie had been engaged. Presumably now they were married. Obviously it would not be safe for either of them to remain if Sophie helped him to escape. It would not be easy to get them back to the British camp but if Sophie could get him out, the rest would have to be left to the inspiration of the moment.

At last the band of sunlight faded and he heard the noises of the villagers settling down for the evening. Children shouted, women's voices rose and fell, gossiping round the well, he guessed. There was a smell of wood smoke as cooking fires were lit, and then the odour of roasting meat. Luke's stomach growled in response. He heard voices outside and gathered that his guard was being relieved; then a woman's voice – Sophie's, he thought – and the clatter of a knife on a plate, followed by a belch. Finally darkness fell and the sounds died away, to be replaced by the high-pitched susurration of crickets.

The minutes dragged by. Then Luke heard a new sound: a steady rhythmic snore. Moments later the bar holding the door was lifted quietly and Sophie beckoned him out. On a stool by the door, his back against the wall of the hut, the guard was sleeping soundly, his mouth gaping, a string of drool hanging from his jaw.

Sophie took Luke's hand and led him through the silent streets. At the door of a house she stopped suddenly and whispered, 'Wait here.' Then she vanished inside and Luke had to fight down a moment's panic in case she had led him into some sort of trap. Seconds later she reappeared, carrying a large bundle wrapped in a dark cloth. He made to take it from her but she shook her head and led him onwards to the edge of the village.

The countryside was quiet. Even the nightingale had stopped and there was no sign of movement. Further down the hillside Luke could make out the line of the reserve trenches and the bulk of gun emplacements but he reminded himself that the sentries there would be looking out towards the British lines, not in their direction.

He turned to Sophie. 'Where's Iannis?'

She frowned at him, then shook her head. 'Iannis is gone – dead.'

'My God! When? How?'

At that moment the bundle in Sophie's arms stirred and gave a low whimper. She rocked it gently and murmured something and it was quiet again.

'You have a child!' Luke said.

'Anton,' she answered. 'That is why you must get us safely to the British camp.'

'But it will make a noise! It will give us away!'

'He will not wake. I have seen to it.'

It took a moment for him to understand. The sleeping

guard, the silent child . . . Sophie had been a nurse, Iannis a doctor . . . He nodded. 'This way. Keep low and follow me.'

He led them across the hillside, navigating by memory, towards the ravine. He misjudged the distance and they almost stumbled into the gun emplacement at the head of the valley and had to backtrack. When they reached the edge of the gully he took the child from her, surprised by how heavy he was, and inched his way downwards, afraid that one of them would start a stone rolling away and alert the men round the gun. Somehow they reached the bottom, where the prickly undergrowth caught at Sophie's skirt. Luke glanced round in time to see her gather it up round her waist, giving him a glimpse of pale legs. He turned away quickly and forged onwards.

It seemed a very long way before he was sure that they had crossed no-man's-land and were behind the British trenches. Then he told Sophie to wait while he scrambled up to the rim of the valley. He was challenged immediately.

'Halt! Who goes there?'

'Pavel, Wellington's. I've been on a recce and I've got a prisoner with me.' It seemed the best way of explaining Sophie's presence.

Ten minutes later they were standing outside the colonel's tent in the first light of dawn, waiting while his orderly went in to wake him. Luke looked at Sophie.

'I don't understand how you come to be here. What happened to Iannis?'

The child in her arms woke up and began to cry. She produced a crust of dry bread from her pocket and gave it to him and he grabbed it in a small, pink fist and gnawed at it.

'When the fighting was over and Adrianople surrendered and there was a peace treaty we thought everything would go back to being as it was. The Turks still held Gallipoli but Krithia had always been mainly Serb and Greek. Iannis's old mother was still here and he felt he should go back. He was the only doctor and he knew people needed him. So we came back, and to begin with it all seemed fine. People were glad to see him. Even the Turks were grateful, because he treated them, too. So we settled down and Anton was born; we opened a dispensary and I acted as nurse and midwife. But then this new war started. To begin with it didn't seem as if it concerned us, but when Turkey declared on the side of the Germans people became suspicious of each other. Then you arrived,' she gestured towards the ships out in the bay, 'and the Turkish garrison was reinforced. Someone, I don't know who, must have had a grudge against Iannis. They went to the commander and told him that Iannis had gone over to the other side in the first war. He was arrested and shot as a traitor.'

Luke put out a hand and touched her arm. She had related the story in such a calm, detached fashion that she might have been talking about someone else. 'Sophie, I am so sorry. When did this happen?'

'Three weeks ago, perhaps a little more. Since then I have lived in fear. I was sure that soon they would come for me. Then, when I saw you being marched into the village, it was like a miracle. I thought if only I could get to you and set you free you would bring me here, away from that place, somewhere safe . . .' Her voice broke at last and he put his arm round her.

'Don't worry. You'll be all right here. I promise you.' She bit her lip and nodded and he said, 'You drugged him, didn't you? The guard?'

'Yes. I still had the key to the dispensary and I knew what to mix into his drink – and what to give Anton, to make sure that he slept all through. It was a risk. I wasn't sure of the dosage for such a young child, but he is all right.' She kissed the child's forehead and he gurgled happily. 'You are all right, my precious. You are safe now.'

The orderly came to the flap of the tent to tell them that the colonel was ready to see them. Malone was heavy-eyed and dyspeptic, annoyed at being dragged out of bed.

'Where the hell have you been, Pavel? We'd made up our minds you were dead or captured. And who the devil is this?'

Luke told his story and before he had finished the child began to cry, a loud, insistent howl.

'For Christ's sake!' Malone exclaimed. 'I can't hear myself think.'

Sophie looked at him with appealing eyes. 'He is hungry, colonel. Is there any milk I could give him?'

Malone harrumphed once or twice, then shouted for his orderly and told him to find some milk for the child. The orderly, an older man with a gentle, almost motherly nature, disappeared and returned a few minutes later with a cup and a spoon.

'It's condensed milk, I'm afraid. That's all we have. But I've diluted it with some boiled water, so I hope it will be all right.'

While Sophie fed the little boy Malone summoned Luke to one side with a jerk of his head.

'This is all very well, Pavel, and I can see why you had to bring her with you, but what am I going to do with her now?'

'Can't we send her back to Wellington, sir?' Luke suggested. 'I'm sure my folks would be happy to take her in.'

'Good God, man! What do you think I'm running here? A passenger cruise line?'

Sophie looked up. 'I am a nurse, colonel. I have seen the boats taking your wounded out to the hospital ship. I think they must need all the help they can get. If you can send me out I promise you I can make myself useful.'

'It's true, sir,' Luke put in. 'I worked with her in the hospital at Adrianople. She is fully qualified and very good at her job.'

A look of relief crossed the colonel's face. 'Excellent! I'll send for the MO and get him to arrange transport.'

The medical officer, when summoned, was clearly delighted to have another pair of hands to help with the work and immediately took charge of Sophie and her child. As he led them out Sophie turned to Luke and put out her hand.

'Thank you . . .' her lips trembled as if she wanted to say more but all she managed was to repeat, 'thank you, thank you!'

Luke squeezed her hand. 'You don't have to thank me. You saved my life. Take care.'

'Will we meet again, I wonder.'

'I'm sure we will, sometime.'

She nodded and gripped his fingers briefly. Then she turned and followed the officer out of the tent.

'Right!' Malone said. 'Now we can get to business. What have you got to report?'

Luke told him what he had seen and when he finished Malone was frowning. 'No weak points anywhere?'

'Not that I could see, sir. The trenches go right across the peninsular and the defences are deep, too. A frontal attack means walking straight into their guns.'

Malone nodded grimly. 'Well, at least we know. You'd better go and get some sleep. You look dead on your feet.'

It was true. Luke suddenly realized that he had not really slept for forty-eight hours. He went to the dugout he shared with the rest of his platoon, lay down in the dust and fell into a deep sleep that even the heat and the flies could not disturb.

Next morning, the order came round that they were to attack that day. There would be an artillery barrage from the ships in the harbour and then the infantry were to go in. Full frontal attack! Luke was on the verge of voicing his incredulity, then thought better of it. What was the point? It was on a par with the way the rest of the operation had been run. Why expect anything to change now?

The Wellingtons stood to at midday, on the left of the line, making their way up through the spider's web of trenches, which had already acquired names given to them by the British contingent – 'Clapham Junction; Holborn Circus; Lancashire Street'. The artillery barrage had gone on all morning. The noise was deafening and it was hard to imagine how anyone could have survived under that intensity of shelling. Some of the men were predicting cheerfully that they would be able to walk into the Turkish lines without firing a shot. Luke was not convinced. As he stood on the fire step, waiting for the order to advance, his throat was parched and his belly burned with the rum ration that had been handed round a few minutes earlier. He knew that he was probably experiencing the last few minutes of his life and he wondered if he should pray, but he had never been religious and right now he saw no reason to appeal to the God of Battles. If God was on their side, and Allah was on the side of the Turks, what sense did that make? Were they not the same deity? He thought he should have written a last letter to his parents, but what could he have said? No heroic, self-sacrificing sentiments came to mind. If he had had time to write it would probably have been 'Here I am, about to chuck my life away, at the order of a high command that cares less for us than we care for the sheep we send to slaughter'.

The whistles blew all along the trenches and Luke launched himself out of the trench.

'Come on, lads! Let's give it to the bastards!'

The illusion that the Turks had been shelled into submission was immediately dispelled by a hail of bullets. Luke ran forward, hearing the zip of bullets passing his ear, the whine of ricochets, the thud as they hit home in living flesh. He was aware of men falling on both sides, but he remained miraculously unscathed. Then a new artillery barrage started up from behind him. He saw shells bursting on the Turkish trenches but many of them were falling short and he saw men from his own unit just ahead of him being felled. He flung himself to the ground behind a low, thorny bush and flattened himself as much as possible. Two others of his platoon crashed down beside him, one of them bleeding profusely from a wound to the side of his head.

'What now, Sarge?' the other one asked breathlessly.

'Dig in here, as well as we can,' Luke replied. 'There's no point in trying to go on any further.'

He squirmed round to look behind him. They had gained about 400 yards and the ground between was littered with casualties. As he turned back he felt a sudden sensation, as if some unseen hand had given him a glancing blow, and realized that his hat had disappeared.

'Streuth, Sarge! Keep your head down. That was a close one!' said his companion.

They scraped a shallow pit with their entrenching tools and lay flat in it. The slightest attempt to raise a head provoked a well-aimed bullet. It was mid-afternoon and the sun beat down. Luke thought he knew what hot weather was, but he had never experienced anything like the ferocity of the sun on this bare hillside. Without his hat he began to feel as if his brain was being fried. The man next to him, with the head wound, became delirious and Luke had to restrain him to prevent him getting up and walking straight into the Turkish fire.

'What do we do now, Sarge?' the other man asked.

'Stay here till dark, then hope we can get back to the trenches.'

At last the sun began to dip but suddenly the barrage started up again and Luke heard a clatter of boots on stones behind him. Lieutenant Franklin threw himself down between the two of them, his head swathed in a blood-soaked bandage.

'Orders from the general. There's to be another attack.'

'Another attack!' Luke stared at the officer incredulously. 'Has he got any idea what it's like out here?'

'The colonel queried the order,' the lieutenant said grimly, 'but we've been told to go ahead. Nothing to be done, I'm afraid.'

Once more the whistles blew, and across the blighted land-scape dusty figures rose up and ran forwards. This time they made another fifty yards before the unremitting fire forced them to the ground. Luke scraped a new pit and lay down, with only one thought in his mind. He was still alive and soon it would be dark.

Twelve

To Leo, the summer at Kragujevac took on an almost idyllic quality. It was true that the work she was doing was very much the same as the work at Lamarck. Most of the patients were typhus cases and required the same intensive care, but there was something about the surroundings that lifted the spirit. In the distance there were mountains, covered in forests of oak and beech and maple. In the valleys, wheat and oats were ripening and as the summer progressed the trees in the orchards bent under the weight of plums and vines clothed the hillsides in between. Above all, she had a sense of home-coming. It was a comfort to hear Serbian spoken again and in the evenings the men who were convalescing sat around the campfire and the inevitable gusla was produced and the old songs sung. And then, those who were well enough would get to their feet and form a circle, linking arms for the solemn steps of the kolo. Leo knew that some of her colleagues groaned when they heard the drone of the gusla but to her it possessed a romance that no other music could evoke, bringing back evenings around the fire at Adrianople when she was still masquerading as an aide-de-camp to Colonel 'Sasha' Malkovic.

Several times she was tempted, when men were being discharged to go back to their units, to ask them to carry a letter, or perhaps to deliver a message. It was on the tip of her tongue to say, 'If you happen to meet Colonel Malkovic, tell him that Leo is here, working as a nurse, and sends her best wishes'. But she never spoke the words. She could not explain to herself what restrained her. Partly it was an honourable reticence, a feeling that he had enough to think about without concerning himself with her presence. Partly it was a much less noble fear that his response would be to tell her to go home, or to disclaim any further connection – or that there would be no response at all. Overlying all this was a sense that, if fate intended them to meet, it would somehow occur without her intervention, so all she had to do was wait.

Meanwhile, there was plenty to occupy her time. Reveille was at five thirty a.m. so that the heavy work of carrying water and cleaning could be done before the heat of the day. Then there were patients to be bathed and dressings to be done before lunch at eleven thirty. Tea was at four p.m., supper at six thirty and all lights were out by nine thirty. Every morning Leo anointed herself from head to toe with paraffin to deter the lice that carried the typhus infection and put on protective overalls and a bathing cap. Every new patient was stripped, washed and coated with paraffin, too, and his clothes were burned before he was given a clean nightshirt and tucked up between clean sheets. All the nurses had been inoculated against the disease before leaving London, but in spite of all precautions some of them contracted the less serious typhoid and most of them, Leo included, habitually suffered from a sore throat and ran a low-level fever.

They were reminded periodically that the Austrians might have changed their minds about invading but the war was still going on. On several occasions they were bombed by Austrian Taube biplanes. Fortunately for the hospital the main target was the nearby town, but they had one or two near misses.

The weather varied between extreme heat and violent storms, which turned the camp into a sea of mud. When this happened Leo reverted to her old habit of discarding her skirt in favour of breeches and boots, and very soon Mabel Stobart and some of the others followed her example.

Although the hospital had been set up to treat the soldiers it soon became known in the villages round about and a steady stream of civilians came to beg for treatment for a variety of diseases. Some had typhus, but others were suffering from diphtheria, TB or even smallpox. Realizing that there were virtually no medical services available to these people, Mabel Stobart decided to set up roadside dispensaries and Leo was often detailed to take charge of one of these, as she was one of the few who could speak the language. It was distressing work because very often the cases that were brought to her were beyond help but among them there were many for whom she was able to provide medication that might cure, or at least alleviate, the sickness; and the gratitude of the families was touching. Often she was invited into their homes to partake of 'slatko', the ceremonial form of hospitality at which the guest was offered a dish of jam, followed by a tumbler of water. Looking around her at the women in their full tartan skirts and coloured bodices and headscarves and the men in their white tunics and trousers she often felt as if she had stepped into the pages of a child's book of fairy tales.

The idyll could not last. In September news came that the Bulgarians had agreed to enter the war on the side of the Central Powers and were once again massing on the borders. Troops had to be withdrawn from the Austrian frontier to meet this new threat and Mabel Stobart was given the command of a field hospital attached to the Schumadier Division. On 30 September they left Kragujevac, leaving a skeleton staff to man the hospital there, and set out for Pirot, near the Bulgarian border. It was an impressive cavalcade, led by Mrs Stobart herself mounted on a black horse, followed by ox-carts and horse-drawn wagons loaded with tents and supplies. Six motor ambulances brought up the rear. Three days later, at three in the morning, they finally arrived at Pirot and set up the tents.

They were not to stay for long. Belgrade had already fallen to the Austrians. Soon they heard that the Serbian forces, hastily withdrawn from the Austrian front, had been unable to hold back the Bulgarians, who had been equipped with heavy weapons by Germany. Initially Stobart and the staff of the field hospital were ordered to retreat towards Nis, but then word came that help was desperately needed further south. After a hasty conference, it was agreed that Leo should lead a small detachment to Leskovac, on the road towards Kumanovo. She would be accompanied by one of the women doctors, Stella Patterson, five nurses, and two ox-carts and a wagon with their Serbian drivers, who would also act as orderlies.

The weather was appalling. Autumn had brought strong winds and endless rain but that could not mask the thunder of the guns to the east. On reaching Leskovac they were directed to a field outside the town, where they struggled against the elements to set up the tents. Before they had even unloaded the wagons, wounded began to arrive, transported as they had been from Chataldzha in jolting ox-carts, with only the primary emergency dressings to cover their wounds. Looking at the faces of her five helpers Leo realized that her previous experience was going to be invaluable.

At dawn next morning, just as they were about to start the daily routine of feeding and bathing, an officer galloped into the camp on a lathered horse.

'You must move at once! Pack up and move! The enemy will be here within hours!'

There followed a period of chaos where one day seemed to blend into the next so that Leo lost track of time. Again and again they set up camp, offloaded the wounded and began the work of caring for them, only to be told within hours that the Bulgarians were close at hand and they must move on again, through Lebane and Medveda to Pristina, along roads clogged with refugees, with their own retreating army at their heels.

Tom swore as the endless rain smudged the line he had just drawn. He rubbed it out and got up from the stool where he was crouching to squint through the periscope that gave him a view of the area beyond the trench. It was an unsatisfactory way of seeing the landscape he was trying to draw, but to raise his head above the parapet was to invite a bullet from a sniper in the enemy lines. He regarded it despondently. It reminded him of Mons: another vista of slag heaps and pithead cranes, with at its centre the huge structure that the troops had nick-named London Bridge, looming out of the mist. The difference was that now, after a year of the war, most of the buildings were ruins and the ground was pitted with water-filled shell-holes, each one a glimmering reflection of the grey sky. Loos, that was the name of the place. The battalion had been redeployed there at the beginning of autumn. The French pronounced it 'Loss'. It struck him as gloomily appropriate.

Tom finished his sketch and turned back through the pages of the pad. They were not all filled with the horror of war. The summer months had passed with a minimum of action on both sides. There had been time to enjoy the sunshine, to listen to the birds, write letters, draw – almost to relax. His pad was full of pictures of men laughing together over a shared joke, playing cards, smoking, mending socks. Their faces were worn and filthy but there was something in their eyes that he had struggled to catch; a look of optimism and hope and the warmth of shared comradeship. He had been touched, over and over again, by the evidence of the close bonds that had grown up, the sense of brotherhood engendered by life in the trenches. But now, the rumour was, that time of relative peace was almost over. There was to be one more big push, one decisive action before the winter set in.

Tom collected his pencils and his stool, said goodbye to the men around him and headed back to the dugout he shared with Ralph. As soon as he entered, he knew that something had happened. Ralph was on his feet, pacing the two or three steps in either direction that the confined space allowed, his face taut.

'What's going on?' Tom asked.

'It's come. We attack tomorrow. The plan is to break through the Boche lines and then circle round to outflank him. Joffre and the French are attacking simultaneously in the Champagne area and along the Vimy ridge. If we can do it, it could end the war.'

'If!' Tom repeated sceptically. 'But it would be marvellous if it works.' He scanned Ralph's face. 'There's something else. What is it?'

Ralph sat down abruptly and let his hands hang idly between his knees. 'We're going to use gas, Tom.'

Tom sat opposite him. 'Oh, God! I thought we were above that.'

They had both seen the effects of chlorine gas when the Germans had employed it at Ypres and the horror of seeing men choking and gasping while others stood by unable to help had made an indelible impression.

'Apparently the thinking is that as the Germans used it first it's all right for us to retaliate in kind,' Ralph said bitterly. He looked up and Tom's heart was wrenched by the despair in his eyes. 'This isn't the sort of fighting I thought I'd signed up for, Tom. I thought there could still be some chivalry, some honour in fighting for your country. But look at us! We sit here, hurling shells at each other, never even seeing each other's faces, and the generals are so far behind the lines they don't even know what's going on. It's a war of machines, not men; and even there we're completely outclassed. Not enough guns, not enough ammunition. Do you know, for a lot of the time our gunners are rationed to one shell every half hour? The men have been making their own grenades out of jam tins filled with gun cotton. And now this. We can't fight them man to man so we're going to try to poison them. How much lower can we sink?'

The stretcher jolted and tilted to one side as one of the bearers stumbled and Luke cried out in spite of himself. The morphia was wearing off and the pain of his shattered leg was like a fire consuming his body. Fire within and fire without, as the sun beat down. At least it was not the merciless sun of midsummer any longer, but even now in October the sky was cloudless and the heat striking up from the rocky earth gave the impression of living in an oven. In his delirium Luke imagined himself spitted like a hog and turning slowly over a fire.

'Water!' he begged, from a throat almost too parched to croak.

'Sorry, mate! There's none left,' was the reply. 'You'll get some when we get you down.'

Luke felt his bowels churn and fought for control, in vain. He whimpered with disgust and humiliation as he realized that he had soiled himself. Dysentery had become a fact of life during the months crouched in shallow trenches on the slopes of Chunuk Bair. They had attacked in August, heading at night up the valley called Chailak Dere to take the height they had called Destroyer Hill. They had cut steps up the sheer cliff with their entrenching tools to reach Table Top, hearing the hakas of the Maori contingent from the adjoining hill. Then, five hundred yards from the summit, the assault had been called off until daylight. By then, the opposing Turks had been reinforced and they had come under fire from a battery on top of the hill. The Auckland brigade had been mown down in their hundreds when they tried to advance and when the orders had been given for the Wellingtons to follow Malone had refused. Luke had heard the row between him and Brigadier General Johnston. 'My men are not going to commit suicide!' Malone had said.

They had made it to the top the following night and found no opposition except a solitary Turkish machine gun crew, who had surrendered. At dawn, they had been able to look across to the glittering waters of the Narrows, between Gallipoli and Asia. But it was impossible to hold the position. The ground was too hard to dig deep trenches and the Turks could creep up on them to within twenty yards without being seen. Luke had fired till his gun was too hot to hold and the front trench was clogged with the dead and dying. There was no water and they had had nothing to eat but salty bully beef, but they fought on. Malone led bayonet charge after bayonet charge until he was killed by shrapnel from one of their own batteries. By the time they retired, after dusk, only two officers and forty-seven men were left.

Luke had been one of the 'lucky' ones that time. For weeks since then he had squatted in a dugout on the slopes below the hilltop, while somewhere, a long way away, faceless men tried to decide what to do next. The hillside was strewn with bodies and the stench as they decomposed was unbearable. In the end a truce was agreed so that men from each side could meet together in no-man's-land to dig pits into which they rolled and dumped the bodies of friend and foe alike. Even after that, the place was still swarming with flies. The only food was bully beef and tins of apricot jam, with hard-tack biscuits, but as soon as anyone opened a tin it was immediately black with flies. It was not long before dysentery struck and none of them were spared. As the weeks passed, the effort of carrying water or moving equipment became almost too much for their weakened bodies.

From time to time the Turks attacked, pouring down the hill yelling 'Allah! Allah!' and screaming and whistling, and the weary Aussies and Kiwis raised their weapons and yelled back 'Come on, you bastards!' and somehow they beat them back.

But it was one of those attacks that had finally done for Luke. A grenade had landed in the trench and Luke had tried to kick it away. The explosion had torn the muscles of his leg. Now, he was on a stretcher, heading down the narrow, winding path, where stretcher-bearers sometimes had to drop their burden and take cover from Turkish snipers; where the ground was so treacherous, and the men so weakened, that it could take three days to reach the beach.

Four days after the attack on Loos Tom and Ralph were back in the same dugout. Ralph was slumped, exhausted, on the edge of his bed with his head in his hands. His uniform was torn and filthy and there was a bloodstained bandage round his left forearm.

'We were there, Tom! In the Jerries' second line! And there was no opposition. It was defended by old men and officers' orderlies. We broke through the first line, even though the bombardment hadn't cut the wire as it was supposed to. We cleared out the opposition there and charged on and found ourselves in total possession of the second line trenches. But by that time our men were exhausted. They'd fought all day and we'd taken a lot of casualties. If the reserves had been on hand they could have passed through us and attacked the Germans from the rear. It could have been the decisive blow. Once the German line was broken they would either have had to pull back or sue for peace.'

'But the reserves weren't there?' Tom queried.

'That bloody fool of a general, Sir John French, had kept them sixteen kilometres behind the lines. Then, when they were told to come forward, they were loaded down with extra rations, extra ammunition, God knows what else, and they marched all night in the pouring rain. They were only boys, Tom, most of them; volunteers – what people are calling 'Kitchener's Army'. They'd never seen action before and by the time they reached us they were as exhausted as we were. They didn't even know for certain where the front line was. Some of them just marched straight into the enemy machine guns.'

'I thought you had cleared the Germans out of that sector.'

'So we had, if the French had kept their part of the bargain.

We didn't know it then, but Joffre had called off his attack because his troops weren't getting anywhere, so the Boche were able to rush reinforcements over to our section. By the time the new lads arrived it was too late.' He ran his hands through his hair. 'That's the whole story of this shambles we are calling a war, Tom. Too little, too late! Not enough guns, not enough shells, men in the wrong place without the supplies they need to keep going. And bloody incompetent generals! We've been betrayed, Tom. That's the long and the short of it.'

Tom looked at him with compassion. He had had no illusions about war, after his experiences in the Balkans, but Ralph had cherished such shining ideals of patriotism and gallantry and it wrung his heart to see him so brought down. He wanted to say, 'But you have survived, that's all that really matters' but he knew it would be the wrong thing for Ralph to hear at that moment. Besides, there was something else that weighed heavily on his mind. He had spent the last days in the forward observation post and had taken no part in the attack. He hated himself for not sharing Ralph's danger. He turned away, folding his arms, and swore to himself that next time they would go into battle side by side.

The following morning he presented himself at battalion headquarters and asked to see the colonel. He had to wait for some time before he was admitted and then the colonel raised his eyes from the maps he was studying and gazed at him abstractedly.

'Well, what is it?'

'I have a request, sir. I want to be transferred to active duties.'

His commanding officer blinked at him as if he was having difficulty focusing and Tom saw that he was on the verge of exhaustion. Then his eyes cleared.

'You're the artist. What do you mean, active duties?'

'I know I have only been given an honorary commission, sir, so that I can document the action in pictures; but I can't stand by and see other men die without sharing the danger. I want to be regarded as a regular officer.'

The colonel sighed. 'You have no training, Devenish. How do you imagine you can function as an officer without training?'

'Then I should like to be trained, if that's possible,' Tom said.

'You want me to send you back to England to undergo officer training, is that it?'

Tom hesitated. 'I can't get the same training here? On the job, as it were?'

'No, you can't! This is a crack regiment. It isn't run by amateurs – though God knows, the way we are losing officers at the moment it may come to that.'

'All the more reason for me to play my full part,' Tom said. 'If I have to go back, then that is what I should like to do. If you agree, of course.'

The CO looked at him for a moment, then he returned to his maps. 'Yes, very well. I'll make the necessary arrangements.'

Thirteen

Leo hoped that when she and her little group reached Pristina they might find Mabel Stobart waiting for them with the rest of the convoy, but there was no sign of them. She asked everyone she could think of, from the mayor to the crowds of refugees flooding into the city, but no one had any news. With the Austrians pressing in from the north and the Bulgarians from the east, it was obvious that her colleagues would have been forced to join the general retreat, so Leo decided to wait as long as possible in the hopes that they would appear; but when three days passed without news she had to conclude that they had either gone on ahead or were taking a different route.

The city was in the grip of panic, besieged from all directions by refugees, and food was getting difficult to find. Leo became familiar with the word *nema* – there is none – as she combed the shops looking for bread and sugar. She became uncomfortably familiar, too, with a question. 'Where are the English and the French? They are supposed to be our allies. When are they coming to help us?' There was a temporary flare of hope when the news arrived that allied contingents had landed at Salonika but it was short-lived. The Bulgarians were surrounding the city and the small allied force did not have the strength to break through. As the first remnants of the defeated Serb army started to appear in the city Leo decided that it would be irresponsible to wait longer. She stopped a cavalry officer and explained her dilemma.

'If I were you, I should move out at once,' he said. 'If the Bulgarians don't take the town in a day or two, the Austrians will.'

'There's no chance of a rally, a fight back?' Leo said.

He shook his head. 'There was talk of a last stand, at Kosovo Polje, but the generals decided against it.'

Leo was touched by the dejection on his face. She knew the significance of that place to the Serbs. It was the locus of every legend and every folk song; the place where in 1389 the Serbs had fought their decisive and ultimately doomed battle against the Turkish army. She knew how many of them would have preferred a gallant last stand on that historic spot to this abject retreat.

'It is better that you should save yourselves and live to fight another day,' she said. 'But where are you heading?'

'Through the mountains. It's the only route left open to us. If we can reach the Adriatic at Durazzo perhaps the allies will send ships to take us off. But it will be a hard journey and the Albanians are not our friends. There will be many who do not survive.'

Leo watched him ride away with a growing sense of despair. It was December now, the worst time of the year to be heading into the mountains. She knew very little about Albania except that it was a poor country and the officer's comment that the Albanians were not their friends sent a chill through her heart. Even if they were disposed to help, how could they be expected to feed the multitude that was about to descend on them? What conditions would be like, up there, she could only guess. But there was nothing for it, they must join the exodus.

The rain was unrelenting and the roads were a sea of mud. Leo grew tired of pinning up the long strands of wet hair that fell around her shoulders, so she resorted to the expedient she had adopted at Chataldzha and hacked it off with a pair of surgical scissors. It occurred to her, in one of her quieter moments, that in her boots and breeches she must look very much as she had done when Sasha first mistook her for a boy. The thought sent a shaft of anguish through her. Where was Sasha now? He would have fought to the last, she was sure of that. Was he now part of this dejected rabble, heading for exile; or was he lying dead somewhere on the borders of the country he loved so much?

At a village outside Prizren, almost on the border of Albania, where they encamped one night, Stella Patterson came to Leo's tent.

'I'm very concerned about Milan, the boy with the shattered foot. Gangrene has set in. If the foot is not amputated immediately he will probably die.'

Milan had been brought to them just before they left Pristina; his foot had been shattered by a shell blast. He was very young – sixteen or seventeen perhaps; he seemed unsure of his exact age.

Leo suspected that this was deliberate and he was actually younger still. He had endured the journey so far with the stoicism typical of these Serbian peasant soldiers and he seemed to her to exemplify the best and the worst of the war.

Leo ran her hand through her hair. The perpetual nagging headache and sore throat, to which she had become accustomed, were getting worse and she suspected that she was running a fever.

'You can't carry out an amputation in these conditions, can you?'

'No. We must find a house, somewhere reasonably clean, with a decent light and a bit of warmth – and a water supply.'

'But we have to keep moving,' Leo said. 'If we stay here we could be overrun by the Bulgarians.'

'I can't help that. It's a risk we shall have to take. If I don't amputate that boy will die.'

Leo hauled herself to her feet. 'Very well. I'll see if there is anyone in the village who will let us use their kitchen.'

She went straight to the home of the mayor, the largest house in the village, though even this consisted of just two rooms with floors of beaten earth. She found the mayor and his family loading their goods on to two mules. When she explained what she needed the response was rapid.

'Use what you like. The house is yours. We are leaving at first light.'

She reported back to Stella. 'There's a table we can scrub clean and enough wood for a fire and a well in the yard for water. But the only light is from candles. We can use our hurricane lamps, but even then you won't really be able to see well enough. Can it wait until morning?'

Reluctantly the doctor agreed that it would be best to wait until dawn. Leo passed a broken night and woke to a new sound. All night she had heard the noise of feet tramping past and the rattle of donkey carts as the refugees pressed doggedly on but this was different. A heavier tread, as of booted men, and the clank and rumble of heavier vehicles. Scrambling out of her tent she realized that the road was full of soldiers, not marching but plodding onwards, followed by horse-drawn limbers carrying guns. The retreating Serb army had overtaken them, which meant that the Bulgarians must be close behind.

The rest of the team were awake and gazing, dumbfounded, at the passing troops. Leo called them together. After a few dizzying seconds, during which she seemed unable to think at all, her mind had cleared and she was quite sure what she had to do.

'I shall stay here with Dr Patterson to assist with the amputation, but the rest of you must go at once. We will follow as soon as Milan is able to travel.'

'But we can't go and leave you behind!' one of the women exclaimed and the others agreed noisily.

'Yes, you can,' Leo insisted. 'You have a duty to the other patients. It is up to you to get them safely across the mountains. I'm sure Dr Patterson and I will be able to join up with another medical team and we will join you at Durazzo.'

'But suppose the Bulgarians get here first,' someone said.

'If that happens, I'm sure we shall be treated with perfect courtesy,' Leo said. 'I have worked with the Bulgarians and I have always found them extremely chivalrous. Now, we don't have time to argue. The men must be given breakfast and dressings seen to and then you must inspan the oxen and be on your way, as soon as possible. Dr Patterson and I will do what needs to be done with Milan.'

They turned away, reluctantly, but training and discipline enforced her orders and within minutes the fire was alight, water was put on to boil and the nurses were bending over their patients. Watching them, Leo felt the confidence she had assumed ebbing away. It was true that the Bulgarian officers she had met had behaved impeccably, but that had been when Bulgaria and Serbia were allies. Now they were on opposite sides and there were old scores to settle. Besides which, it was likely that the first Bulgars they would encounter would be common soldiers, not high-ranking officers, and she had heard terrible stories of the way they had treated helpless civilians in the villages they had overrun.

She called two orderlies to carry Milan over to the mayor's house and found Stella Patterson already there, boiling up water over the fire and scrubbing the wooden table in the centre of the main room. Milan was laid on the mayor's bed and Leo went back to see off the rest of the convoy. The tents had been struck and the patients loaded into the ox-carts and the nurses gathered round Leo, some of them in tears. She hugged them all in turn.

'Be brave! It's going to be a long, hard journey but we will get through – all of us. You are with the army, so you'll be safe enough. There will be plenty of men to help if you need it. Just keep going, that's all you have to do.'

The drivers and orderlies kissed her hands as she wished them God speed. '*Sbogom!* Goodbye! We'll meet again soon.'

The wagons creaked into motion but the road was so congested with men and vehicles that it was almost impossible to join it. It was not until an officer in charge of an artillery company saw their difficulty and halted his men that they were able to filter in. Leo watched them moving away until they disappeared into the curtain of rain that veiled the mountains. Then she turned and hurried back to the mayor's house.

Dr Patterson looked up from arranging her instruments. 'Good, you're here. I'm ready to start. Help me to lift him on to the table.'

He was not a big man, fortunately, and short rations had reduced them all to skin and bone. Even so, Leo found it took all her strength to help the doctor heave him from the bed on to the table, which she had covered with a sheet from the small store of clean linen. Her head was pounding and her throat so sore that she had been unable to swallow the day-old bread which was all that was available for breakfast. Milan was semi-conscious, but when he saw the doctor advancing with the mask and the bottle of chloroform he began to struggle and tried to get up.

'No, no! Not that, not that!'

Leo took him by the shoulders and pressed him back on to the table. Then she took hold of his hands and held them tightly. 'Milan, listen to me! You are quite safe. The chloroform will send you to sleep for a while, that's all. The doctor has explained to you, she has to remove your foot or you will die. But if you are asleep you will feel no pain. I promise you! And when you wake up it will be all over.'

He looked up into her eyes. '*Maika*, you will stay with me?'

Maika – it meant mother. Leo swallowed. 'Yes, Milan, I will be here all the time. There's nothing to worry about.'

His eyes swivelled from her to Patterson, standing ready with the anaesthetic, and he nodded. She put the mask over his nose and mouth and dripped on the chloroform. For a moment he struggled against it, then Leo felt the grip on her hands relax.

'Now, we must be as quick as we can,' Patterson said.

Leo had assisted at operations before, but never at an amputation and the sight, combined with the rotten/sweet smell of the gangrene, turned her stomach. Once or twice she was afraid that she was going to faint or vomit, but she managed to keep control and hand the necessary instruments when requested. Even her inexpert eyes could see that Patterson was good at her job and in a remarkably short time the wound was sutured and dressed and the gangrenous foot disposed of in the midden in the back yard. Leo leaned over Milan as he began to come round, stroking his face and murmuring reassuring words, ready with a bowl for the inevitable attack of vomiting.

'*Maika*, when will it be over?' he whispered, when he could speak.

'It is over, Milan,' she answered. 'It is all done and now you will get well.'

When he had been put back to bed and the instruments cleaned and packed away Stella drew the big cauldron off the fire and poured water into two mugs.

'You look as if you need a coffee,' she commented. 'It's a pity there's no milk or sugar but at least it's hot.'

Leo became aware again of the endless tramp of feet past the door of the house. 'When will he be able to travel?'

'In an ideal world, not for several days. But as this is not an ideal world – tomorrow, at the earliest.'

There was nothing to do, then, but wait. Leo sat by the fire, lulled into a kind of stupor until another sound roused her. At first she thought it was a child crying. Then she realized it was the bleating of a goat. In the backyard she found a nanny goat tethered. It was a poor, thin creature but its udder was swollen with milk. Leo hurried back to the house and found a large bowl. She had never milked a goat, or a cow for that matter, and it took some time to master the technique but she was eventually rewarded with half a pint of milk. She had kept back a small amount of the dwindling supply of food which the convoy possessed, including a little bag of oats, and from those and the milk she concocted a thin gruel. They fed most of it to Milan when he woke, but she and Stella shared what was left and agreed that it was the best meal they had had in days.

By dawn the next morning the endless procession of soldiers and civilians had begun again. Leo stopped an officer and asked him how close the Bulgarian army was.

'Not more than a day behind,' he said. 'If I were you I should get on the road as fast as you can.'

Leo reported the conversation to Stella Patterson and they agreed that Milan would have to travel, weak as he was. While Stella attended to her patient, Leo stood by the road watching for some form of transport. She stopped several wagons but the answer was always the same. They were full, either with wounded men or with essential supplies. Eventually, about midday, she waved down a wagon marked with red crosses and pleaded with the driver to find room for them.

'We are a doctor and a nurse. Surely we could be useful on the road, if you have other injured men on board.'

The sergeant in charge scowled at her. 'Where's the doctor, then?'

'There!' Leo indicated Stella, who had come to the door of the house.

'A woman!' he snorted with derision.

'Yes, a woman!' Leo retorted. 'And a fine doctor, who has just saved the life of one of your soldiers.'

He looked from her to Stella and grunted. 'I'll take the doctor. No room for anyone else.'

Stella came forward. 'You'll have to take all of us, or I don't come.'

'I've told you, no room. Now, I'm blocking the road. I've got to move on.'

'Look!' Leo said desperately. 'Take the doctor and the patient. I'll find someone else to take me.'

Stella was inclined to argue but Leo was insistent. 'It will be easy for me to hitch a lift, on my own. You go, with Milan. Don't worry about me.'

Milan was carried out and lifted into the wagon and Stella climbed up on to the tail board. The driver cracked his whip and called to the animals and the wagon forced its way back into the stream of traffic.

'Look after yourself! See you in Durazzo!' Stella called.

'Yes, see you there!' Leo shouted back.

She waited a while longer, trying unsuccessfully to hitch a ride. Then one of the drivers shouted at her, 'What's wrong with your legs, boy? Walk, like the rest!' and she realized that her appearance was against her. Her skirt had gone with the convoy so, short of standing by the roadside shouting 'I'm a woman, help me!' there was nothing she could do. She reminded herself that the whole purpose behind the FANY and Mabel Stobart's Sick and Wounded Convoy was to prove that women could be as brave and as resilient as men. Now was the time to prove it. She gathered up the few scraps of bread and a little twist of coffee – all that remained of her supplies, and joined the throng of people plodding along the road.

Very soon the road began to climb, following the course of a river, and the air grew colder. The rain turned to sleet and then to snow. Leo had bought a sheepskin coat from an old shepherd when the retreat began. It stank of badly cured leather but at least it was warm and reasonably weather proof and she was thankful for her good English boots. Even so, it was not long before the wet soaked into her breeches and crept up to her waist, while the snow managed to filter down inside her collar and dampened her tunic. Her head burned and throbbed, she shivered convulsively and her legs felt like lead.

The passing of so many heavy wagons had churned the unsurfaced road to mud and she passed several that had become stuck axle-deep while the drivers yelled and cursed at their beasts. Apart from that and the occasional thin wail of a child she was struck by the absence of human voices. None of the soldiers sang or joked. The whole vast army trudged on in silence. The mountains closed in around them as they climbed, so that the river ran in a narrow valley and the road, such as it was, clung to the side, sometimes a hundred or more feet above the river, at others dropping down to cross it on shaky bridges. At one of these Leo saw that a gun limber had overturned, throwing the gun into the water and dragging the whole equipage with it. The men in charge of it were struggling to cut the traces to free the horses, which were plunging and struggling in the rapid current.

As the early winter dusk drew in the various units began to pull off into the pine forest beside the road. Here, at least, there was wood for fires and soon the whole hillside was starred with twinkling lights. Seeing one company gathering around their fire Leo hesitated. She knew that, if she was to survive the night, she must find some warmth but she was afraid to ask if she could join them. As a boy, which they would take her to be, they might feel she should be able to fend for herself. But at the same time, there was a certain security in her disguise. Instinct told her that this was no time to present herself as a helpless female. In the end, she plucked up enough courage to creep to within a few yards of the group round the fire and huddled down on the pine needles that covered the ground. A cauldron had been set to boil over the flames and her nostrils caught a faint savoury smell that brought the saliva welling up in her mouth. She took out her scraps of bread and gnawed at them and became aware that one of the men from the other side of the fire was looking at her. When the cook came round to fill his tin mug he said something to him and when all the men had been served the cook came over and held out a mug half full of steaming liquid.

'Make the most of it,' he said. 'It's the last any of us will get this side of the mountains.'

The savoury smell had been deceptive. The liquid in the mug was mainly hot water with a few scraps of vegetable floating in it, but at least it was warm. Leo swallowed it thankfully and one of the men moved over and beckoned her closer to the fire. They did not ask her any questions. She got the impression that they, like her, were too tired to talk. Before long, they curled themselves up, three or four together for warmth, and fell asleep. Leo slept too but intermittently, disturbed by vivid dreams and repeated fits of shivering.

The next morning she was given a cup of bitter black coffee, which was all any of them had for breakfast, and then there was nothing for it but to drag herself to her feet and set off again. The men she had shared with that night, exhausted as they were, could still walk faster than she could and soon pulled ahead. She put her head down and plodded on, aware that from time to time she was overtaken by other groups or by carts or wagons. She paid no heed to them. She had almost passed beyond the capability of conscious thought, her brain instead filled with strange imaginings. If she looked up, the trees and the mountain crags seemed to whirl around her so that she almost fell. Only by keeping her eyes on the ground was she able to stay on her feet. As the hours passed the snow grew deeper and the road narrower, so that often it became so congested that the whole procession came to a halt. It only needed one wagon to stick in a rut, or one donkey to lie down and refuse to get up to keep them standing in the cold for what seemed like an hour.

As the day wore on Leo began to hear voices. She heard her grandmother scolding her for going out in such inclement weather; once she was certain that Victoria was shouting to her, needing help, but she could not find her in the crowd. Again and again she fancied she heard Sasha's voice, urging her on, telling her that she must keep walking. As the light began to fade again she heard him calling to her, as he had called that day at Chataldzha. '*You, boy! Come here!*'

'You, boy! Wait!' It was a real voice, though it was hard to distinguish it from the clamour in her head. A horse was urged alongside her, a grey horse, and she looked up.

Sasha stared down at her. 'My God! It is you! I thought I was dreaming. What in the name of Christ are you doing here?'

She gazed back at him. Her head was swimming but she felt herself smiling from pure joy. 'Trying to escape, like you,' she croaked and grasped at his stirrup leather for support.

He was beside her, although she had not seen him dismount, his arm round her waist. Above her head she heard his voice raised to give an order.

'Bring Shadow up, Michaelo. Quickly now.'

There was movement round her and she was lifted bodily into the black horse's saddle. 'Oh, Shadow!' she murmured ecstatically. 'Dear old Shadow!' She slumped forward on to the horse's neck and tangled her icy fingers in his mane. There was a jolt as he started forward and then the steady rocking movement of his walk. Leo closed her eyes and let herself drift.

She came to as they turned off the road again and saw that they were preparing to make camp. Sasha lifted her down and wrapped her in his cloak, then settled her between the roots of a great pine tree with her back against the trunk. Crouching in front of her he brushed the hair off her forehead with his fingertips.

'I don't understand. How did you get here?'

She struggled to make coherent sentences and gave up the effort. 'Nursing . . . Kragujevac . . . Stobart . . . got separated.'

'Where are the others?'

She made a vague movement indicating the road ahead. 'Up there, somewhere.'

He stared at her in silence for a moment longer, as if he wanted to question her further, then nodded and got to his feet. 'Stay still. We have very little food left. I'll bring you what I can.'

He came back after a while with a mug of tea and a small piece of bread. There was sugar in the tea and Leo felt as if every nerve in her body responded to the intense sweetness. He watched her eat and as her head cleared she saw that his face was drawn with fatigue and he was frowning.

'Don't worry about me,' she whispered. 'I didn't mean to add to your burdens.'

He reached out and touched her face. 'Oh, my dear,' he murmured, and left it at that.

She was dimly aware after that that he was going among his men, encouraging, reassuring. Once she even heard him laugh. Then he came back to her.

'Time to sleep.'

He moved her so that she lay down, then curled himself against her back and wrapped the cloak around them both. Leo closed her eyes. Death was very close, but it no longer mattered. She was lying in the arms of the man she loved above all others. Slowly, his comforting warmth seeped into her body and she gave herself up to the darkness.

Luke opened his eyes and closed them again. Somewhere above him a voice was saying, 'It's all right, you're going to be fine. Lie still.' Something about the words puzzled him, then he realized that they were spoken in Macedonian Serb. He opened his eyes again. Sophie was leaning over him.

'So, you are awake. Do you want some water? Just a sip now. You can have more later.'

She lifted his head and held a cup to his lips. He swallowed and fought back nausea.

'Where am I?'

'On the hospital ship. You've had an operation.'

He remembered then: the explosion, the pain, the endless jolting as the stretcher was manoeuvred down the hillside, and the fear that had been uppermost in his mind.

'Is it still there?'

'Is what still there?'

'My leg. Have they taken it off?'

She smiled and stroked his cheek. 'No, no your leg is still there. The doctor has set it. It will take time but one day it will be as good as new.'

'Thank you.'

'Not me. Thank the doctor when you see him. Now I must go. I have other patients to attend to. I will come back and see you in a little while.'

She moved away and for a while he drifted back into unconsciousness. When he woke again it was a new sensation that roused him. He was being tipped to one side, and then to the other. For a moment he thought he was still on the stretcher and the interlude with Sophie had been a hallucination. He had experienced plenty of those on the journey down. He opened his eyes and saw that he was lying on a mattress on the floor. Close beside him was another mattress on which a man was lying. Beyond that was a bed. He turned his head and saw the same pattern repeated on his other side and above him was a ceiling of polished planks. The tipping sensation repeated itself and he became aware of a steady throbbing that transmitted itself from the floor on which he lay. Little by little these isolated perceptions coalesced into a comprehensible pattern. He was on board ship, and the ship was under weigh.

He raised his head cautiously, and had to fight back nausea again. When it subsided he saw that the opposite side of the deck was as crowded with beds and mattresses as his own. Nurses were busy with dressings and medicines, but there was hardly enough room for them to walk between them. Luke lay back. In the confined space the heat was stifling and the whole place stank of sweat and urine and shit; but he was used to that. He had lived with it in the trenches for months.

He looked at the man next to him. He was lying on his back with his hands behind his head. 'Where are we bound for, mate?'

Blue eyes swivelled slowly in his direction. 'No bloody idea, mate. But who cares? As long as it's away from there.'

Away from there! Away from Gallipoli, from the heat and the flies and the bloated corpses. 'Too right!' Luke agreed.

'You know, you're one lucky bastard,' his companion said. 'When they brought you in, we all thought you were a gonner. If it hadn't been for that little dago nurse you would have been. She stayed by you for hours, bathing your face, feeding you sips of water. Word is, the surgeons wanted to take your leg off, but she wouldn't let them. Reckon she's pretty sweet on you.'

'She's not a dago,' Luke muttered, 'she's Macedonian Serb – like me.'

'No kidding? I thought you were a kiwi.'

'Yeah, that too,' Luke agreed, and closed his eyes.

Fourteen

Leo turned over and stretched and shivered. The warm presence that had comforted her all night had gone. She opened her eyes and looked around. Men were moving around, stoking the fire, boiling water, saddling horses. There was no sign of Sasha. For a moment she wondered if she had dreamed him, then she became aware of the cloak that still covered her. She pulled it up to her face and buried her nose in it. It smelt of him. It was unmistakable, yet she had never realized before that she could recognize his smell.

He spoke from behind her. 'Good, you're awake. We have to move on soon.'

She struggled into a sitting position. 'Sasha?'

He crouched beside her and touched her face. 'You look better. I believe the fever has broken. Last night I was afraid for you.'

She rubbed her eyes and realized that her throat was hurting less and her headache had almost gone. 'You're real! I was afraid I'd imagined you.'

He smiled briefly. 'I thought I was going mad when I saw you trudging along the road with the rest. I told myself you must be a real boy and it was just my fevered brain that saw a resemblance. What, in God's name, has brought you back to Serbia?'

'You,' she answered.

He looked as if he was going to say more, but he shook his head in despair, or exasperation. An orderly appeared at his side with a steaming mug and a small piece of dry bread.

'Would the young gentleman like some coffee, sir?'

He looked so puzzled that Leo felt a stab of concern, but Malkovic laughed. 'This "young gentleman" is actually a young lady. You can call her Gospodica Leo. Yes, give her the coffee.'

The confusion on the young man's face was so great that Leo almost laughed too, in spite of the fact that her head was swimming. Sasha held the cup out to her. It contained the usual brew of bitter black coffee, without which, it seemed, no Serbian could start the day.

'No sugar this time, I'm afraid,' Sasha said. 'You had the last few grains in the bag last night.'

Leo sipped the drink and although it contained no nourishment the warmth and the caffeine helped to raise her spirits. Before long she knew that she must answer a call of nature – but where, in the middle of all these men?'

She struggled to her feet. 'Sasha, I must . . . I need to . . .'

He understood. 'I'll show you where.' He led her across the clearing to where a tumble of rocks offered some shelter. 'Don't worry. I'll see you are not disturbed.'

When she had finished she found him standing with his back scrupulously turned.

'We must get on the road,' he said. 'Come.'

The orderly was holding Cloud, Sasha's grey gelding, and Shadow ready, but as they approached them Leo gave a cry.

'Oh, Sasha, they're skin and bones! Poor creatures!'

'I know,' he replied. 'We haven't been able to find fodder for them for days. They are surviving on dried leaves. But there's no help for it. We must hope that they will keep going until we reach the other side of the mountains.'

He helped her into the saddle and she felt Shadow sag for a moment under her weight. It crossed her mind that it was cruel to expect him to carry her, but she knew that she would never survive the journey on foot. If Sasha had not come upon her when he did, she would probably be lying helpless by the road now, like others she had seen as she trudged past.

All day the road wound on, higher and higher, the horses stumbling in the mud and slush. The river now ran in a ravine, far below them, and at one point Leo saw the snow flattened and discoloured at the edge of the track and, looking down, saw that a wagon had overturned and tumbled into the abyss, dragging the oxen that pulled it down with it. A little later they heard the sound of sawing and hammering and passed a group of wagons that had pulled off into a clearing. The oxen had been outspanned and the drivers were apparently cutting the wagons in half. Sasha called out to ask them what they were doing and received the answer that the bridges ahead were too narrow for the wagons to pass, so the men were converting them into two-wheeled carts. Further on they came upon the contents of several vehicles in a heap at the side of the track. Guns and ammunition, cooking pots, tents – all the impedimenta that the army carried with it – had been offloaded so that essential supplies could be carried. Sasha shook his head, grimly.

'If we get through alive we shall be a rabble, not an army!'

Worse was to come. In a little valley Leo saw ahead of them a crowd of moving shapes, wraith-like in the drifting snow. Coming closer, she saw that they were soldiers but not in Serbian uniform.

'Austrian prisoners of war,' Sasha said.

'Do you mean they have just been abandoned, left to fend for themselves?' Leo responded.

'We can't feed our own people,' Sasha said. 'Why should we use up our last essential supplies on them?'

As they rode past the men stood and stared in silence. Leo bent her head and did not return their gaze. To leave them seemed inhuman, but she saw the strength of Sasha's argument and reminded herself that it was the Austrians who had started the war. Nevertheless, she was ashamed.

Soon after that they began to pass bodies lying in the snow. Civilians, men, women and children, who had finally given up the struggle; and soldiers, too, many of them wounded. Some of them were still alive and called out for help. Sasha reached out and gripped Shadow's reins, urging the horse on.

'There's nothing we can do, Leo. Those of us who have the strength must survive. Otherwise we all die. The Austrians are behind us and the Bulgarians are said to be moving in from the east. If they reach the far end of this valley before we do, we shall be bottled up here and forced to fight for our lives.'

Leo thought of her own convoy of patients and nurses. They would have had to abandon the ox-carts like everyone else. Were they still somewhere up ahead, struggling onwards? Or had she ridden past them, without recognizing them? What of Milan and Stella Patterson? There was no way Milan could have walked. Was he one of those lying in the snow by the roadside?

That night they ate the last of the bread and huddled together round the fire, trying to sleep.

'How much further?' Leo asked.

Sasha shook his head. 'A day? Two days? I don't know.'

It was sometime around the middle of the next day that Shadow suddenly staggered and went down on his knees. Leo just had time to throw herself to one side before he collapsed. Sasha dismounted and went to the horse's head, clicking his tongue and pulling at the reins. Shadow lifted his head once and made a feeble effort to bring his hind legs under him, then sank back, his breath whistling through dilated nostrils. Sasha was still for a moment, then he drew his revolver.

'Leo, turn your back.'

'No!' She knelt and stroked the black neck that had once been so sleek and powerful. 'Is there nothing we can give him?'

'You know there isn't. It's kinder to put him out of his misery than leave him to die. Turn away – please!'

She shook her head obstinately and after a brief hesitation he shrugged and put the muzzle of the gun against the horse's head. There was a crack, Shadow convulsed once and was still. Sasha got up and pulled Leo with him.

'Now you will do as I ask and come away.'

But she had already seen two of the men advancing with knives in their hands. That night the cauldron over the fire gave off an odour that filled her mouth with saliva and the resulting stew was rich with gobbets of meat seasoned with the fiery paprika the company cook had carried with him. Leo thought that the first mouthful would choke her but as soon as she tasted it sentiment was swamped by sheer physical need and she devoured everything that was given to her.

That night they all slept better but Leo woke to the sound of lamentation. One of the men had died during the hours of darkness and his companions were mourning him. Sasha's face was taut with grief.

'He's the fourth to die since we left Pristina,' he said. 'And two others have just disappeared, left behind somewhere. God knows, we lost enough men in the fighting, but to see them dying from cold and hunger . . .'

He broke off and turned away. The ground was too hard

to attempt to bury the dead man. They covered him with his greatcoat and someone fashioned a rough cross from two bits of wood, and then they set out again on their journey.

Sasha wanted Leo to ride Cloud, but she shook her head. 'He's your horse, and your men need you. I don't belong here.'

He gripped her arm tightly. 'You belong with me, and either we live together or we die together. Now get up on the horse! He hasn't the strength to carry us both.'

She rode for a couple of hours, then made the excuse that her feet were freezing and she needed to walk for a while. So he looped the reins over his arm and took her hand.

'We'll walk together. Cloud needs the rest.'

At that moment they heard the crack of a rifle and a scream of pain. Swinging round, Leo saw one of Sasha's men drop to the ground, clutching his shoulder. A second later she was forced down on to the snow herself, with Sasha on top of her.

'Stay still! Stay down!'

'What is it?'

'Bandits! Albanians, out for all they can steal.'

Twisting round she saw him reach up and grab his rifle from where it hung on his saddle. There were other shots, now, closer at hand, and she realized that their own men were returning fire. Sasha's rifle cracked close to her ear. She raised her head and saw figures among the trees, dodging from trunk to trunk. There was a cacophony of shots and screams, then sudden silence. She could hear Sasha breathing hard, then one more shot and a cry of triumph from one of his men. He got cautiously to his feet.

'Cease fire, men. They've made a run for it. They'll be looking for easier pickings somewhere else.'

Leo got up and grabbed her pack. There was little in it but she still had a few field dressings. The man who had been wounded by the first shot was groaning and swearing and a brief examination showed her that the bullet was still lodged in his shoulder.

'We can't probe for it here,' she told Sasha. 'All I can do is dress the wound to stop the bleeding and give him some morphia for the pain.'

'Do it,' he agreed, adding with a wry smile, 'I had forgotten how useful it could be to have a nurse with us.'

They pressed on, along a track that grew narrower and narrower, towards the head of the valley. The way ran closer to the river again here, and they frequently had to cross it on bridges that consisted of nothing more than a few rough-hewn planks. More than once the whole column was held up because a pack mule or a handcart had slipped and fallen into the water. Then, towards midday, they heard a confused noise from the crowd ahead of them.

'Is it another attack?' Leo asked.

Sasha shook his head, screwing up his eyes. 'It sounds more like cheering.'

The word began to spread back along the line. 'The sea! We can see the sea!'

A distant memory stirred in Leo's mind of her Greek lessons with her father. 'Thalassa! Thalassa!' she murmured, and Sasha grinned and squeezed her hand. 'Zenophon. But it was the Black Sea in that case.'

Leo glanced sideways at him. 'You're the only person I know who would immediately recognize that.'

His grip tightened. 'It's only one of the many things we share.'

When their turn came to crest the last rise Leo strained her eyes into the distance. At last the snow had stopped and far below them she could just make out the sea, like a band of pewter along the horizon. Looking ahead and behind from this vantage point she was amazed to see how the line of people stretched out of sight in both directions. It was clear that they must number in their thousands.

'It's still a very long way,' she murmured.

'But we shall get there,' he replied. 'Now I have no doubt.'

She stumbled and he caught her arm again. 'Now you will ride.'

This time she did not argue.

At evening they came to a small village, a collection of poor, circular huts straggling along a muddy street. The inhabitants stood in their doorways watching them pass with hostile faces. Sasha called out to one or two, asking if they would sell him some bread, but they turned away without answering until they came to a house that stood slightly apart at the end of the village, where an ancient woman responded with a toothless smile.

'Yes, I have bread. How much will you give?'

Sasha named a price twice what Leo had been paying, even when the shortages began to bite. The old crone cackled and asked for double. He offered a figure somewhere between the two and eventually she hobbled off into the hut and returned with four loaves of rough black bread. That night there was more horse stew and this time they each had a small piece of bread to dip into it. When they had eaten Leo went to check on the wounded man. Until that time she had been too absorbed in her own struggle for survival to pay much attention to the rest of the company, but now she saw that several of them had minor wounds which were beginning to fester for lack of treatment. She spent an hour cleaning and dressing them and responding to their shy questions. It was plain that they were consumed with curiosity about her sudden appearance and her relationship with their commander but they had too much natural courtesy to ask her directly. She told them about the Sick and Wounded Convoy and how she had become separated from it. As to the rest, she left them to draw their own conclusions.

To Leo, the following day seemed the longest of all, even though they were going down hill and the snow had given way to a persistent drizzle. The bright strip of sea seemed to get no closer, and sometimes it disappeared from sight altogether and she began to think that it would take days rather than hours to reach it. But as the light faded they came at last to a proper road and turned south towards the port of Durazzo. A messenger rode along the ranks towards them and stopped to speak to Sasha, who turned and shouted to his men.

'Keep going, lads. There's a camp waiting to receive us outside the town. Not far now.'

Starving and exhausted, they raised a ragged cheer and plodded on.

The camp, when they reached it at midnight, was in a field already churned to mud by the earlier arrivals. There were a

few tents, but not enough by a long way to accommodate
everyone and they were already full, and there was no wood
for fires. They spent a miserable night huddled together on
the wet ground with nothing to eat.

Soon after dawn an officer rode into the camp, followed by
three wagons. Leo took one look at his uniform and ran to
greet him.

'Good morning! I can't tell you how glad I am to see a
British officer! Oh, by the way, I'm Leonora Malham Brown.
How do you do?'

He stared down at her and she suddenly realized how she
must look to him: a filthy, ragged urchin. She ran a hand
through her hair and said lamely, 'I don't usually look like this.'

He found his voice and said, 'You're English?'

'Yes.'

'And you're – forgive me, you are a woman?'

'Yes. I came out to help nurse the wounded, but I got
separated from the rest of the convoy. But listen! These people
are starving. I mean, quite literally dying of hunger. Do you
have food in those wagons?'

'Yes, some. But we had no idea that there would be so
many. It won't be enough to go round, but I will come back
with more.'

She had been joined by Sasha and officers from the other
units. The strongest men were called for and the wagons were
rapidly unloaded and their contents, tins of bully beef and
packets of hard biscuits, divided as equitably as possible. Leo
watched Sasha going round his men, ensuring that the weakest
were fed first. There were no arguments and she marvelled,
not for the first time, at the uncomplaining endurance of these
peasant soldiers. He insisted on giving her an equal ration but
when he came back to her she saw that he had reserved only
a small portion for himself.

'Here, you eat this. I've finished,' she said, offering him the
last biscuit with its smear of beef jelly.

He refused and they bickered for a few moments. Then he
laughed and said, 'I'd forgotten what an obstinate creature you
can be. Here!' and he broke the biscuit in two and put half in
his mouth.

When the British officer returned he came to find Leo.

'Forgive me, I completely forgot my manners this morning. My name is Robert Johnson. I have a message for you. There is a Red Cross mission in town with a number of English and American nurses. I've made some enquiries and they would be very happy to accommodate you until arrangements can be made for you to return to England. I can take you there on my way back.'

For a moment Leo was taken by surprise. The idea that she might leave Sasha and his men had never crossed her mind. She shook her head. 'That's very kind of you, but I have no plans to return to England at the moment.'

The officer looked nonplussed. 'Well, at least let me take you to the mission until we are able to discover what has happened to your friends. I assume you will want to rejoin them?'

'You should go, Leo,' Sasha said quietly.

She turned to him. 'You want me to leave you?'

'I'm trying to do what is best for you.'

'The colonel is right,' the British captain said. 'After all, this is really no place for a lady.'

Leo set her jaw. 'Then perhaps I am no lady. I am staying here.'

The captain looked at Sasha. 'Cannot you persuade her, sir?'

Sasha raised his eyes heavenwards. 'I know that look. I might as well try to persuade the sun not to set.'

The captain frowned. 'Very well. The offer is there, if you should change your mind.'

As he turned away, Sasha said, 'What is going to happen to us? We can't sit here indefinitely.'

'Ships have been chartered to take you off and transport you to Corfu. The first should arrive tomorrow, but it will be some time before we can accommodate so many of you. I'm afraid I must ask you to be patient.'

Leo had been thinking. Now she said quickly, 'Captain, I'm sorry to have been so ungracious. I should like to accept your offer after all. But I should like to bring one of the men with me. He has a bullet in the shoulder and he needs a doctor urgently.' Then she added in Serbian to Sasha, 'Stefan will be better off in the hospital but I shall come back, before dark. You won't go anywhere without me, will you?'

'We shall be here,' he said. 'But you should go home, you know.'

'Oh, no,' she replied. 'I'm coming to Corfu with you.'

'Leo! Leo, it's you! Thank God! We thought you had been taken prisoner, or . . . well, we didn't know where you were. It's such a relief to see you!'

Stella Patterson caught her by the arms and hugged her as she entered the hallway of the building where the Red Cross mission was housed.

'It's a blessed relief to see you, too,' Leo responded. 'I was so afraid that you hadn't made it over the mountains. How did you manage?'

'It was thanks to our wonderful drivers. When the road got too narrow for the wagons they cut them up and made two-wheeled hand carts and dragged the patients along in them. We lost two of them on the way, sadly, but three survived.'

'Including Milan? Tell me Milan survived!'

'Yes, he did and he's hobbling about on crutches. Come on in and see. The others are here, too. They will be so glad to see you.'

Stefan, the man who had been shot during the Albanian ambush, was taken up to one of the wards and minutes later Leo was reunited with the rest of her small team. They were all thin and tired but otherwise in good health. Having started out ahead of the main body of the army they had been able to buy supplies and had acquired three pack mules to carry them.

'And the best news is,' Stella said, 'Stobart and the rest have reached Scutari, north of here and are heading for Medua. We've all been promised a ship to take us to Brindisi and from there it will be easy to get the train to Rome and then back to London. Have you realized what the date is?'

Leo shook her head. 'I've no idea.'

'It's the twenty-third of December! Two days to Christmas. Of course, it isn't Christmas by the calendar they use here, but that's not the point. Just think! We shan't make it home for Christmas, but we might get there for New Year.'

For a moment Leo's imagination conjured a vivid image of the drawing room at Sussex Gardens; a blazing fire in the grate and Beavis bringing in tea with toasted crumpets. She dismissed it and smiled at the others.

'I hope you do. You've all done a marvellous job out here.'

'What do you mean?' Stella asked. 'Surely you are coming with us.'

Leo shook her head. 'I'm going back to be with . . . with the people who brought me over the mountains. They're old friends and I want to stay with them.'

She resisted all their attempts to persuade her to change her mind, but accepted the offer of a hot bath and a meal. The Red Cross nurses gave her a set of clean underwear but she declined the offer of a linen uniform dress and insisted instead on sponging the worst of the dirt off her breeches and tunic. She did, however, agree to exchange her smelly sheepskin coat for a thick woollen cloak with a hood. Lunch was the inevitable bully beef hash but it was followed by bread with real butter and apricot jam and coffee sweetened with condensed milk. The sudden rush of sweetness made her feel almost light-headed.

When they had eaten she thanked the nursing sister in charge, a cheerfully efficient American, and added: 'I wonder if I could ask you a really big favour. The men I came over the mountains with are almost starving. They are getting food now, though not really enough, but what they miss most is sugar for their coffee. It seems as though they can face almost anything as long as they get their hot, sweet coffee in the morning. Is there any chance you could let me have some sugar to take back to them? I probably owe them my life and I should like to repay them in some small way.'

As a result, she set off back to the camp in a donkey cart carrying the equivalent of a year's ration of sugar for one nurse and several tins of jam. Her leave-taking was a tearful affair, and her companions still begged her to change her mind and go home with them, but she never wavered. The comforts of home were a distant illusion, compared with the real prospect of returning to Sasha and his men.

* * *

Back at the camp conditions had improved. There were still not enough tents, but rough shelters had been constructed with sheets of tarpaulin and the men had scoured the countryside for wood, so that each company now had its vital campfire. Hay had even been procured for the horses and Leo found Sasha at the horse lines, stroking Cloud's emaciated flanks as the horse champed at the fodder. He greeted her with a frown.

'What are you doing back here?'

She felt as if he had struck her. 'I told you I was coming back.'

'You should have stayed in the town. As the English captain said, this is no place for a woman.'

Leo swallowed. 'Perhaps not. But it's where I want to be. You sent me away once before. This time I won't go.'

He turned to look at her and clasped both hands to his head in a gesture of self-mocking despair. 'Dear God! What have I done to be punished with this insubordinate female?'

In the space of a breath they were in each other's arms, not kissing but clinging together like the survivors of a shipwreck. She felt her tears soaking into the shoulder of his cloak. Voices nearby made them draw apart at length and as they looked at each other she saw that there were tears on his cheeks as well.

He ran the back of his hand across his eyes and then over her cheek. 'You smell good. What is it?'

'Soap and water,' she answered. 'Come and see what I have brought back with me.'

When she showed him the jam he called his men together and she went along the line giving each one a spoonful, which they received with almost religious solemnity, as if it had been the Holy Sacrament. After that, they had beef stew fiery with paprika and finished with mugs of thick, dark sweet coffee. The sugar raised their spirits to such an extent that one man produced a gusla and began to play and sing and two others even attempted the kolo; but they were quickly exhausted and sank down again on to the ground.

Sasha's face was still gaunt with anxiety. 'Some of them are so weak,' he confided. 'I thought if I could get them this far all would be well, but now I am afraid that we shall lose more unless they get better care soon.'

It was not long before the men moved back into their improvised shelters and began to roll themselves in their blankets and settle down to sleep. Leo looked at Sasha. On the mountains it had been a matter of survival to snuggle together, but now that excuse had vanished. She longed to feel his arms round her but he led her to a small space at the back of the tent, where a groundsheet had been suspended across the corner.

'It's not very comfortable, I'm afraid, but it will give you a bit of privacy.' He touched her cheek and turned away to stretch out near his men.

She understood that he was concerned for her honour but as she settled down, covering herself with her newly acquired cloak, she could not help feeling abandoned.

All next day they waited for news of the ships that would take them to Corfu, but there was no sign of them. Around noon two Austrian Taube biplanes came over and dropped bombs on the harbour. None fell on the camp but the sight increased the sense of despair that had settled over the refugees. However, as the sun was setting, Captain Johnson returned to tell them that ships were expected the next day. They must make their way to the harbour at dawn, to be ready to embark.

In the morning, as they prepared to leave after a hastily brewed cup of coffee, Leo looked for Sasha and could not see him. She found him down by the horse lines, standing by Cloud with his revolver in his hand.

'What are you doing?' she exclaimed, aghast.

He looked round at her, his eyes sunk so deep into their sockets that the flesh around them appeared bruised. 'We can't take horses on the ship. I won't leave him here to be worked to death by some peasant.'

'You can't!' she whispered. 'Sasha, you can't!'

'What else am I to do? Stay here with him?'

He turned away and held his hand to the horse's muzzle and Leo saw Cloud's tongue flick over his palm and guessed that he had kept his share of the sugar ration as a last treat for him. Then he put his arm round the animal's neck and whispered in his ear, and pressed the revolver against his head. Leo heard the report and saw the horse's legs buckle beneath him. Sasha put a second bullet into his head to make sure and turned away.

'Are the men ready?'

'Yes, they are waiting for you.'

'Let's go, then.'

When they reached the harbour it was empty of ships, though the quayside was already crowded with men. The hours passed and they waited without food or shelter from the biting cold. Around midday a cheer went up and two Italian ferries steamed into sight. They were too large to moor up to the quayside, so small boats put off to carry the troops out to them. They had just taken on their first load when the Taubes came over again. There was nowhere to shelter, so all they could do was huddle together on the quay and watch as the bombs dropped. Most of them fell harmlessly into the water, but one hit one of the ferries amidships. Within minutes she split in two and sank. The men in the small boats had to climb back on to the quay, while the boats went to rescue the survivors who were thrashing about in the harbour.

Eventually some of the waiting troops were loaded on to the second ship but it was clear that there would not be room for all of them. As the evening darkened Leo looked at Sasha.

'Should we head back to the camp, do you think?'

'What would be the point? The men still waiting there will have eaten all the rations. We can starve here as easily as anywhere else.'

She had never seen him so dispirited and it hurt like a stab to the heart. But as she struggled to think of words to cheer him another cry went up and they saw a rusty freighter steaming into the harbour. By midnight they were all aboard and the ship, so low in the water that Leo feared the slightest swell might swamp her, set sail for Corfu.

Fifteen

'Ladies, I have some really excellent news!'

Victoria put down her cup of cocoa and looked at Lilian Franklin with interest. It was not like Boss to get excited. Around her in the fuggy common room at the top of Lamarck the other FANYs stopped chatting and turned to their leader in anticipation.

'I don't have to remind you that our original intention was to provide an ambulance service for our own troops. It is not from choice that we have spent the last fifteen months caring for the Belgian and French wounded, although I know how much our efforts have been appreciated. Now, at last, it seems the powers-that-be have relented and we are to be allowed to do what we set out to do.'

There was an excited buzz of questions and exclamations, above which Marian Gamwell's voice rose decisively. 'How is this going to happen, Boss?'

'The British Red Cross Society will commission us to provide transport for the sick and wounded. They will provide the vehicles and all the necessary accommodation, stores etc. and we will do the driving.'

'Does that mean we are becoming part of the Red Cross?' Beryl Hutchinson asked.

'No. Mac has managed to negotiate a deal whereby we retain our independence and our identity. We shall wear our own uniform but be entitled to the same privileges as members of the BRCS.'

'Where are we going to be based?' Gamwell asked.

'Here, in Calais. The BRCS are setting up a camp for us.'

'Will we all be going?' someone asked.

'No. We can't abandon our work here, so some of you will remain. Eighteen of us will move to the new base. The people I have selected are as follows . . .'

Victoria gripped her hands so that the nails bit into her

palms. She wanted, more than anything she could remember, to be one of those chosen. Driving was her passion, she almost felt it as her vocation. She had done her bit as a nurse in Lamarck, but now at last there seemed to be a chance to concentrate all her efforts as an ambulance driver. Franklin was reading out the list of names: Baxter Ellis, Gamwell, Hutchinson, Lowson . . . and there it was, at last! Langford. Victoria gasped with relief and realized she had been holding her breath.

'When do we start?' she asked.

'January the first,' was the reply.

Luke hobbled along the hospital corridor in search of Sophie. It was evening and the windows were open to catch the cooling breeze from the Nile. He had been at the hospital for almost two months and his leg was nearly healed; and he was bored almost to insanity. But now, at last, something was about to happen.

He found Sophie in the sluice room, washing out bedpans. She glanced round as he came in and then went on with her work, keeping her face turned away from him.

'Hey!' he said. 'I've got some good news.'

'What news is that?'

'Well, first, the rest of the guys are being evacuated from Gallipoli. The generals in London have finally realized that all they are doing is getting thousands of good men slaughtered for nothing. The whole thing has been a shambles from the very beginning. Thank God it's over now.'

'So now you will all be able to go home,' she said.

'I don't know about that. Rumour is that the troops are going to be redeployed to the Western Front. It can't be worse than Gallipoli. At least they'll be away from the heat and the flies.'

'But not you,' Sophie said. 'Not with that leg.'

'No,' he agreed, 'not yet, anyway. Guess I'm due for a spot of home leave.'

He was not sure himself whether to feel relief at the prospect or a sense of disappointment at missing out on the next scene of the drama, whatever that might be. He had developed close bonds with the men in his unit and he felt a sense of duty to go with the survivors, wherever they were sent. However, it was clearly not to be – at least, as he had said to Sophie, not yet – so he might as well enjoy his luck while it lasted. 'The other bit of news is there's a ship leaving the day after tomorrow to take guys like me home. So it won't be long now before I can show you the farm and introduce you to the family.'

She turned to look at him then and he saw that she had been crying. 'Luke, I know about the ship. But I can't come with you.'

'Why not?' He moved closer and reached for her hand. 'Sophie, I know you miss your home and you want to go back, but it's impossible right now. You know that, as well as I do. Maybe in a few months or a year, when we've finally routed the Turks out of the area, you'll be able to go back, but it's too dangerous now. You have to think of little Anton.'

He saw the tears well up in her eyes again. 'I don't want to go back, Luke. But I can't come to New Zealand with you. I asked the adjutant to post me to the ship as a nurse, but he says the immigration people at Wellington would just send me straight back because I have no papers.'

Luke stared at her. 'That can't be right. You saved my life. Wait right there, I'm going to talk to the adjutant myself.'

The adjutant, however, simply reiterated what he had said to Sophie. 'I'm sorry, old man, but it would be irresponsible of me to let her board the ship, knowing she'll be turned back at the port. There's only one thing I can suggest, and that is that you go and see the consul. He might be able to provide some kind of emergency paperwork that would allow the young lady to stay in New Zealand for a while, at least. I'm afraid that's the best chance I can offer.'

Luke went straight out of the hospital, jumped into one of the horse-drawn gharries that waited at the gate and asked to be taken to the New Zealand consulate. There he insisted on an immediate audience with the consul, declaring that the situation was an emergency and using his status as a soldier wounded in the service of his country to press his case. The consul listened to his story and agreed with him that it showed remarkable heroism on Sophie's part, which deserved its reward, but his final verdict was the same.

'I'm sorry, Sergeant, but I don't have the authority to produce papers for a resident of what is, for better or worse, an enemy country. Whether we like it or not, the lady is in law a Turkish citizen.'

Luke ground his teeth in frustration. 'What about natural justice?' he demanded.

'Not within my remit, I'm afraid,' the consul replied.

At that moment Luke had an inspiration. 'Would it make a difference if we were married?'

'You and this young lady?'

'Me and Sophie, yes.'

'Well, of course that would be different. As your wife she would have the right of residence.'

'And she wouldn't be turned away by immigration?'

'I don't see how she could be.'

'Then that's the answer.' Luke got up, thanked the consul, and took his leave.

He found Sophie about to go off duty and persuaded her to come and sit with him in the garden. They found a bench under the shade of a palm tree at the edge of a dusty patch of grass.

'I went to see the adjutant,' he began, 'and he told me to go and talk to the consul.'

She gave him a weary smile. 'You should not wear yourself out like that. You are still not strong and it will do no good.'

'I'm not so sure about that. There is a way, but I'm a bit doubtful about suggesting it. I don't know what you will think about it.'

'A way I can come to New Zealand, with you, and bring Anton with me?'

'Yes.'

'Tell me. I will do anything I can.'

'It isn't anything difficult. All you have to do is marry me.'

She stared at him. 'Marry you?'

'Yes. I know it's a big step. You're still grieving for Iannis and obviously you're not in love with me. But it would be a formality, that's all. I wouldn't expect you to – well, you know.

We might have to share a cabin on the ship, but I'd respect your privacy. Am I making sense?'

For a long moment she sat looking down at her hands, which were clasped in her lap. Then she said, without looking up, 'You would do this for me?'

For the first time the full implications of what he was suggesting came home to Luke. It had seemed so obvious when the consul had mentioned the idea but now he realized that he was offering to commit himself to what was in essence a legal deception. Presumably he would be able to escape from the marriage in due course; words like divorce and annulment floated through his mind. If that was what he wanted . . . But what did he want? Why was it so important that Sophie should come home with him?

He answered in the only way that seemed to make sense at that moment. 'You saved my life. It's the least I can do in return.'

Slowly she raised her eyes and the expression in them was unfathomable. 'Then, if you are prepared to do this thing for me, I accept. And I thank you.'

Luke and Sophie were married by the hospital chaplain the following morning and the next day they took ship for New Zealand.

'Stand to! Stand to!' The hoarse whispers of the NCOs ran along the trench and men tumbled out of bunks hollowed in its sides, bleary-eyed but with their rifles in their hands.

Tom yawned and shivered. It was almost the end of his three-hour watch. Soon he would be able to go back to the dugout for breakfast. Orderlies came along the trench with the morning ration of tea and rum. Tom headed for company HQ to wake the other officers, pausing on the way to exchange a few words with a man here and there. He knew all his platoon personally now, and consciously modelled himself on Ralph in taking an interest in their backgrounds and their problems. Besides which, he had sketched most of them and handed them the results, which had earned him the nickname of 'Doodles'. He was not supposed to know that, but he had heard it whispered along the trench at his approach.

He had returned from England just in time to see the New Year in with Ralph. The regiment had been in reserve in the village of Poperinghe but now they were back in the trenches and in many ways that was a relief. He had survived his officer training, but only just. It had put him at the mercy of some of the regiment's 'old hands' – both officers and NCOs. Some of these men had served in the Boer War and were intent on preserving what they called 'the traditions of the regiment'; traditions which, in Tom's opinion, were merely a continuation of the bullying and meaningless rituals of public school. Junior officers were regarded as some kind of inferior being, to be humiliated at every opportunity. Tom, being a volunteer rather than a regular soldier, was a particular subject of contempt. When it was discovered that he was an artist, to boot, he became the target of every disciplinarian in the battalion. He was punished for failing to salute in precisely the prescribed manner, sent for riding lessons during which he was made to jump fences bareback on a particularly intractable mare, and forbidden, along with all the other junior officers, from drinking anything stronger than beer in the mess. Before the war he had not been particularly aware of snobbery and class divisions, but his time in the army had brought home to him the patent absurdity of such attitudes. In civilian life he would have been regarded as a social equal by even the most senior officers, because he was the son of a baronet. In barracks, he was treated worse than an errand boy.

At the end of his training he had been given two weeks' leave, which he had spent at Denham Hall with his parents. If he had found his training a time of trial, this period of so-called relaxation had made him more eager than ever to get back to France. His father, always fond of a drink and a gamble, spent most of his time carousing with the red-faced local squires who were only too happy to accept his hospitality, or at his London club. His mother, meanwhile, whom he had always found chilly and aloof, seemed to have withdrawn almost completely from family life. Neither of them seemed to have any concept of conditions on the Western Front and his father's only response to the information that

Tom had volunteered for active duty and officer training was a derisive snort.

Returning to France, he had seen Ralph with fresh eyes and realized how much he had changed. The bright gloss of youth had gone, both physically and mentally. Even his hair was no longer the colour of a freshly fallen chestnut; instead it was more like the dulled relic of the previous autumn. The devil-may-care courage had gone, too, replaced by a bitter endurance.

At company headquarters, a two-roomed dugout in the side of a trench connecting the forward and support lines, he woke his fellow officers but found that Ralph was missing.

'Called back to battalion HQ, sir,' his batman informed him. 'Some kind of a flap on, I expect.'

Ralph had been promoted to captain and was now in command of the company, a transition that seemed to put a distance between them. Tom was sitting down to a breakfast of bacon, eggs, coffee, toast and marmalade with the others when he came in.

'Good morning, gentlemen. No, don't get up. Finish your breakfasts. HQ have intelligence that Fritz is digging a sap out towards our front line. They want us to go out and verify it. It means going out after dark and locating the area, then lying up in a shell-hole for the day, listening for sounds of digging. I need a volunteer to come with me.'

'I'll come,' Tom said at once.

Ralph turned to him with a frown. 'No, not you, Tom. You're needed back here.'

'But . . .' Tom protested, but at the same time a young sub-lieutenant called Carver, who had only been with them for a few weeks, piped up.

'I'll come with you, sir.'

Ralph nodded. 'Thank you. Be ready immediately after stand-to this evening. Now, is there any of that bacon left?'

Tom opened his mouth to argue and then thought better of it. At worst it would be insubordination; and even if Ralph could be persuaded he could not go back on what he had said in front of the others. He must wait until after he had carried out his routine morning duties: inspecting the men's rifles, checking that the trench was kept clean, and organizing work parties to repair and improve the defences. The trench system had developed by this time into an underground village, with a network of communication trenches and support trenches, where it was quite easy to get lost. The trenches were protected by a revetment of sandbags and broken into sections by traverses, to impede any enemy forces that might get into them. There was always work to be done to keep these in good repair.

When he was sure that all this was in hand Tom went back to the HQ dugout. By good luck, he found Ralph alone except for another officer who was fast asleep in the inner room. He launched into his argument without preamble.

'Ralph, this has got to stop.'

'The war? I quite agree with you, but it isn't going to – not for a long time yet.'

'You know quite well that I'm not referring to the war in general.'

'What, then?'

'The way you are behaving towards me.'

'Have I been less than correct in my behaviour?'

'No. I'm not talking about manners or military correctness! I'm talking about the way you turn me down every time I volunteer for anything with the slightest risk.'

'I simply feel that you are better employed here rather than out there between the lines.'

'Are you afraid that I'll panic? Do you think I haven't got the guts for operations like that?'

At last Ralph looked up from the maps he was studying. 'Good God, no, Tom! I know you're as brave as any man here.'

'Then why are you giving everyone else the impression that you think I'm not up to the job?'

'That's not my intention.' He paused and looked at Tom with an intentness that made him feel uncomfortable. 'It's just . . . Look, you've got more to give the world than some of us. You're an artist. In all this mindless slaughter some people have to be preserved, and you're one of them.'

'Codswallop!' Tom said energetically. 'If I was Reubens or da Vinci there might be some justification, but my talent, if I

have any, is a very minor one. There are plenty of other men
out here with far more to offer in that line than me. What
about some of the poetry that's being written? That fellow
Graves is writing some brilliant stuff but I bet his CO doesn't
go out of his way to keep him out of danger.'

'Well, I'm not his CO,' Ralph replied. 'It's my decision,
Tom, and you'll just have to live with it – *live* being the opera-
tive word.'

Tom stared at him in despair for a moment, then he used
his last ammunition.

'You know what people are saying, don't you?'

'What do you mean?'

'People know that we were at school together. They think
you are giving me special treatment because . . . well, because
we have a certain kind of relationship.'

He saw the colour rise in Ralph's face. 'Who is saying that?
Tell me his name and, by God, I'll call him out!'

'Don't be ridiculous, Ralph! What century do you think
we're living in – the seventeenth? You can't fight a duel these
days. If you even suggested it you would be in contravention
of the King's regulations. You'd be cashiered. Anyway, it isn't
one particular person. It's just a vague rumour, a series of
innuendoes. But it isn't good for morale.'

That was his trump card. 'Morale' was all important and
Ralph would go to great lengths to maintain it. Ralph glared
at him for a moment, then he got up and turned his back.
'Very well, come if you want to. Come and get your stupid
head blown off, for all I care. Tell young Carver that I've
changed my mind.'

As darkness fell Tom stood with Ralph at the corner of a
traverse and heard the whispered word passed along the line:
'Officer's patrol going out.' This was an essential precaution in
case a sentry, seeing movement in the dark, took a pot shot at
them. Ralph got up on the firing step and raised his head
cautiously above the parapet. After studying the expanse of
no-man's-land for a few moments he glanced back at Tom and
made a forward gesture with one arm. Then he wriggled over
the top and disappeared. Tom hoisted himself up, his heart

pounding, and followed. Flat on their bellies they inched forward, under their own barbed wire, and out into the shell-pocked land beyond. There was no moon and the sky was overcast, so the darkness was absolute. Every few yards they stopped and lay motionless, watching and listening for any movement. It was well known that the Germans also sent out patrols during the night. Then they crawled on again, sometimes skirting the shell-holes, sometimes finding no way forward but by descending into their waterlogged depths and then climbing out on the far side. Once a German flare went up, casting an unearthly light over the whole expanse, and they lay still, shamming dead, until it went out. Once Tom felt something slimy under his hand and recognized with horror that he had put it on the face of a corpse that had been left lying there for months.

After crawling for what felt like miles Ralph beckoned him close and breathed in his ear, 'This is roughly where they think the sap has got to. We'll get down into this shell crater and hope we're near enough.'

The bottom of the crater was covered in a couple of inches of icy water. Tom tried crouching, so that only his boots were in it, but that position soon became untenable. It hit him that they were going to be there all through the next day until darkness fell again. He told himself that wounded men survived in similar conditions, so there was no reason why two healthy ones should not do the same. Nevertheless, the prospect was grim. A hand nudged his arm, and a flask was pressed into his hand. It contained strong coffee, well laced with rum. Tom drank and felt a little better.

Dawn came at last but once the protective veil of darkness was withdrawn he felt dangerously exposed. Ralph wriggled carefully to the edge of the crater and peered over.

'We're about twenty yards from the German wire,' he whispered. 'If we're in the right place we should be able to hear them working on the sap.'

They hunkered down, keeping well below the rim of the crater, and drank more coffee and ate some of their iron rations. Tom eased his position with a suppressed groan and caught Ralph's eye. Suddenly they both grinned and Ralph whispered, 'Well, you wanted to come.'

It was a quiet morning. There was no bombardment and except for the occasional crack of a sniper's rifle no firing of any sort. Then Tom's ears caught a faint sound. He tapped Ralph's knee to get his attention and cocked his head in an attitude of listening. From somewhere a short way to his right he could hear the unmistakable noise of a pick striking earth. Moments later it was joined by the muffled sound of voices. Ralph caught his eye and nodded triumphantly. He inched his way up the side of the crater until he could just peer over the rim, then slid back again.

'Got a pencil and paper with you?'

'As always.'

'See if you can identify any landmarks to pinpoint the area where the noise is coming from.'

In his turn, Tom squirmed to the rim of the crater and peered over. The whole area had been reduced to an almost featureless waste ground but a short way off a broken tree stump stuck up out of the mud. Nearer at hand, there was a more gruesome landmark, the skeleton of a dead horse. Tom's eyes raked the scene, estimating the distance from the German wire, and the angle of their travel from their own base, committing the details to memory. He slid back into the crater, got out his sketch pad, which he carried in a waterproof pouch slung round his neck under his tunic, and rapidly laid out all the salient features. When he had done he handed the pad to Ralph, who returned it with a gleam in his eyes.

'You were right. You're the right man for the job.'

There was nothing to do after that but wait out the daylight, listening to the sounds of work nearby and eating and drinking sparingly from the supplies they had brought with them. Tom thanked heaven it was winter and the days were short, even if the cold had penetrated to his very bones. When darkness fell again and all was quiet they hauled themselves out of the shell-hole and began the crawl back. Stiff and chilled, they found it harder going than on the way out, though Tom was amazed to see, from his reconnoitre earlier, how short the actual distance was. It took them nearly two hours to regain their own trench. When they reached it Ralph beckoned Tom forward and he slid over the rim and dropped on to the fire step, where his platoon sergeant was waiting to welcome them.

'Well done, sir! Good to see you back . . .'

His words were lost in the crack of a sniper's rifle. Tom turned to say, 'That was a close one . . .' and was just in time to catch Ralph as he fell into the trench.

Sixteen

'Forty-eight, forty-nine – start, damn you!' Victoria muttered breathlessly as she cranked the starting handle of the Napier. 'Fifty, fifty-one – oh, thank God!' as the engine coughed into reluctant life.

The new base for what was being called 'the Calais convoy' was on the top of a windswept hill just outside the town. The accommodation was in tents, set round an open square in which the ambulances, all converted motor cars, were parked. It was a bitterly cold January and Victoria had grown accustomed to waking in the morning to find icicles on the outside of her sleeping bag; but it was the cars that caused the most problems. They had been filled, supposedly, with antifreeze, but still starting them in the mornings was a nightmare. Start they must, because every morning a hospital train, marked with red crosses, came into the Gare Centrale loaded with wounded who must be conveyed either to one of the hospitals in the area or, when the hospitals were full, as they often were, to ships in the harbour.

As soon as all the vehicles had been started a procession formed behind Lilian Franklin's car and they drove through the town to the station. When the train came in the casualties were sorted by the duty medical officers and then allocated to different vehicles. Victoria helped to carry two stretchers to the Napier and load them in. One of the men was writhing and groaning in pain; the other was silent and so pale that Victoria wondered if he was still alive. She placed her fingers on his neck and found a faint, unsteady pulse. Climbing into the driver's seat, she wondered if he would survive the journey.

As carefully as possible she eased the car out of the station yard and over several sets of railway lines. The inevitable jolting provoked a stream of obscenities from the man who was conscious, and then a shamefaced apology.

'Never mind me, miss,' he called. 'Just go as fast as you can and get it over with.'

Victoria paid no heed and nursed the car along the potholed road as gently as she could. When they finally reached the hospital the man apologized again and thanked her. One of the nurses bent over the second man and felt his pulse.

'Is he still alive?' Victoria asked.

The nurse looked up. 'Just. Any longer and we would have been too late.'

Victoria turned the car and set off back towards the camp. Now that there was no need to avoid the bumps she drove flat out, using all her skill to cover the distance as quickly as possible. It concentrated her mind and helped to wipe out the memory of those screams of pain.

She was almost there when the engine lost power, choked once or twice and died. Cursing under her breath, she climbed out and swung the handle. It took her a long time to get the Napier going again and by the time she got back to camp all the other ambulances were parked in their allotted places. Victoria ignored the friendly jibes of her fellow drivers and went to find Beryl Hutchinson, who was in charge of the mechanical upkeep of the cars. In passing she paused to pat Sparky's bonnet. He had been deemed too small for ambulance duty and was kept as a general run-about, but she felt sure he would not have let her down.

She explained what had happened to Hutchinson. 'It's probably a fuel blockage, I should think.'

Hutchinson grimaced. 'That means it'll have to go into the depot for an overhaul, and I've just been warned that Captain Goff, who's in charge, gets almost apoplectic at the very idea of women drivers.'

Victoria groaned. 'You know what that means. Our job will go to the back of the queue and every vehicle that comes in with a male driver will get done first. Wretched man! Why should it be a male prerogative to drive? Most of them haven't the foggiest idea how to maintain a car.'

'Because it's a male prerogative to do most things that are fun,' Hutchinson responded. 'But you've given me an idea. We'll show him that we do know how to look after our cars.

We'll clean the engine up till it looks as if it has only just come out of the showroom and we'll oil all the bolts that might have to be undone and loosen them off and then do them up just tight enough to get us to the depot. That way, they will have the minimum amount of work to do and Goff won't be able to find anything to complain about.'

'Brilliant!' Victoria said with a grin. 'Right, let's get to work.'

An hour later she wriggled out from under the car and got to her feet, rubbing her back. 'Well, I reckon you could go under there in full evening dress without having to worry about getting dirty.'

Hutchinson was wrestling with a spanner. 'I've slackened off every one except this and I can't move the beastly thing.'

'Let me try,' Victoria offered. She took the spanner but after a few minutes she, too, had to admit defeat. 'Wait a mo! I've got an idea.'

A number of bathing machines had been parked around the site and served various useful purposes. She went to the one which Hutchinson used as an office and came back a few minutes later carrying a label. Hutchinson took it and read out 'I'm afraid this one was too hard for a poor weak woman to undo. It needs a man's touch.'

'That is brilliant!' she declared. 'Clever you!'

'Well, it never does any harm to flatter the poor creatures' egos, in my experience,' Victoria said with a chuckle. 'And they never seem to realize that we're laughing behind their backs.'

They drove the Napier to the depot and reported to Captain Goff. He looked them up and down and blew through his nostrils – like an impatient horse, Victoria thought.

'You'll be two of these Fannies I've heard tell of. Why some fool thought it would be a good idea to put women behind the wheel of a car I shall never understand.'

'We're here to do a job, sir, like you,' Hutchinson said. 'We do a lot of our own maintenance but I'm afraid this is a bit beyond our resources.' She detailed the symptoms and added: 'We think it may be a fuel blockage.'

'Oh, you do, do you?' The sneer in the captain's voice was barely hidden. 'Well, leave it here. I'll see when we can get round to it.'

Victoria had been patient long enough. 'We need it back by the end of the day, Captain. Tomorrow we have to collect more wounded from the train and we have barely enough vehicles for the job as it is. A man nearly died in my ambulance today. If it had broken down on the way to the hospital, instead of on the way back, he would have done. So, if you care about the lives of our boys, please do your best to get the repairs done quickly.'

Goff looked at her, nostrils quivering. Then he turned away. 'I'll see what can be done but I make no promises. Come back later on this afternoon.'

When they returned, the Napier was standing ready and Goff's face bore a grudging smile. 'Well, I'll have to give you credit. I've never seen an engine so well maintained.' He patted the Napier's bonnet. 'She'll give you no more trouble, I'll guarantee it. And I'll see all your vehicles get priority treatment in future.'

Once in the cab and away from the depot, Victoria and Hutchinson gave way to a fit of giggling that lasted all the way back to the camp.

Later, in the mess tent, someone came in waving a newspaper. 'I say, chaps, has anyone else seen this?'

'Seen what?' several voices enquired.

'This article. It's about women who drive cars. Hang on, I'll read you a bit. "The uncongenial atmosphere of the garage, yard and workshops, the alien companionship of mechanics and chauffeurs, the ceaseless days and dull monotony of labour will not only rob her of much feminine charm but will instil into her mind bitterness that will eat from her heart all capacity for joy". How about it, girls? Have we lost all capacity for joy?'

A roar of laughter gave her her answer, but when it died down a plaintive voice remarked, 'I can see his point in one way. I don't think I shall ever be presentable enough to show my face in a London drawing room again. Driving around in the snow and the rain and the wind, I'm going to have a complexion like an old washerwoman by the time we're finished.'

Victoria rubbed her cheeks and recognized the truth of the comment. None of the vehicles had windscreens and as a result her face was chapped and her lips were cracked, and she had run out of cold cream to put on them.

'Never mind faces,' someone said. 'Look at my hands!'

'Snap!' Victoria said, holding out her own. 'I've scrubbed and scrubbed but I can't get the grease out of my fingernails.'

'Never mind,' Hutchinson said, 'when the war is over we'll start a new fashion. We'll call it *washerwoman chic!*'

Next evening, coming into the mess tent, Victoria found a small group standing in front of the noticeboard, on which was pinned a sheet of paper torn from a notebook. Over their shoulders she read:

I wish my mother could see me now, with a grease-gun under my car,
Filling my differential 'ere I start for the camp afar,
Atop a sheet of frozen iron, in cold that would make you cry.
'Why do we do it?' you ask.
'Why? We're the F.A.N.Y.'
I used to be in society once;
Danced and hunted and flirted once;
Had white hands and complexion – once.
Now I'm F.A.N.Y.

The daily routine continued: the hospital train convoy went out every morning and often, later in the day, the cry would go up, 'Barges!' and everyone would drop what they were doing and run for the ambulances. Barges were used to convey the most seriously wounded along the canals, because they caused less jolting than the train journey. But there were lighter moments. Calais was always full of troops, either passing through or based there as part of the garrison, and the officers were glad to have female company – even with 'washerwoman' complexions. There were frequent invitations to dinners and dances and a number of flirtatious liaisons were begun. Victoria's first impulse was to steer clear of all such involvements. Her affair with Luke was still a very present memory and she had no intention of letting anything similar happen now. What changed her mind was the realization that these officers had horses at their disposal and were happy to lend them. A good gallop along the sands was second only to driving a racing car flat out in her estimation and so she began to accept the invitations, though she was careful to make it clear that all she was offering in return was a cheerful comradeship.

When she started work at Lamarck she had sometimes wondered how long it would be before she found herself treating someone she recognized. She had had a wide circle of friends in London before the war and many of the men were now serving in the army. It was something she dreaded, but as the days passed she forgot about it and now the blanket shrouded figures she loaded into her ambulance had acquired a kind of anonymity. They were patients, some more seriously wounded than others, some noisy, some quiet – but just patients. One morning, stooping to pick up a stretcher, she suddenly found herself looking down at a face she knew. As she stared, momentarily caught off-guard, the man opened his eyes.

'Oh, bloody hell! Not you, of all people!' said Ralph, and shut his eyes again.

Seventeen

As the overloaded ship ploughed southwards towards Corfu Leo convinced herself that all their troubles were over. There was no food on the ship, and very little drinking water, but once they reached Corfu they would be on friendly territory and their allies would provide for all their needs. In her imagination the island was a paradise, bathed in constant sunshine.

When they eventually docked it was dark and still raining and there was no one on the quayside to welcome them or to tell them where to go. The warehouses were closed and the streets deserted. For eight hours the pathetic remnants of the Serbian army sat huddled on the dock without food or shelter. Eventually, when it grew light, a French officer appeared and asked to speak to the senior officer.

It seemed that in all the confusion of the journey most of the units had lost their officers and Malkovic was the most senior of those that remained. He stepped forward, saying to Leo, 'Come and translate for me. Ask him why we have been left sitting like this all night.'

It seemed that their ship had not been expected. Others had arrived, in the last few days, but it had been assumed that they carried the only survivors. However, a camp had been prepared for them, some twelve kilometres outside the town.

Sasha looked around at the empty dockside. 'How are we to get there? Where is the transport?'

Leo translated the question and turned back to him with bitter resignation. 'There is no transport. We have to walk.'

So they set off again, not marching but shuffling and limping, the stronger among them supporting their weaker comrades, a rag-tag army of ghosts plodding through the rain. The camp, when they reached it, was another collection of tents in another muddy field and there was neither food nor firewood. Sasha called the junior officers and NCOs from the other units together and told them to take a roll-call. Each one reported back that less than a third of their men had survived. Of his own regiment, two more had died on the ship and three others were too weak to stand. He dispersed them to find what shelter they could and disappeared into one of the tents. Leo followed and found him huddled on the ground with his head buried in his arms. When she touched his shoulder he turned a haggard face towards her.

'We were one thousand strong when we left Prizren. Now there are just over three hundred left. How many others have died from other battalions? And what have we struggled for? So we can die here, instead of on the mountains? Where are our so-called allies? Where are the British?'

Unable to answer, Leo turned away. She had never seen him like this and his despair dragged at her heart. She left the tent and as she stood gazing around her in a desperate search for inspiration she saw a lorry pass along the road, heading for the city. It was quickly followed by another. She wiped her hand across her eyes and went to find Janachko, Sasha's orderly.

'I am going into the town to look for help. Don't tell the colonel, unless he asks for me. He is resting, so don't disturb him.'

She did not have long to wait at the roadside before another truck came into sight and she saw that it was flying a small union jack from the bonnet. She stepped into the road and held up her hand. The driver sounded the horn and made to drive past but she stood resolutely in his path so that he had to skid to a halt.

'What the hell are you playing at, boy?' he demanded. 'Bugger off out of it! Go on! Imshi! Vamoose!'

Leo summoned her most ladylike tones. 'I don't know who you think you are addressing, Corporal, but you shouldn't be deceived by appearances. My name is Leonora Malham Brown. I am an officer in the First Aid Nursing Yeomanry and I require immediate transport into Corfu Town.' Then, ignoring his half-throttled exclamation of 'Blimey', she swung herself up on to the seat beside him.

'Beg pardon, ma'am,' he mumbled. 'I thought you was one of them peasant boys. I didn't mean no offence.'

'And I have taken none,' Leo assured him. 'I quite understand

that I don't look as you might expect. But I have had a very
long and difficult journey and now I must see someone in
authority. Who is in control here?'

The driver gave her a sideways glance as he put the engine
into gear. 'That's a very good question, ma'am, if you don't
mind my saying so. Officially it's the French. They've taken
over the island for the duration and we're here as back-up. But
then there's the Greek government and the Eyeties. If you ask
me, nobody knows who's in charge.'

'But there is a British military mission here?'

'Oh, yes.'

'Then please take me to the British attaché.'

Ten minutes later she was dropped outside the building
housing the British military mission. The sentry at the gate
was not as easily persuaded as the lorry driver so Leo produced
what she regarded as her trump card. Fortunately, before leaving
England the previous April she had obtained one of the new
passports, with a photograph and a description. She had kept
it securely buttoned in a pocket of her tunic all through her
journey and held it out to the man with a flourish. He peered
at it, and then at her, and turned his head towards a small
building just inside the gates.

'Sarge! Something here I think you'd better see.'

The sergeant appeared, chewing and clearly annoyed at
having his lunch disturbed.

'Lad here trying to pass himself off as the owner of this
document,' the sentry said.

The sergeant examined the passport and then looked at Leo.
'How did you come by this, eh? Did you steal it? Where's the
owner?'

Leo drew a long breath. She was almost at the end of her
strength. 'I am the owner. I am Leonora Malham Brown and
I must see the attaché immediately. If you don't believe me
I'm quite prepared to take off my clothes here in the street,
so you can see that I am a woman.'

She began to fumble with the buttons of her tunic and saw
the sergeant's face turn red.

'Now then, that's enough of that! You'd better come with
me and get this sorted out inside.' Leo followed him into the

house, where they were met by a Greek in civilian clothes who appeared to be the butler. 'Someone here to see the major,' the sergeant said, neatly bypassing the question of Leo's sex.

'Major Frobisher is at lunch,' the butler responded. 'You will have to wait.'

'I can't wait,' Leo said. 'I am an English woman and I have some vital information which the major must hear at once.' The statement was not exactly accurate but she judged that it was an approach that would strike a chord with the military mind.

At that moment a servant passed through the hallway where they stood carrying a tray and disappeared through one of the doors. Guessing that this was the door of the dining room Leo marched across to it and went in. The major was having lunch with a lady, but Leo paid no attention to her. Instead her eyes went to the plates on the table, which bore the remains of their meal. Beyond them, on a sideboard, was what was left of a chicken and a joint of beef.

Frobisher looked up sharply. 'What the . . . ? What do you mean by barging in like this? Sergeant, who is this ragamuffin?'

'Lady says she has vital information,' the sergeant mumbled.

'Lady? What lady?'

Leo found she was unable to withdraw her eyes from the food on the sideboard. 'I am Leonora Malham Brown,' she intoned, addressing the joint of beef. 'I have just walked through the mountains of Albania with the Serbian army and I haven't had anything to eat since . . .' She tried to remember when she had last eaten and found that she could not. 'We need your help. You must give us some food.' The floor seemed to be rocking under her feet. She groped around her for support, found nothing and lost consciousness.

She came round to a pungent smell and the sensation of being supported on someone's arm. The major's companion was kneeling by her and holding a phial of smelling salts under her nose, murmuring in Greek, 'Oh, the poor child! Poor little thing.' Then, in English: 'Don't worry, my dear, you are quite safe now.'

'Here, give her this.' A glass of red wine was held to Leo's lips. She sipped, choked, and sat up, struggling against the urge to sink back into oblivion.

'Please, Major Frobisher, we need your help. We arrived last night and we were sent to a camp, but there is no food. Nothing! Men are dying, Major, dying by the dozens. You must send food, at once.'

'We?' he queried. 'Who are you talking about?'

'I came with a shipload of men from the Serbian army. Other ships have come, too. So many died in the mountains and the rest are starving. Why is there no food for them?'

She staggered to her feet and the major's lady friend caught her by the arm. 'Sergeant, a chair, quickly!'

Leo sat and Frobisher seated himself at the table again. 'I'm sorry, but I can't answer that question. The French are officially in charge here. I know a supply ship docked yesterday and I assumed that the food was being transported to the camps, but that is not part of my remit.'

'Then take me to whoever is responsible,' Leo begged. 'Where is the French commander's office?'

'No, no, my dear,' the lady protested. 'You cannot go anywhere in your present state. The major will go and talk to his opposite number and sort everything out, won't you, Major? You must stay here and have something to eat. Then you can have a bath and we will find you some more suitable clothes.'

Leo shook her head. 'No, I can't eat until I know my friends have food, too. Please, Major Frobisher, can we go at once?'

'Not until you have eaten!' the lady said. 'What good can you be to your friends if you are going to faint again? Dimitri, a plate for the young lady.'

'Give her some of that chicken,' Frobisher ordered.

'No! If she has not eaten for several days her stomach will not be able to digest it. Some soup, Dimitri. That will be best.'

Leo saw the sense of what she said and allowed herself to be moved to a place at the table. A bowl of soup was set in front of her and she had difficulty in restraining herself from falling on it like an animal. But before she had swallowed half her stomach rebelled.

'I'm sorry, I can't eat any more,' she said. 'Can we go now?'

'Very well. But you must promise to come back and let us look after you.'

'I . . . I will come as soon as I can,' Leo agreed evasively, getting to her feet.

While she was eating the major had called for his car and they were soon winding through the narrow streets of the town to the headquarters of the French mission. The man at the desk in the foyer informed them that M. le Colonel was not in his office.

'*Mais, c'est le midi, n'est pas?*'

Bypassing Frobisher's inadequate French Leo, emboldened by the red wine, told him that midday or not the colonel must be summoned, if he did not wish to be responsible for the deaths of hundreds of men. The colonel, arriving rumpled and flush-faced from his interrupted siesta, gazed at her in horror as Frobisher introduced her, and then spread his hands as the problem was explained.

'But, my dear madame, it is all in hand. You must understand it is a question of priorities. There is a limited amount of transport available and many demands to be met. But the food will be delivered, in due course. *C'est la guerre, n'est pas?*'

'Yes, we are at war – and these people are supposed to be your allies!' Leo exclaimed passionately. 'Is this the way France behaves towards those who are prepared to lay down their lives in her cause? If more men die in that camp it will be your responsibility and you will not be forgiven.'

Suddenly she found herself in tears, tears that grew from fury and a sense of helplessness. At once, she was led to a chair, a clean handkerchief was pressed into her hand, and the colonel was saying that of course something must be done at once and he would summon the officer in charge of organizing transport. Weakened as she was, it crossed her mind as she mopped her face to reflect on the irony of her position. She had always despised what she regarded as 'women's wiles': fainting and bursting into tears. Now she saw that they had their uses.

Twenty minutes later Leo, Frobisher and the French transport officer arrived at the docks to find a scene of chaos. Crates of supplies were stacked on the quayside, while a Royal Navy petty officer and a French sergeant were shouting at each other in their respective languages and the Greek stevedores sat in the shelter of a doorway, eating pistachio nuts and playing backgammon. It was clear that none of the three elements in the equation was able to understand the other and all were equally taken aback when a filthy urchin appeared in their midst, demanding first in English, then French and finally in Greek, to know what the problem was. It took only minutes for Leo's identity to be explained and for her to elucidate that the cause of the hold-up was a bureaucratic muddle over paperwork.

As the sun set, Leo arrived back at the camp in the passenger seat of a lorry loaded with food. She jumped down triumphantly and was met by a furious Sasha.

'Where have you been? How dare you go off without asking my permission? Have you any idea how much anxiety you have caused me?'

She looked at him and felt tears rising again in her throat. She forced them back and said faintly, 'But look. I have brought you food.'

Already the lorry was surrounded by hungry men, their eyes huge with hope in their skeletal faces. Sasha swung away from her and began issuing orders. What might have turned into a chaotic scramble became instead a disciplined process by which the crates were unloaded and their contents distributed amongst the various different units. While this was happening, Frobisher looked around him and turned to Leo.

'I had no idea . . . I'm sorry. When we heard that the Serbian army was being evacuated we assumed . . . well, that it would have the usual support systems, supplies, cooking facilities, medical care and so forth. What happened?'

Leo shook her head. 'You can have no idea what it was like. There are no roads through those mountains. The track is too narrow for wagons and the bridges too weak. The animals died from lack of forage. We had to abandon everything – guns, ammunition, cooking pots . . . Men died from cold and starvation, and they will go on dying unless you help us.'

'I will do all I can, I promise,' he said. 'But I don't understand how you came to be with them.'

'It would take too long to explain,' Leo said. 'I will tell you one day, when there is not so much to do.'

Sasha came back and she introduced him to Frobisher, who saluted and said, 'I must apologize, Colonel. I was not aware how bad your situation was until this young lady arrived in my dining room.' He glanced from her to Sasha and added: 'I must congratulate you. I don't know how Miss Malham Brown came to be in your company, but if she had not been around to ginger us all up you might have waited days for your supplies. Now, I must get back to town, but I'll come along again tomorrow. Is there anything you particularly need?'

'Firewood!' Sasha said at once. 'We are desperate for some means to warm ourselves.'

'I will see to it,' Frobisher promised. He saluted again. 'Good night, sir. Goodnight, ma'am. Till tomorrow.'

They watched him get back into the lorry and neither of them spoke until it had turned around and left the camp. Then Leo held out her hands to Sasha.

'I'm sorry you were worried. You were exhausted and I knew I had to do something, but I was afraid that if I told you what I intended you would forbid it.'

He took her hands in his and held them tightly. 'My lioness! What would I have done without you? You have saved us all.'

'You saved me,' she replied. 'Without you I should have died on the mountain.'

They gazed at each other in silence and she saw how worn and thin his face was, but his eyes burned into hers. She felt his desire and it drew her like a magnet. She longed to lean to him and press her lips to his, but at the same time she was aware that they stood in the open field, in full view of his men and she knew that he recognized it, too. She squeezed his fingers and stepped back.

'Have all the men been fed?'

'Yes, all who are capable of eating. Misha died today, while you were gone and I fear two more will not make it through the night.'

'Is there anything I can do?'

'No. They are being cared for. You have done enough. Have you eaten?'

'Yes, earlier. The major insisted. How about you?'

'Janachko has put something in my tent. Come and join me. I told him to leave enough for you, too.'

There was less food than either of them would have liked but the immediate hunger pangs were assuaged. As soon as she had finished Leo was overcome with a feeling of intense exhaustion. She wrapped herself in her cloak and, without a second thought, stretched herself on the ground beside him and fell asleep.

Leo woke to the smell of wood smoke and coffee. Crawling out of the tent she saw that every company now had its camp-fire and the men were busy brewing up the last remnants of their precious coffee. Sasha was sitting nearby on an upturned crate and as soon as he saw her he filled a tin mug from the jug at his side and held it out to her.

'There is even sugar, thanks to your friends in Durazzo.'

'When did this happen?' Leo asked, indicating the fires.

'Soon after dawn this morning. You slept though it all, but I presume it was arranged by your Major Frobisher.'

'Good for him!' Leo said, sipping the hot drink.

'Yes.' Sasha gazed into his cup for a moment in silence and Leo saw that he was brooding over something.

'What is it?'

'Ten more men died during the night – including two of mine. The food came too late for them. And there are others who are terribly weak and will go the same way.'

'We must talk to the major about getting proper medical care,' Leo said.

Frobisher himself appeared soon afterwards and Leo tackled him at once.

'It is in hand,' he responded. 'We are setting up a hospital on the island of Vido, out there in the bay.'

'Why on an island?' Sasha queried sharply. 'Why not some-where closer – easier to get to?'

'The Greek authorities are concerned about the possible spread of infection.'

'We are dying of starvation and exposure, not some kind of plague!' Sasha exclaimed angrily.

'I can understand the authorities' point of view,' Leo put in reasonably. 'There is typhus and dysentery in the army. I know that from experience. It is sensible for them to take precautions.'

'I assure you they will have the best possible care,' Frobisher added. 'Some of your own medical teams are already there. Tell me how many men you have here in need of urgent care and I will see that transport is sent for them.'

'There are others here, then?' Sasha asked eagerly. 'Other Serbs?'

'Oh, yes. Soldiers and civilian refugees. There are camps all round the city. We estimate around one hundred and fifty thousand all together.'

'One hundred and fifty thousand?' Sasha repeated. 'There should be twice that number.'

Frobisher looked at him sympathetically. 'I can only express my condolences. It is becoming obvious that what you have all suffered is beyond anything we can imagine. But the fact that you are all here at all bears witness to your heroic determination. I salute you.'

Sasha thanked him and turned away, Leo guessed to hide tears that he was too weak to repress. Frobisher addressed her.

'Miss Malham Brown, I have two messages for you. The first is this. We are setting up a committee to coordinate the relief effort. But as you have already seen, there is a difficulty of communication. There are French, Greeks, and Italians involved, apart from ourselves and the Serbs. You obviously speak most of the languages required. Will you join the committee and act as our interpreter?'

Leo glanced at Sasha, who had recovered himself and nodded. 'Yes,' she said, 'of course. I shall be glad to help in any way I can. And the second message?'

'That is from Melinda – Madame Papadakis – whom you met yesterday. She asks me to remind you of your promise. She invites you to her home, where you can bathe and rest and be well fed.'

Leo's first impulse was to thank him and refuse. To accept seemed like a betrayal of Sasha and his men. But then it occurred to her that if she was to serve on the committee she

must make herself reasonably acceptable and she was desperately in need of a bath and clean clothes. She smiled at Frobisher. 'That is very kind. I shall be very pleased to accept her offer.'

'I can take you there as soon as I have finished my business here, if you like,' he said.

Sasha touched her arm. 'Go. You should go.'

Frobisher was temporarily distracted by a query from one of his men, which gave Leo the chance to say, 'I shall come back later today; this evening if not before.'

Sasha frowned. 'No, you should stay with this lady who is offering you a home.'

'I can get a bath and a change of clothes,' Leo said, 'but then I will come back here.'

He shook his head. 'Do you not see? It is not fitting for you to sleep in my tent now. On the mountains it was different, but here there is no excuse. God knows, I should prefer to have you with me, but the fact is I am a married man and you are an unmarried woman. My men love you for what you have done for them, but they all have very strict ideas about morality. Already there is gossip. It is bad for morale.'

Leo felt herself flush. It had not crossed her mind that her relationship with Sasha could be interpreted as anything other than innocent, but now she saw how it must look to outsiders. 'I'm so sorry,' she stammered. 'I didn't think. Of course, if that is what you think is best . . .'

He looked into her eyes. 'You know what I should wish, if it were only up to me – but we have to think of what the rest of the world will say.'

She nodded and swallowed. Frobisher returned to say, 'If you will show me which men need to be evacuated to the hospital . . .'

An hour later, Leo found herself being ushered into the house of Melinda Papadakis, where she was received, quite literally, with open arms.

Eighteen

'I'm afraid it's me again.' Victoria stood at the end of the bed in the Calais Casino, which had been turned into a hospital for the duration.

Ralph opened his eyes. 'Victoria? It really was you, then? At the station?'

'Oh, yes. It was me all right.'

He frowned. 'I'm afraid I was abominably rude.'

'Well, you didn't seem all that pleased to see me.'

'I'm sorry. It was unforgivable. I should have been thanking you.'

'I don't expect thanks. I'm just doing my job.' She sat down on the chair by the bed. 'How are you feeling?'

'A lot better than I did when I arrived here. The medics seem to have patched me up pretty well.'

'Was it . . . ? I never had a chance to find out how badly you were wounded.'

'Could have been worse; a sniper's bullet. Got me between the ribs and the pelvis but missed anything vital. I was lucky.'

'Yes, you were. I'm glad it's not too serious.'

'Me, too. The doc says I should be able to get back to active service after a few weeks convalescence.'

'Most of the patients I deal with are just happy to have got a 'blighty'; a wound that will get them back to England and away from the trenches.'

'I know. But I'm a regular officer. I've got responsibilities.'

They were both silent for a moment. Victoria was remembering how much she had disliked Ralph before the war, with his confident swagger and his assumption of masculine superiority. She guessed that he was thinking along the same lines. They both spoke at once.

'I really wanted to ask you . . .'

'Have you by any chance heard from Leo?'

'That's what I was going to ask you.'

Ralph shook his head fretfully. 'Not a word since last October, and then it was weeks out of date.'

'Same here.'

Their eyes met. Ralph said, 'From what I've seen in the papers, the Serbs have had a pretty rough time.'

'Yes, I read it, too. But Leo wouldn't have been involved in the fighting. From what she wrote to me I gather she was working in a hospital run by Mabel Stobart, well back from the front line.'

'But if the whole country has been overrun . . .'

'Leo's a non-combatant. She was under the protection of the Red Cross. Surely all sides would respect that. Do you think she's been taken prisoner?'

'It seems a possibility. But if so, her name should have been listed and handed over to the War Office, and I should have been notified, as her next of kin.' He rubbed his hand across his face. 'That damned girl! Why couldn't she stay at home, like other women?'

'You blame me for that, don't you?' Victoria said.

Their eyes met again and he gave a rueful laugh. 'I used to. But now I think if Leo hadn't met you and joined the FANY, she would have found some other way of getting into danger. If only she'd stayed with you, I shouldn't be so worried about her.'

'I wish she had, too,' Victoria said. 'I tried to persuade her.'

'What made her so determined to go back to Serbia, anyway?' he asked. 'I mean, I know she made friends when we were in Belgrade but I can't for the life of me understand why she felt it necessary to go and nurse them instead of looking after her own people.'

Victoria looked at him, wondering if he guessed something about Leo's relationship with Sasha Malkovic and was trying to probe her for details, but his expression showed only puzzled irritation and she felt a momentary exasperation. His own sister had had her heart broken, right under his nose, and he had sensed nothing. She could see no way of explaining Leo's decision without giving too much away, so she simply shrugged and remained silent.

After a moment he said, 'I wonder if you could do

something for me. I want to get a message to Tom Devenish. He was with me when I got wounded and he'll be wondering what's happened. I've written him a note. Could you see if you can get it sent up the line for me?'

'Yes, of course. I'll do my best. How was he, when you last saw him?'

'Doing incredibly well. I've always thought of Tom as the most unsoldierly chap I've ever met, but he's been a tower of strength. It's extraordinary what war brings out in some people. I just wish he'd had the sense to marry Leo while they had the chance. Then perhaps he could have stopped her going off like that.'

Victoria confined herself to a non-committal grunt and got up. 'I must be getting back. I have to report in half an hour. I'm glad to see you are getting better.'

'Thanks for coming in.'

'That's all right. I had to find out how you were. 'Bye for now.'

'Cheerio.' Then, as she turned away: 'Victoria?'

'Yes?'

'If you get the chance . . . do drop by again. It's nice to see a familiar face.'

She paused and looked at him, and saw for the first time how young he looked and how pain had hollowed his cheeks and smudged dark shadows under his eyes. She nodded. 'I come here most days, bringing wounded in from the train. I'll call in when I have time.'

'Thanks. And you'll try to get my letter to Tom?'

'Yes. I'll do my best.'

Tom came to an abrupt halt and swore under his breath as the roll of barbed wire he was helping to carry struck him in the back of the neck. The roll was suspended on an iron stanchion, which rested on his shoulder and that of the man behind him. It was almost pitch dark, but he could just make out a hunched shape blocking the trench in front of him.

'Traffic jam!' he whispered hoarsely, to explain his sudden stop.

The man following him groaned and hitched the stanchion

to a less painful position, causing the wire to cut into Tom's shoulder. The company had been withdrawn from the front line, ostensibly 'for a rest', but there was little chance of that. While billeted some six miles back from the line it was their job to bring up essential supplies and, since all movement during daylight hours attracted a barrage of shells from the Germans, the work had to be done at night. This meant a two-mile tramp along a cobbled road, carrying the huge variety of items required by the men manning the trenches; apart from barbed wire, and the metal posts to support it, there were sandbags to repair trench parapets, duckboards for the worst flooded areas, balks of timber, ammunition, grenades, and the daily rations of bread and jam and tea and sugar and bully beef. At the end of the two miles, they reached the beginning of the communication trench. From here, it was a further three miles along a narrow, muddy ditch, often up to the tops of their boots in water, with frequent right-angled bends designed to make the progress of an attacker more difficult but which also rendered the manoeuvring of cumbersome loads even more exhausting. On top of this, they were not the only company on the same errand, with the result that there were frequent hold-ups while the party ahead negotiated a particularly difficult obstacle.

This time, the jam had a different cause. Word was whispered from man to man: 'Stretcher party coming back.' There was no way a stretcher could be carried past in the narrow trench, so there was only one solution. Tom turned, with difficulty, and gave his order, sotto voce: 'Up!' With a struggle, they heaved the wire up out of the trench and scrambled after it. All along the edge, Tom could see the shadowy figures of waiting men. He knew what they were feeling. In spite of the darkness, the sense of exposure was inescapable. At any moment he expected to hear the whistle of an incoming shell. It seemed a long time before he saw the men ahead slipping back into the trench and then heard the panting and splashing of the stretcher-bearers passing his position. He looked behind him and gestured his company down again into the muddy darkness.

They reached their designated area sometime after midnight,

handed over the supplies and set off back to their billets. The going was easier without their loads but they had to climb out twice to make way for groups heading in the opposite direction. By the time they finally reached the road and could make out the dim shapes of shattered trees and ruined houses after the total blackness of the trench, Tom was exhausted and he knew his men were in the same condition, but they still had a two-mile slog ahead of them. Tramping along, with nothing particular to focus on, his thoughts turned as always to the two most important people in his life: Ralph and Leo. He had heard no news of Ralph since he was carried away unconscious after their night expedition into no-man's-land. He had made repeated enquiries, but to no avail. He could only comfort himself with the thought that Ralph had still been breathing and the wound, as far as he could tell, did not appear to have struck any vital organ, but the uncertainty was a perpetual torture. Occasionally, at moments like this, he allowed himself a comforting fantasy. If Ralph recovered, he would undoubtedly be given leave to convalesce. If he, Tom, could only wangle some leave at the same time . . . But he knew it was improbable. He had had two weeks after finishing his officer training, not long ago. A man was lucky to get that once in a year. Putting the thought aside, his mind turned to Leo, but there was little comfort there. Since a letter which had reached him last November he had heard nothing, but the newspapers had carried reports of the Serbian defeat and he could only fear the worst. While he was on leave he had made a point of calling at Sussex Gardens, but the staff there had heard nothing. He had also contacted the solicitor who handled Leo's affairs, but he was as much at a loss as the rest. The situation in Serbia was chaotic and somewhere in the middle of it Leo had simply disappeared.

Dawn was breaking as the weary men shambled into the village. Tom dismissed them and went to his own billet, which was in the house of an elderly man who had once been the village schoolmaster. He was an irritable character who appeared to find Tom's inability to speak French a personal affront; but in compensation, his housekeeper was a motherly woman who made it her mission to provide her English lodger with whatever little treats were available. Neither of them were up when Tom let himself in, but the old range in the kitchen had been stoked up and only required raking to glow into life and the big iron kettle was ready on the hob. Tom drew it over on to the hotplate and fetched his tea ration from his room. It was only then that he noticed two parcels and a small packet of letters on the table. The long-awaited post must have come up during the hours of darkness and his batman had collected it and left it for him. His stomach clenched with anxiety as he sorted through the envelopes. None was addressed in the handwriting he longed to see. There was one from his mother, one from a distant cousin who seemed to have decided it was her duty to send him uplifting quotations from the Bible, one from a newspaper editor presumably regarding some drawings Tom had sent him; and a fourth that appeared to have origi-nated in Calais, addressed in a hand he did not recognize. He tore it open with shaking hands.

Inside was another envelope, and there, at last, was the familiar script. He ignored the covering letter and opened it.

My Dear Tom,

I hope this letter will get to you quickly, because I know you will be wondering what has happened to me. Well, you can stop worrying! It seems I have been very lucky. The sniper's bullet went straight through without touching anything vital and the docs say I shall be fit to leave hospital quite soon. They will be sending me home for a bit, of course, but I shall make sure that I get a medical board asap so I can be passed fit and get back to you and the rest of the chaps. I don't suppose there's any chance of you getting a spot of home leave so you can join me?

Don't worry about me. I'm being well looked after by some really lovely nurses. Oh, and on that topic, guess who picked me up from the train and drove me here in her ambulance. None other than Victoria! It seems she and the other FANYs are established as regular ambulance drivers and doing a rather splendid job. It wasn't the first face I should have wanted to open my eyes to, in an ideal world, as you can imagine. Still, I suppose I have to admit that the whole FANY set-up has

turned out to be not as crazy as I first thought. If only Leo
had stayed in France with them! I asked Victoria if she has any
news, but she has heard nothing.

   My main worry is what you may be getting up to while I
am not there to keep an eye on you. Please try not to do
anything silly. You are much too valuable to go risking your life
on some daft escapade. I mean it, Tom! I expect you to be
there, hale and hearty, when I get back.

   I shall have to stop now. I get tired rather quickly. If you
want to write, it is probably best to send it to Sussex Gardens,
as I hope to be back there soon.
Take care, old fellow.
Your affectionate friend,
Ralph

Tom laid the letter on the table and rested his cheek on it.
In his exhausted state the sudden relief almost reduced him to
tears. The sound of the kettle coming to the boil roused him,
or he might have fallen asleep where he sat. He got up and
made himself a mug of tea, then resumed his place and began
to look through the rest of his mail.

Victoria's covering letter was brief and told him no more
than he had already learned from Ralph. His mother's letter
was almost as short, simply informing him that she had ordered
a hamper of food for him from Fortnum and Mason. Tom had
long ago given up expecting any kind of emotional sustenance
from his mother's communications, so he turned his attention
to the parcel, which contained the hamper itself. Pate de foie
gras, chocolate and strawberry jam had to substitute for maternal
affection. He drank his tea, ate some chocolate and dragged
himself off to bed.

Nineteen

Victoria was on leave. It was the first time she had been back in London since she had set off to join the FANYs at Lamarck, and she was finding it a disquieting experience. After the unrelenting effort of dealing with the constant stream of casualties, the primitive living conditions and the tedious rations, it seemed unbelievable that life in London continued almost unchanged. The streets were full of servicemen home on leave, determined to have a good time; the theatres and music halls were booming. It was true that there was a certain sense of constraints being loosened and old taboos overthrown; but the men and women of the upper middle class among which Victoria had grown up continued to live much as they always had done. There were complaints about shortages of staff and the unavailability of certain luxuries but no sense, as far as she could see, of the cataclysmic events taking place across the Channel.

It did not help that there were very few of her contemporaries in town. Victoria had always been a rebel, uncomfortable in drawing-room society, and most of her friends had either been men whom she had met during her career as a racing driver or women in the FANY. Now they were all engaged in the fighting, in one capacity or another, and she found herself at a loose end. One morning she was strolling along Bond Street, idly looking in the windows of jewellers and dress shops, when a voice hailed her.

'Victoria! Over here!'

She turned and saw across the street a woman with a familiar face but one she could not immediately place. The woman crossed the street, dodging between the hansom cabs and the motor cars that clogged it, and caught Victoria's hand.

'It is you! I was sure it was. Don't you remember me? Lozengrad!'

'Of course!' Recollection flooded back. 'Sylvia Wallace! How are you?'

'I'm well, thank you. And actually it's Sylvia Vincent now. I've been married for . . . gosh! . . . it's nearly a year now. And how are you? What are you doing with yourself these days?'

'Look,' Victoria said, 'we can't talk standing in the street. Let's go into Fenwick's coffee shop. Then we can have a proper gossip.'

Once settled over cups of coffee and a plate of fancy cakes Victoria began by describing her work in France.

Sylvia shook her head regretfully. 'You're doing such a wonderful job! And I'm just sitting at home, being useless. After working with Mabel Stobart in Lozengrad I feel ashamed not to be doing something. I wanted to go with her to Serbia, but Martin – that's my husband – wouldn't hear of it.'

'It's probably lucky for you he wouldn't,' Victoria said. 'Goodness knows what has happened to them.'

'Oh, but they are all back in England!' her companion exclaimed. 'Didn't you know?'

'Back? When?' Victoria demanded. 'How do you know? How did they get out of Serbia?'

'I had tea with Georgina MacIntosh last week. You remember her from Lozengrad? She went with Stobart this time, too. The poor things had a terrible time. They had to retreat through the mountains in awful conditions, but they finally made it to somewhere called Medua, on the Albanian coast, and got a boat to Brindisi. Poor Georgie looked worn to an absolute shadow . . .'

'Did she mention Leo Malham Brown?' Victoria interrupted. 'You remember Leo. She was at Lozengrad with us.'

'Wasn't she the girl who dressed like a boy? I didn't know she went on this last expedition.'

'Well, she did. I haven't heard from her for months and I've been assuming the worst. But if all the others got back, she must be with them.'

'Well, I suppose so,' Sylvia said. 'Georgina didn't mention her by name, but she did say that the whole party got through, thanks to Stobart.'

Victoria gathered her gloves and handbag. 'I must go! It's

been lovely meeting you again, but if Leo is home I must go and call on her and find out if she's all right. I can't think why she hasn't been in touch.' She fumbled in her bag. 'Here's my card. Do give me a call and we'll get together for a proper chinwag – but please excuse me now.'

Leaving Sylvia looking slightly bemused, Victoria hurried out of the shop and called a taxi. A few minutes later she was ringing the bell at 31 Sussex Gardens. Beavis, slightly greyer, slightly plumper, answered it.

'Beavis! Is Miss Malham Brown at home?'

'Miss Leonora, madam? No, I'm afraid not. But Captain Malham Brown is here. Shall I announce you?'

Ralph was in the library, smoking a cigarette and reading *The Times*. He got up stiffly when Victoria entered.

'Victoria! This is an unexpected pleasure. Come in, please. Beavis, bring some coffee, please. I'm sure Miss Langford would like a cup.'

'No, really, thank you. I've just had coffee with an old acquaintance. Ralph, is Leo home?'

Ralph nodded dismissal at the butler and indicated a chair opposite his own. 'Sit down, please. No, she isn't. What makes you think she might be?'

Victoria dropped into the chair, her excitement ebbing. 'This friend I met, she was with us at Lozengrad. She told me Mabel Stobart and all her party were back in England. I felt sure Leo must be with them.'

'No,' Ralph said. 'Leo is in Corfu.'

'Corfu! How do you know?'

Ralph reached into his pocket. 'This letter arrived yesterday. Here, you can read it if you like.'

Victoria scanned the letter eagerly. It was not long. Leo explained how she had come to be separated from the rest of her group, described briefly the privations of the trek through the mountains and said that she probably owed her life to the kindness of 'a Serbian officer'. She went on to outline the work she was doing with the international committee on Corfu and finished by expressing the hope that the letter would reach her brother and find him 'in good health and spirits'.

'She doesn't say anything about coming home,' Victoria commented, when she had finished.

Ralph responded with a wry smile. 'No, she doesn't, does she. But you know my sister. Never happier than when she's organizing people. I expect she's in her element out there.'

'She's obviously been through a terrible ordeal,' Victoria pointed out. 'Aren't you worried about her?'

Ralph hesitated a moment, frowning. 'To be quite honest, I've got to the point where I've given up worrying about her. For the last six months I haven't known whether she was alive or dead. Neither has poor old Tom. She insists on going off on these mad expeditions and she seems to have a remarkable talent for survival, so I've come to the conclusion that I just have to let her go her own way.'

'But you must be thankful to know that she's all right.'

'Yes, of course I am! I just wish she'd come home and marry Tom and behave like any other decent woman.'

'Present company excepted, of course!' Victoria said waspishly.

He gave her a crooked smile. 'All right. I know you're doing a wonderful job out there, and I suppose she is, too. I'm just tired of wondering what she's going to get up to next.'

Victoria studied his face for a moment and saw the faint lines around his mouth and the shadows under his eyes. She remembered making a cruel joke to Leo about his shiny boots and felt contrite. She softened her tone.

'Anyway, what about you? How is the wound healing?'

'Pretty well, thanks. It still gives me a stab if I move too quickly, but the medics say I should be able to go before a board in a week or two. I'm just praying they will pass me fit to go back to the trenches. Frankly, I'm going out of my mind here. It all seems so . . . so unreal, pointless . . .'

'I know exactly what you mean,' Victoria said. 'People here don't seem to understand what it's like over there.'

'They don't want to understand,' Ralph said bitterly. 'They just want to think of it as a glorious sacrifice. Have you seen these houses with photographs in the windows, draped in black crêpe, just so everyone knows that their son or husband or brother has died for his country? It makes me sick!'

'Some of the letters to the papers are pretty mawkish, too,' Victoria agreed.

'I want to shout at people that there's nothing glorious about it! What's glorious about thousands of men dying for the sake of a few yards of muddy ground?' Ralph hitched himself up in his chair and winced. 'Mind you, I'm as much at fault as anyone, I suppose. When I have to write home to some grieving mother or wife I don't tell them their son or husband died in agony after lying up to his waist in mud all day with half his face shot off. I tell them he was shot while bravely doing his duty and let them think it was quick and virtually painless.'

'What else can you do?' Victoria said. 'Why make their suffering worse? But I sometimes think that if some of those wives and mothers could spend a day or two with me, and see the casualties coming off the trains and the barges, the war would be over by the end of the week. People wouldn't stand for it, if they could see the reality.'

Ralph sighed and they were both silent for a moment. Then he said, 'Look here. What we both need is to be taken out of ourselves. How do you fancy a night out?'

'A night out? Where?'

'Oh, anywhere you like – as long as it's not the opera! I can't offer to take you dancing, I'm afraid. How about the music hall? I feel like some good, rowdy entertainment. What do you say?'

Victoria hesitated. Once upon a time she would have laughed out loud at the notion of a date with Ralph. But he did seem to have mellowed and was not the bumptious, self-satisfied prig she had thought him before the war. 'All right,' she said. 'Music hall it is.'

'Excellent! I'll pick you up around seven, and we'll have a bite of supper afterwards.'

The evening was more enjoyable than Victoria had expected. She had never been to the music hall before and initially the rowdy voices and the haze of tobacco smoke that hung over the long tables and the crowded benches gave her

reason to doubt the wisdom of agreeing to Ralph's suggestion. But she had developed a taste for gin during her service
in France, as an antidote to the stresses of the job, and Ralph
saw to it that her glass was frequently refilled, while he kept
pace with her in pints of beer. Very soon they both relaxed
and allowed the convivial atmosphere to sweep them along.
The chairman kept the evening going with a swing,
summoning act after act on to the tiny stage. There were
comics and singers and magicians and conjurers and Victoria
found herself applauding and joining in the choruses with
the rest. Top of the bill was Marie Lloyd, resplendent in a
huge hat and a frilled parasol. Her sly innuendo, pressed home
with winks and nudges, had Victoria giggling helplessly during
songs like 'A Little of What You Fancy' and 'She Sits Among
the Cabbages and Peas'. Ralph roared with laughter, too, but
they both sobered up and glanced at each other ruefully when
she sang her well-known recruiting song, 'I Didn't Like You
Much Before You Joined the Army . . .' The mood passed,
however, and they left the hall humming and holding on to
each other's arms.

Ralph took her to the Café de Paris for supper. They ate
oysters and drank white wine and Victoria began to feel a
languorous euphoria enveloping her. Ralph, she decided, was
good company and not nearly as objectionable as she had found
him before the war, and it was pleasant to be seen on the arm
of a handsome man in uniform. When the taxi stopped outside
her flat it seemed just common good manners to invite him
in for coffee. Anyway, she told herself with a suppressed giggle,
he was perfectly harmless. 'I might as well be with my maiden
aunt!'

Quite how it happened that she found herself kissing him,
she was never sure; but then suddenly she was flat on her back
on the sofa with Ralph on top of her. There was a brief,
undignified scuffle with underwear, a moment of violent
thrusting and then he pulled away with a choking sound and
turned his back on her.

Muzzy-headed, she pulled herself together and straightened
her clothes, but he was already heading for the door.

'Ralph!' she called. 'It's OK! Come back.'

'It's not!' he replied, his voice strangled. 'It's not. I'm sorry!' And the door of the flat banged behind him.

Next morning Victoria telephoned Sussex Gardens, to be informed by Beavis that Captain Malham Brown had gone to the country for a few days. He was still away when her leave came to an end.

Twenty

Leo sat beside Sasha Malkovic on a bench overlooking Corfu harbour. Almost two months had passed since their arrival and at last the rain had stopped and the sun was warm on her shoulders. In the crystalline air the rocky shores below them dropped sharply into sea that shaded from turquoise to sapphire, while the slopes above were silvered with olive groves and punctuated with the sharp exclamation marks of Cyprus trees.

'It's beautiful, isn't it?' she said.

Sasha stirred and grunted. 'Is it? For me, rocks and water and those twisted trees don't constitute real beauty. That requires green pastures and tumbling rivers and rich orchards.'

Leo sighed. 'I know. You're pining for Serbia.' She touched his sleeve. 'Don't give up hope. We will go back, one day.'

'We?' He looked at her.

'Yes, of course. I miss it, too.'

He looked away again. 'You should go home.'

'Why? There's nothing there that matters to me.'

'What about your family? They must be worried about you.'

'I have no family, except my brother'.

'And your fiancé. What about him?'

The question gave her a shock. She had not mentioned Tom since meeting Sasha again. 'You know about that?'

'Naturally. You became quite a celebrity in Belgrade, when you were there. The local papers soon picked up on the announcement of your engagement. It did not come as a surprise. It was obvious that Tom was in love with you.'

'You're wrong!' Leo exclaimed. 'It was a ruse, a deception. I had to get out of Belgrade after . . . well, you know why. I was still underage and Ralph was my guardian. He would not allow me to go home alone, so Tom agreed to the engagement. It suited us both, but we never had any intention of marrying. You must know that! I could never have considered marrying anyone . . .'

'I assumed,' he said, 'that you had decided that marriage to an old friend would be preferable to the life of a single woman.'

She stared at him. 'How could you think that? How could you believe that I would do something so . . . so venal? Did you really think that I was unable to face life independently, without a man to support me?'

He glanced at her and then away again. 'What else was I to think?' The tone was abrupt, but she saw the colour rising in his cheeks.

'I thought you knew me better than that,' she answered.

He was silent for a moment. Then he turned and took her hand. 'Of course I should have done. Forgive me.'

'I understand,' she conceded. 'It was a difficult time, for both of us.'

He frowned. 'I don't understand why Tom agreed to the deception.'

'It suited us both. You were wrong to think he was in love with me. A platonic relationship was all he wanted. Tom has no interest in women.'

He looked surprised, even slightly shocked, and she realized that he was uncomfortable with the idea that she even knew about such matters. But he recovered himself and continued. 'All the same, he must be worried about you – and your brother, too.'

'I have written to both of them,' she said. 'But I assume they are both in France somewhere – that is if they are . . .'

He pressed her hand lightly. 'We must hope for the best.'

'Anyway,' she went on, 'I have no idea how long my letters might take to reach them. I have not had any reply so far.'

'There is still time,' he said. 'Don't be downcast.'

The conversation had brought to her mind a subject she had been avoiding since their meeting in the mountains. She decided the moment had come to put it into words.

'And you? Have you been in touch with your wife? Where is she?'

'In Athens, I hope. When the fighting started I sent word to my mother that they should both head south immediately. I can only hope that they reached the border before the roads were cut off by the Bulgarians. I have spoken to our consul here and asked him to make enquiries through his counterpart in Athens, but, like you, I have not had any response so far.'

'Well,' she said, trying to express a sympathy she did not feel, 'as you say, there is still time. We must hope for the best.'

He gave her a quick glance, an acknowledgement that neither of them was saying what they really meant.

They were both silent for a while, then he stirred himself and murmured, 'You are right, of course. There is beauty of a kind out there. But I shall never be able to look at this scene without sorrow.'

She followed the direction of his gaze, to where the island of Vido rose from the blue waters. 'Of course, I didn't think. I'm sorry.'

For the first weeks after their arrival Serbian soldiers, sick and starving after the journey through the mountains, had died on the island at the rate of three hundred a day. One thousand had been buried on the island itself; then, when space ran out, they were buried at sea in the deep waters around. Already, the Serbs who survived were referring to them as 'the blue graveyard'. But there was room for optimism. The death rate had reduced now, and for the survivors who were camped around Corfu conditions had improved. Food and fuel were adequately provided, and the men's tattered clothes had been replaced by good English boots and woollen underwear and French uniforms. Leo had worked tirelessly with the committee, interpreting and cajoling, seeking to iron out the endless bureaucratic misunderstandings, resorting at times to foot-stamping fury, and she knew that she could take some credit for the improvement.

The Corfiotes themselves had taken the refugees to their hearts and invited many of them into their homes. Increasingly, Serbs displaced from their homeland congregated on the island. Serbian government ministers had established themselves in the White Venice Hotel and the National Assembly now met in the National Theatre. Certain churches, such as St Archangel and Holy Trinity, had been set aside for Serbian Orthodox worship. There was even talk of producing a Serb-language newspaper.

Leo herself was being spoilt and pampered in a way she had

never before experienced. Melinda Papadakis was a childless widow, who had been left comfortably off by her late husband, and she treated Leo as if she were her own daughter. Horrified by her skeletal appearance, her hollow eyes and unkempt hair, she set out to tempt her appetite with all sorts of delicacies and put her in the hands of her own lady's maid, who gave her hot baths and massaged her body and her hair with scented oils. Leo accepted these attentions gratefully, though she had pangs of guilt when she considered the hardships still suffered by Sasha and his men. There was one point of dispute, however, between her and her hostess. Melinda had a wardrobe full of elegant and fashionable dresses, which she was eager to have altered by her dressmaker to fit Leo, so that she could show her off in local society; but Leo insisted on choosing the plainest and most serviceable garments. Melinda complained that they made her look like a governess, but Leo pointed out that she could hardly conduct her work with the committee dressed as if she was on her way to an embassy garden party.

One of her first acts on her arrival at Melinda's, apart from writing to Ralph and Tom, had been to contact the London solicitor who managed her affairs. He had set up a facility for her to draw money from a local bank. No longer dependent on Melinda's generosity, she went to a tailor in the town and ordered a replica of her FANY uniform. Clad once again in breeches and boots she felt more like her old self, though she had to bow to society's rules by donning the divided skirt that covered them. It irritated her to feel it flapping round her ankles, but at least she could stride out freely. She remembered, with a pang, how her grandmother had despaired of her mannish gait. She had even sent her to a finishing school where they had tried to teach her to walk 'like a lady', with a book balanced on her head. She had tried to conform; but what a relief it had been to join the FANY!

One thing that did bother her was her shorn hair. This time she had not kept the locks she had hacked off to form a switch, so she had no way of disguising their lack. But it was beginning to grow again, and most of the time it could be hidden under a hat.

Sasha stood up and stretched. 'I must get back to camp.'

Leo rose also. 'And I have another meeting of the committee. There are rumours that Crown Prince Alexander is going to visit us and people are talking about organizing a ball or a concert in his honour.'

'He will not want any ceremony, if I know him,' Sasha responded. 'What he will want is to review his troops and discuss how soon we can reform and prepare to counter-attack. That is all that matters.'

'I know,' Leo agreed. 'But it will take time to re-equip the army. I hear all the time about shortages on the Western Front. It is not going to be easy to persuade the British and the French to part with weapons for us.'

He sighed and nodded. 'I know – and I know we have a staunch advocate in you. I will try to be patient.'

'Will you dine at Mme Papadakis's tonight?' Leo asked. Sasha had become a regular guest at the house.

He hesitated and then gave her his rare grin. 'Why not? The food is good and the company . . . has its attractions.' He took her hand and kissed it, then saluted and walked away.

Twenty-One

Victoria peered out of the door of the latrine block. No one was about yet in the compound, where the ambulances stood in line. She had been back in France for nearly six weeks and, opposite her, a long building housed the individual cabins which had replaced the bell tents, where the members of the convoy had originally slept. She thought grimly that when the new huts had arrived she had never imagined how grateful she would be for the privacy they conferred. At that moment the doors were closed, but soon the reveille would sound and the occupants would come tumbling out for roll-call. She had just enough time to get back to her own room without having to explain why she was up so early. She took a deep breath and prayed that she was not going to be sick again. As she crossed the compound, the morning breeze wafted the smell of cooking from the cookhouse at one corner, triggering another wave of nausea. She fought it down and hurried into her room.

Scrambling into her uniform, she cursed herself for the hundredth time. What a fool, to let herself fall pregnant after all this – and to Ralph of all people! She had been lucky with Luke, and since then she had made sure that her relationship with the various officers passing through Calais had never gone beyond a chaste kiss on the cheek. She had been so sure that she was safe with Ralph. She was drunk, of course. They both were. But that was no comfort now.

Buttoning her tunic, she forced herself to assess the situation. There were three options, for a woman in her situation. One was to confront the man and ask him to 'do the decent thing'. And she was fairly sure that Ralph would feel obliged to comply. It would be a matter of honour. But what a prospect, for both of them! She remembered how he had torn himself away, almost before the act was completed, and rushed out of the flat. She was certain, now, that he was homosexual, even if he did not admit it to himself, and their brief coupling had sickened him. To be locked into marriage would be torture for both of them, to say nothing of the unwanted child. It was not to be contemplated.

Option two was to confess to her superiors, suffer the opprobrium visited on single mothers, let the pregnancy go to full term and have the child adopted. She had no doubt that it would be the end of her career with the FANY. Neither Mac nor Franklin would be prepared to tolerate such a scandal. What she would do with herself after the birth she could not imagine, but she knew that she was not prepared to bring up a child on her own.

There remained one further resort. She remembered the woman who had spoken of doctors in London who could arrange matters, for a fee. She had given Victoria a card with the name of one such. At the time, Victoria had tried to refuse, certain that it was something she would never need, but she had tucked the information away . . . 'just in case'. Now the time had come to use it.

But to do that meant going to London, and she had only just come back from leave. There was no possibility of another spell for months. And she could not pretend that there was a close relative who needed her presence at the bedside, because she had often told people, proudly, that she had no close family and therefore no ties. The only other possibility was to feign illness, but that required a sickness that was serious enough to get her sent back to England and she was doubtful that she could convince the doctors at the local hospital that it was genuine. She seemed to have hit a dead end.

Outside, the whistle summoning her to roll-call sounded. She dragged a comb through her hair, grimacing at the pallor of her face, and hurried out of her cabin. All along the corridor doors were banging open and women were appearing buttoning tunics, pushing hair under caps. One or two were wearing top coats and boots and Victoria suspected that underneath they were still in their pyjamas. It was not surprising. An ambulance train had been scheduled for eight o'clock the previous night but had been delayed until ten. After each ambulance had made three round trips lasting about an hour, none of them had got back to camp until after one a.m., exhausted from driving their casualties over roads full of potholes by the light of one dimmed headlight. In addition to her other ills, Victoria felt light-headed from lack of sleep.

After roll-call they had a hasty breakfast, which she was unable to stomach, and then it was time to get the ambulances started. They were all Napiers now and Victoria had named hers Nancy. As she cranked the starting wheel the three possible solutions to her dilemma went round and round in her head. She was checking the oil pressure and the fuel gauge when the cry went up, 'Barges!' and all around her colleagues scrambled into the driving seats. Victoria followed the rest down the long road from the camp and on to the wharf beside the canal. She had just backed her vehicle up to the edge of the water when the first barge came slipping gently under the bridge. The stretchers came up on lifts and were placed in the back of the waiting ambulances and for the next hour her mind was fully occupied as she eased the Napier over bumps and culverts on the way to the hospital. But on the return drive to camp her predicament came back to her in full force.

She managed to keep some lunch down, but as she left the mess tent Beryl Hutchinson stopped her.

'I say, old thing, you look a bit green about the gills. Are you all right?'

'No, actually. I'm feeling a bit under the weather,' Victoria admitted. 'I think I may have picked up some kind of tummy bug.'

'Why don't you go and ask Boss to give you the rest of the day off?' Hutchinson asked. 'There's no shame in going sick, if you're really not up to the job, you know.'

'I know,' Victoria agreed. 'But I'll keep going for the time being. Don't worry about me. I'll be fine.' If she was going to go for the sickness option, it had to be something more serious than an attack of diarrhoea.

As she crossed the compound Lilian Franklin called her over.

'Colonel Martin needs someone to drive him to Pont du Beurre this afternoon. I thought it would be a good job for you and Sparky.'

Victoria's heart sank. She had been looking forward to an

hour's rest in her cabin but she could only nod and respond cheerfully, 'Righto, Boss. What time does he want me?'

'Right away. He's waiting at HQ for you to pick him up.'

Victoria made her way to where Sparky was parked and pulled out the starting handle. The little car was usually very cooperative and started on the second or third turn, but on this occasion he refused to oblige. Victoria cranked and cranked, swearing under her breath. Suddenly, there was an explosion and she felt a violent, wrenching pain in her arm and was thrown bodily sideways to land on the bonnet. Her cry of pain and the subsequent extremely unparliamentary language brought Hutchinson out of her office.

'What happened?'

'Sparky backfired.'

'I heard. Are you all right? Let's have a look at that arm.'

She ran expert hands over Victoria's right arm and grimaced. 'If you ask me, that's broken. I'll get someone to run you to the hospital.'

'But what about the colonel?' Victoria protested. 'I'm supposed to pick him up.'

'Someone else can do that. Come on, let's get you settled.'

Victoria reached into the front seat with her good arm and grabbed the haversack that held her first aid kit and a few personal possessions. She patted the steering wheel and whispered, 'Good old Sparky! You never let me down!'

After that, events took on a momentum that left little time for reflection. The doctor at the hospital confirmed that the arm was indeed broken, but it was a clean break that could be set without surgery, and by dinner time Victoria was back in camp, standing in front of the CO's desk with her arm in a sling.

'Boss' Franklin looked her up and down and remarked, 'Well, you're not going to be much use to us here, in that condition. You'd better go home until the arm is usable again. I'm sure the London office can find plenty for you to do. There's a hospital ship leaving tomorrow morning. I'll see if I can get you on board.'

By the following afternoon Victoria was letting herself into her flat in Mayfair. Next day, she reported to the London HQ in the Earls Court Road. Janette Lean, the Secretary of the Corps, regarded her sympathetically.

'Oh, poor you! What rotten luck! Well, we can certainly use some extra help. There's a flood of new recruits coming through, and great loads of comforts for the troops to be dealt with, apart from the general effort to raise funds. But you look really done up. Why don't you take a few days off and have a good rest? Then you can come back and really make yourself useful.'

By mid-afternoon, Victoria was sitting in the comfortably appointed consulting room of the doctor whose name she had been given all those years ago. She had changed out of her FANY uniform and put on a dove-grey coat and skirt, the soberest items in her wardrobe. She had decided that she was likely to get a more sympathetic hearing if the doctor did not know how she had spent the last two years, and she had her story ready.

After a cursory examination and a few routine questions he said, 'So, you are quite sure that you really don't want this baby?'

'Quite sure,' she replied.

'And the child's father? Have you consulted him?'

'I can't. He was killed by a sniper's bullet a month ago. He'd just been home on leave. That's when . . .'

'When the child was conceived. And you are not married to this man?'

'No. We were engaged. We wanted to wait until the war was over before we got married, but then . . . it seemed cruel to let him go back without . . . you know.'

'It's a story I am hearing far too often these days,' the doctor said. 'And your family? What do they think?'

'I have no family, really. My parents are both dead and I'm an only child.' That part, at least, was true.

He put his elbows on the desk and steepled his fingers. 'There are only two grounds upon which a pregnancy can be legally terminated. One, that the physical health of the woman would be in danger if it was allowed to continue. The second is that her mental health would suffer irreparable damage. You seem to me to be in good physical health. Tell me, if I were to refer you to a colleague of mine who is a psychiatrist, do you think he might conclude that your mental health was at risk?'

'Oh, yes!' Victoria said earnestly. 'I really think I might have a nervous breakdown.'

He nodded. 'There is one further point. I have a nursing home, quite small but well equipped and very discreet. I am sure we could find a room for you there, but it is not cheap.'

'That won't be a problem,' she assured him. 'My father left me quite well off.'

He smiled. 'Then I will get my secretary to make an appointment for you with my colleague.'

The psychiatrist had consulting rooms a few doors away in Harley Street. His manner was less unctuous than the first doctor's but it was clear to Victoria that the interview was purely a matter of form. After a few questions he said, 'What happened to your arm?'

'I fell down some stairs.'

'Really?'

'Yes, I . . . I suppose I wasn't looking where I was going.' If he thought that she had thrown herself down the stairs in an attempt to produce a miscarriage, so much the better.

'Dr Congreve is of the opinion that to be forced to continue this unwanted pregnancy would severely damage your mental health. Is he right?'

Victoria stretched her eyes wide until she felt tears pricking them and when she spoke the tremor in her voice was only partly assumed. 'Oh, yes! I'm sure I couldn't go through with it. I think I should go mad.'

The next morning she checked into the nursing home in a quiet street in St John's Wood. Three days later she presented herself again at the Corps HQ.

'Oh, you look better,' Janette said. 'Do you feel it?'

'Oh, yes,' Victoria replied. '*Much* better.'

Twenty-Two

Leo was relaxing at the Papadakis house. Melinda had given her a small suite of rooms to herself and she was in the sitting room, reading by an open window. Summer had come, and the day had been oppressively hot, but now there was a faint breeze off the sea, carrying the smell of jasmine and roses from the garden. She had exchanged her FANY uniform for a dress of white linen so fine that it was almost transparent, cut low enough in the neck to reveal the swell of her breasts. Melinda had succeeded in her aim of feeding her up to the extent that she now had breasts that would make it very hard for her to disguise herself as a boy again.

There was a tap on the door and Melinda's maid came in. 'Excuse me, madam, but Colonel Malkovic is here. He says he has something important to tell you. Shall I send him up?'

Leo felt a momentary confusion. She was not dressed for receiving visitors. She took up a light shawl and put it round her shoulders. 'Yes, ask him to come up, please.'

Sasha came into the room with a rapid step and a light in his eyes that told her he had good news. 'It's come! We're on the move at last.'

'Where to?'

'Salonika. The whole force is being transported there to join the garrison of French and British troops. Once there, we can make plans for a joint attack. With our allies' help we shall be able to break though the Bulgarian lines and then the way is clear for an advance on Belgrade.'

Leo smiled at him. For months he had been morose and withdrawn and it was good to see him so animated. 'That's excellent news. When do we leave?'

'We can begin embarking an advance guard before the end of the week. French ships are on their way to pick us up.' He stopped and looked at her, his face darkening. 'Now, you must go back to England.'

'Why?' His words struck her like a physical blow.

His brows drew together. 'There is no place for you with the army. You have no role to play. It is not fitting for a respectable single woman to trail round Europe like a camp follower.'

Leo rose and drew herself up. 'Is that all you think of me?'

'I am concerned for your reputation.'

'What do I care about my reputation? Don't you know that, wed or unwed, I would follow you to the ends of the earth? All that matters to me is that we should be together.'

For a moment he stood gazing at her with an intensity that frightened her. Then he reached out and took hold of her hands. 'Very well, then, so be it. Let us be . . . together.'

The next instant she was folded in the embrace she had dreamed of for four long years. But this time his kiss was not the tender farewell she remembered from the first occasion. It was fierce and urgent and after a moment he swept her up in his arms and carried her through into the bedroom. There he set her on her feet and began to struggle with the fastenings of her dress. Realizing that he would rip it in his haste she took a step backwards.

'Let me.'

He drew back then, but instead of turning away, as she had expected, he stood watching her, devouring her with his eyes. For a brief moment she felt ashamed. Then she remembered that it was courage he admired and it was courage he expected of her now. Swiftly she discarded her clothes until she stood naked in front of him. He reached out and touched her cheek.

'My lioness! Come!'

He carried her to the bed and stripped himself in a few rapid movements. Once in his arms she forgot all doubts and hesitation. She had dreamed, of course, of a moment like this, and feared it a little; but his hands were skilful and her body opened to him like a flower. He came with a great sobbing groan, and she knew that he had waited and longed for this just as she had.

Later they lay looking into each other's faces and she recalled the first time she had seen him. Those dark eyes that seemed now to caress her face had been full of pride and contempt barely veiled by formal courtesy, and yet even then she had known, in some deep half-conscious part of her mind, that she had found her soulmate.

As if his mind had been running along the same lines he touched her cheek and murmured, 'So, at last, we are one, as fate intended.'

'You didn't think like that when we first met,' she reminded him.

'You forget. For months I thought you were a boy. It was a great relief to discover you were not.' His hand slid downwards to cup her breast, triggering a new upsurge of desire. 'How could I have been so blind?'

He kissed her throat, then lifted his head and looked into her eyes, his expression suddenly grave. 'I want to tell you something.'

'Tell me what?' she asked, with a tremor of fear.

'My marriage to Eudoxie was never consummated.'

'What?'

'It was not that I did not try to honour my obligation as a husband. But every time I approached her it brought on an attack of asthma. After a while, I realized that it was distressing her and I left her alone. Then I was recalled to my regiment and we have not met since.'

'I see,' Leo murmured, keeping her voice neutral to suppress the laugh of pure triumph that rose in her throat.

His smile gave licence to her delight. 'When this war is over, I shall apply to have the marriage annulled and then we can be wed. That is, if you can reconcile yourself to life as the wife of a Serbian country gentleman, which is what I intend to be.'

She smoothed the thick dark hair on his brow. 'Oh, Sasha! There is nothing in the world I should like more than that.'

They made love again then, this time slowly and with infinite tenderness.

A week later Leo stood beside Sasha on the foredeck of the French warship as it steamed towards the Greek coast.

'Salonika!' she murmured. 'Again! Strange how fate seems to lay down certain pathways for one's life, so that you keep returning to the same places. Was it really only four years ago? It feels like a lifetime.'

'When did you come here first?' he asked.

'The day we met for the first time, when we walked into your hotel and demanded to be sent to Chataldzha. What a silly, naïve pair you must have thought us!'

He lifted an eyebrow. 'Naïve? Yes, I suppose so. But silly? I'm not so sure about that. I do remember thinking that one of you could be quite attractive, if only she was more suitably dressed, and not so damned arrogant!'

Leo laughed. 'Arrogant? Talk about pots and kettles!' She slipped her hand into his. 'Never mind. They say like calls to like. Perhaps we've both met our match – to coin a phrase.'

He squeezed her fingers. 'And what a pair we make! Look, we're entering the harbour. This is the end of the long retreat. From now on we go forward. And nothing less than victory will do.'

She leaned into him and looked up at his face, fired with pride and determination. She thought, *This is the only victory that I really need*, but she did not voice the thought. Instead she said, 'We may have a long road ahead of us. But as long as we can travel it together nothing else matters.'